Finding Tess

A Viv Fraser Mystery

V. Clifford

Published by Inverardoch Press
Copyright © Vicki Clifford 2014

Chapter One

Friday. Viv Fraser woke with her arm draped over the smooth latte-coloured shoulders of a young man she'd met ten hours before. She cursed under her breath, stealthily rolled onto her back, and manoeuvred toward the edge of the bed. A hint of streetlight prised its way through ill-fitting curtains, and she glanced back at his serene face. Viv stretched her hand towards almond shaped eyes where a wisp of hair was caught on long dark lashes. The eyelids twitched and Viv withdrew her hand. She tiptoed through to the next room, retrieved her jodhpurs, a shirt and one sock from the polished wooden floor.

Viv ruffled her hair, unable to see any sign of her underwear and quietly groaned at the memory of the previous evening. She spotted her second sock peeking out from the side of a large cushion but when she lifted it she unearthed nothing more. Resigned to go without, she pulled on her jodhpurs and socks then slid through into a large square hallway, which doubled as a study. She prayed that the vision left in bed remained lost in slumber. A black anglepoise lamp sat on one side of a scuffed partner's desk; to the right of this lay a stack of books, each with a sheet of A4 sticking out. Viv spotted her own recently published work with its bold black title on a white background. Unable to resist, she glanced at the notes wedged in the introduction. She whispered, 'Not bad!' and replaced the paper, keen to make her departure. An oak coat-stand wobbled as she reached for her tweed jacket. The echo of wood on wood made her even more anxious to be gone. Her leather boots stood like sentinels at the front door. She hauled them on, thinking at least things had been orderly at the beginning of her visit. She shrugged into her jacket and gently closed the door behind her.

Both the outer and inner gates of the Victorian lift glided apart then clunked reassuringly when she drew them together. Viv pressed G and the ancient mechanism rumbled into action. Her eyelids fell as she recalled the persistent journey of the young man's soft mouth; their ambitious, searching tongues. She shuffled her feet, to rid her loins of the memory. The taste in her mouth was a rude reminder of how unkind the night's booze had been to her gut. With her forehead rested against the cool tinted mirror on the back wall of the lift carriage, she sighed again and whispered, 'Damn, damn, damn' as it crept towards ground level.

Leaving the gates slightly apart she strode out through a heavy mahogany door onto Moray Place and enveloped by the dark unnerving silence of the morning checked her watch. It read ten to six, in reality it was only half past five. Had she looked back she'd have caught a shadow behind the curtain at the top floor window. Oblivious, Viv buttoned her jacket up to her chin and set out at a jogging pace, for once impervious to Edinburgh's magnificent Georgian architecture, up to Charlotte Square, across Princes Street to the bottom of Lothian Road, then left along King's Stables Road trailing the high wall of St Cuthbert's church graveyard marking the western boundary of the Old Town. Moss had fallen from the top of the wall and lay in little piles on the pavement. Viv imagined tortured ghosts jostling for territory, scrabbling to rejoin the outside world.

Fifteen minutes and she was back in her tiny flat in Edinburgh's West Bow. Beneath a torrent of near scalding water, Viv attempted to wash the night's casualty down the drain. The nauseating words, 'I have always admired you from afar', echoed in her ear. She blew out a stream of water, groaned, added a dollop of shampoo to her scalp and scrubbed. Viv Fraser regarded guilt as one of life's overused accessories: a loud decorative way of avoiding action. But what was she to do to limit the damage? The seductive almond eyes belonged to a student. She squeezed her eyes closed and shook her head wishing the catastrophizing would cease.

Viv was seeing, or at least lunching with, someone. Or was she? She, like most, could hoodwink herself into or out of anything. What had possessed her? She'd already deluded herself into believing that the cocktails were responsible. A conversation about 'Freud's Women' couldn't have been that seductive, even if the guy had quoted from her book more eloquently than she could herself. They had argued about it, but as the night progressed a small frisson of sexual tension had cranked up a few notches.

She rubbed her hair with a towel, threw it into the laundry basket, and padded through to the sittingroom where the gentle face of Sal Chapman floated into her frontal lobe. Then Viv pressed play on her answering machine and her belly lurched as Sal's voice echoed out across the room. 'Hi Viv, sorry to ring so late. I'll try you again if I get a spare minute. It's crazy here. Wall-to-wall discussion panels. Blokes boring for Britain. Speak soon hopefully.'

'Shit!' Viv hadn't expected to hear from her. The next message, from Margo, sounded anxious, her request totally uncharacteristic. Viv was intrigued but didn't ring either back and justified her delay with, 'far too early'.

After industrial strength coffee and a scan of her emails, Viv headed out to visit her first client. It was an April morning, fresh with a nip in the air, and no sign of the promised rain. She found her car, squeezed into a motorcycle bay, with a ticket on the windscreen. Blaspheming, she ripped it off and tossed it onto the passenger seat. As she drove west out of the Grassmarket towards the Forth Road Bridge, she felt grateful that she wasn't in the opposite lane, where cars sat nose to tail with their lights dipped: a sign of dark skies to the north.

The turn-off before the Bridge was signposted to Kirkliston MOD base. At the end of the slip road she turned right, passing back over the top of the motorway. After continuing for a couple of miles, on one of those country roads with so many dips that oncoming drivers appear out of nowhere, she finally indicated left and entered through the highest, most ornate gates in lowland Scotland.

Thurza Weston, otherwise known as the Countess of Newhall, kept the same appointment at 10am on the last Friday of the month. The stately home came courtesy of her husband, Toddy, the Earl of Newhall, who everyone regarded as 'a lovely man'. An Etonian, whose drinking hadn't aged him well, Toddy was probably bullied as a boy and didn't see anything wrong in continuing school traditions at home. Viv, having once had to stand between Thurza's already swollen cheek and his attempt at a second punch, was less than enthusiastic about him.

Viv skipped up the front steps and was greeted by Roy the head guide. He tipped the cap of his gaudy and now too large uniform exposing a balding head peppered with age spots. 'How's my young lovely today then?'

'Great, Roy. And yourself, how's that knee?'

'Doing away m'dear, doing away. You're expected.' He nodded in the direction of a side door marked 'Private' in bold gold letters. The sign wasn't enough to deter public curiosity so there was a rope with a larger sign dangling from it, also saying 'Private'. But even this was insufficient, and a security lock with a number pad had been installed six months ago.

Viv typed in the code and entered the sacred domain of some of Scotland's senior aristos. She crossed the hallway, toeing a dog bone off the crested rug onto the flagstone edge. Above a panelled dado rail hung Toddy's collection of nineteenth- century Scottish landscapes. Beattie Brown's *Falls of Dochart* took a prominent position. Viv loved it. The unremitting force of peaty water roaring down a gorge, backed by peaks of high hills obscured by a foreboding sky could make her reach for a sou'wester.

She heard the anxious but overly upbeat voice of Thurza coming from the kitchen. Viv smiled, knowing that this could change in a trice, but continued her advance. Thurza, an American, had told Viv of her early elocution lessons. A governess had been employed to ensure Thurza had an accent more English than Ishiguro or any English person Viv'd ever known. The heiress of a corrugated paper manufacturer, with mills and factories spanning the east coast of America, Thurza had, like many before her, exchanged dollars for a title which allowed her to masquerade with British gentry who, while regarding her as a fake, never refused her lavish entertaining.

Although Thurza and Viv had had a bit of a rocky start, Viv soon got the measure of the bored intelligent preppy, besides Americans love anyone who rises through merit. Viv's conversation went some way to softening Thurza's defences, and once she'd experienced the consistent quality of Viv's haircuts she became her greatest evangelist.

Mabel, Thurza's very cute, but over-fed and under-exercised, Border terrier, waddled up to Viv and sniffed her kit bag. Viv bent and tickled her chin just as Thurza said goodbye, tossed her phone onto the worktop, and grabbed a packet of cigarettes. 'My stepbrother,' she, pointed her thumb at the telephone. Then with a dramatic change in her tone, 'God! Am I glad to see you. This white tie do we're hosting tonight is such hard work. You've no idea . . . ' She stopped, seeing Viv's raised eyebrows.

Viv held up her hand and laughed, 'Spare me the histrionics.' She began pulling the essentials of her trade from her case. 'You've got an army of runners; all you have to do is chill out, turn up looking bonny, and keep smiling.'

Thurza laughed and unable to find her lighter, stuck the end of the fag onto the hotplate of the range. 'D'you mind?' She drew in a lungful of nicotine, the question completely rhetorical. Viv shrugged and continued sorting out her scissors, brushes and combs.

Thurza pulled a chair out from beneath a long rectory table strewn with magazines, letters and the general scraps of the life of a modern countess, available for all who cared to see. 'Have you heard . . .?'

Viv shook her head. 'You're incorrigible. Even if I had . . . I wouldn't give you ammunition.'

'No. No, it's too recent for you to have heard it.'

Viv put her hands over her ears and started clicking her tongue until Thurza brushed away an imaginary interloper and plonked herself on a chair. 'You're no fun.' They giggled.

Viv arranged her large green gardener's sheet on the floor, plugged in her dryer above the worktop, and wrapped a gown round Thurza's shoulders. 'You wearing it up or down?'

Thurza looked nonplussed. 'I don't care.'

Only people who really care say that they don't. Viv lifted the back of Thurza's long blonde hair off her neck, and piled it on top of her head, instantly taking a decade off a sagging jaw line.

'Think gravity T, when biology picks up its pace use all the engineering available to arrest it.'

Thurza was a handsome woman who had been on the wrong side of nicotine for long enough to lose her bloom. But on such a day as this, Viv, Marie-Therese the manicurist, and Rosanna the beauty therapist were all booked in to perform their miracles.

Thurza, stealing a peek at her reflection in the door of the microwave said, 'It looks better up. Let's have it up. Have you seen Petrea recently?'

Viv hesitated. What was at stake here? 'We'll get to Petrea. But let's get this hair sorted out first. What are you wearing? High neck? Low neck? No neck? Are the jewels coming out? They must be. White tie isn't exactly for the discreet.'

Thurza chuckled and began to describe what she was wearing. 'It has no real neck but a lace thingy across the top.' She stood and beckoned. 'Follow me.' And before Viv had the chance to answer they were marching back past Beattie Brown and upstairs to Thurza's bedroom. The dress, wrapped in acid-free paper, was draped over the mahogany four-poster. Thurza whipped off the paper and with no little effort, held the bejewelled spectacle up against her body.

Viv reached out to touch it. 'May I?'

'Sure. Toddy's mother wore this to Elizabeth's coronation.'

There were more pearls and jewels on the fabric than you'd find in Garrard's. 'My God, T, it must weigh a ton. How could she stand up?' Toddy's mother, the old countess, must have shrunk in her last years, because this bit of kit had been made for a sturdy frame.

'Oh, she wasn't always frail Viv. Even when I first knew her she could out run me on the tennis court.'

Viv caught Thurza's slightly defensive tone, and, ever keen not to get caught up in family politics, concentrated on the dress. Its heavy, pale golden silk was barely visible beneath rows of gleaming stones following the cut of the fabric. 'Okay. I've got the measure. The dress is the star of the show tonight, so we'll have your hair up as inconspicuously as possible.'

Thurza carefully laid the dress back on the bed. 'My family in

Pennsylvania wouldn't believe it if I told them where that dress has been. Think of all the titled people that it has encountered. It's quite something, isn't it? Oh, by the way, you won't mention that it's in the house . . . '

Viv shook her head. 'You should know me by now. Besides, I won't need to. It'll be all over the press tomorrow. But by that time I'm guessing it'll be back in the bank.' Viv visualised Jules, her editor, cocking a snook at those she called 'Scotland's Tinea Corpus'. Jules hated 'freeloaders', banishing any news of them, that wasn't damaging, to a left hand page between car sales and sport.

Thurza grinned. 'It comes with an armed guard.'

Viv laughed, but then realised that she was serious. 'No?'

'Yes. Look at this.' She pointed to a particularly large pink stone placed at the centre of the detail on the bodice. 'This diamond was given to Toddy's great grandmother when her husband was the Viceroy of India. It's called the 'Vicereine Stone'. Queen Victoria made a huge fuss about it at the time. She believed it belonged to her because, as Viceroy, he was her 'representative', but the Maharaja insisted it was for the Vicereine. Victoria never forgave them for not gifting it to her and dropped them from favour, like a rock – no pun intended.' She chuckled.

Viv stretched her hand out and gently touched the cool surface of the stone, and wondered why, if the Newhalls had these jewels to sell, did they force their sons across the pond to find wives within the families of American industrialists. 'Come on, let's get your hair started. I take it you washed it before I came?'

Thurza laughed, bringing on her smoker's cough. 'Of course. Do you think I'd be seen by anyone but you looking like this?' She lifted her limp locks and dropped them.

Viv shook her head. 'How many times have I said if there's a chance that you'll want to have it put up to leave it, however grubby it is. Clean hair is the hairdresser's enemy. At least when we're trying to defy gravity.' Viv set to work, first spraying it with water, then cutting a centimetre off the baseline, before graduating the front sections. She'd learned that less really was more when it came to fine hair like this, and without the benefit of her two monthly tint, to swell the cortex, Thurza's hair would have been even more of a challenge. Viv used enough pins and hairspray to survive a hurricane, but knew Thurza well enough that even with her army of helpers, she wouldn't be able to resist meddling in the plans downstairs. Viv imagined the new hairdo rushing between the kitchen and the ballroom, and applied another layer of spray. Pleased to leave a vision more glamorous than she could have believed possible, she didn't envy those left caught up in Thurza's frenetic spin. With a cheque for sixty quid in her hand Viv's parting shot was, 'Don't, whatever you do, go anywhere near a magnet.'

Thurza laughed. 'Wish me luck.'

Down in the main hallway, Roy had been replaced by a group of tall, broadly built men wearing black suits, earpieces, and postures that would put the FBI to shame. They couldn't all be there to look after the dress.

Chapter Two

On the short journey to her next client Viv reflected on how much Thurza reminded her of her own sister: two women with no notion of the traps they'd made for themselves, or the vacuousness of their values. Lynn couldn't be more different from them, but was connected to Thurza by circumstance. Lynn used to live in a cottage with Ben, one of the gamekeepers at Newhall. But after his death she moved to the edge of South Queensferry, a lone parent, whose children went to the local primary school with Thurza's boys. Viv didn't know the details but when Ben died, Lynn left the tied cottage, and moved to a little modern block of flats within walking distance of the village, and with panoramic views over both Forth Bridges.

As soon as Viv buzzed, the door clicked open and Lynn's voice came through the entry phone. 'Come on up.'

Viv took the stairs two at a time to the first floor. 'Hiya. I can never get over that view. It's breathtaking.'

'Glad you think so. I sometimes wonder if I'm mad to be so enthusiastic about bridges.' She beamed and gestured to take Viv's jacket. 'Good to see you, Viv. I'm guessing you've just come from the House.' Lynn nodded in the direction of Newhall. 'Big do on tonight. They haven't had a white tie event for years. It'll be the real deal for Thurza.'

Whatever had happened between Lynn and the estate she remained generous about Thurza. Viv had often wondered about Ben's death but Lynn actively avoided speaking about it, and Viv hadn't asked.

Lynn took Viv's jacket out to a hook in the passage and called over her shoulder. 'Fancy a cuppa?'

Viv replied as she moved a small coffee table to make space for her sheet. 'That'd be great. The possibility of coffee at the House faded in all the excitement.'

'Give me two minutes.'

She really did take two minutes. Viv sipped her coffee and winced. Lynn didn't do 'real' and added two sugars as a matter of course. But Viv smiled, grateful for a little hot sustenance, as she set up in Lynn's tiny living room. Everything was immaculate and matching, a total contrast to the mock confident shambles in Thurza's kitchen. Lynn, out of habit, ran a brush through her reddish brown, slightly frizzy, shoulder length hair before she took a seat.

'The boys are helping with the parking tonight. Thurza rang earlier in the week. She's worried about the events guys not knowing the lie of the land.'

Viv rolled her eyes. She'd spotted pantechnicons as she left, with the same company logo on them as those who do rock concerts at Murrayfield and the Festival fireworks. 'Yeah. I'm sure she has cause to be worried. The blokes she's got only happen to be the best in the business.'

Lynn nodded and smiled. 'You know what she's like. Everything has to be just so.'

This description of Thurza's off the scale, control freakery was typical of Lynn's understatement; her loyalty did her credit.

Lynn rubbed her upper arm. 'I was decorating and pulled a muscle in my shoulder, about three weeks ago, and my hair has been a nightmare. I haven't been able to reach the back properly.'

'I have the very thing . . . ' Viv scrabbled about in her case and pulled out a tiny set of straightening irons.

'It's all right, Viv. I was going to say it's much better now.'

Too late. By the time Viv had finished cutting Lynn's wavy layers, the rods were hot and her hair had almost dried off. 'Watch this.' Viv gave the hair a quick blast with the drier then deftly slid the slim titanium plates down the hair shaft from roots to tips, careful to keep them slightly curved, then released and let the hair cool before taking up another section.

Lynn sat erect and motionless with her feet planted shoulder width apart. 'I thought those things were lethal.'

Viv shook her head. 'God almighty. What next?' She suddenly had a vision, 'Imagine the Scottish countryside becoming a grid system because of boy-racers from . . . Falkirk. Dangerous roads are not dangerous. People who drive dangerously are the hazard. A road is a road is a road, and entirely benign. Ditto, straightening irons. If you leave them lying on the duvet without switching them off, there's a chance that you'll have a hole in your duvet. But that would mean you were at fault, not the irons.' Viv glimpsed Lynn's confusion. 'Not that you would do such a thing. Besides, these come with a stand.' She held up the straighteners and their stand.

Lynn chuckled. 'I'm getting it . . . Let me have a go.' She took the irons and copied Viv: smooth, straight hair in an instant. 'Reeesult! How good is that?'

'If you get it right first time you shouldn't get too much static.' Viv stood back. 'That looks great. I wish I'd thought of these for your hair ages ago.'

'How much are they?'

Lynn was one of the few of Viv customers on a tight budget, or rather that she cared about being on a tight budget.

'Actually, you can take these off my hands. I've been carrying them in this case for months and never used them. I got them free with a couple of Wigos.'

Lynn screwed up her face. 'And Wigos are . . . ?'

'Professional hairdryers.'

She looked doubtful. 'You sure you're not just saying that?'

Viv grinned. 'If you don't want them someone else will.'

'As long as you're sure.'

As Viv started her car and waved back up to a delighted Lynn swinging new silky locks at her first floor window, she grinned and sighed with satisfaction. What was not to like about being able to transform the way people looked and felt? Lynn wore her gratitude for all to see.

Friday night. In her bedroom with its coombed ceilings and views to the Pentland hills, Viv gave her own hair a quick blast with a dryer. She was on her way to see Margo but hadn't yet had the courage to ring Sal back. Viv realised that Sal's tone had been fine; it was her own remorse that made her think otherwise. Even the voice of Walter Sessions had sounded anxious as it floated through her head. Was he anxious or was it just her? Perception was everything. Whatever. Sal had touched something way deep inside Viv. Not a good thing.

Walter Sessions had been Viv's psychotherapist for five years, and apart from a couple of appointments after Dawn had been killed, when Viv couldn't drag herself out of the mire, she hadn't seen him. Dawn Rhodes had been an exceptional classical double bass player with the RSO, and Viv's lover. Their relationship had been turbulent but death had camouflaged the horrors or their last six months together. Distraught she'd returned to Walter.

But why would he ever want to employ her? If she agreed, there'd be a few ethical issues to contend with, although he'd gone more than the contracted mile for Viv on more than one occasion. She recalled his gentle Irish voice, his impeccable professional track record and swithered. Viv was fond of private investigations but preferred when they resulted in news headlines. But for Walter she felt obliged, and more than a tiny bit intrigued.

Walter's message, 'Trouble with an ex patient,' could mean a myriad of things. 'Trouble' was the meat of psychotherapy. After all, if people were treading a steady path to happiness they didn't seek out the likes of Walter. Viv wondered if it could be a transference gone wrong. That was a common issue, but disproportionate emotions were what Walter was used to. He was a pro. She heaved a sigh. No point in speculating. He'd tell her in his own words.

Viv switched the dryer off and tossed it onto an old tartan rug that had belonged to her dad and she now kept at the end of her bed. She groaned, wishing he hadn't called at all, and slipped on a new, pale blue linen shirt, tucked it into her jodhpurs. She pondered the notion that his patient might be in love, and love, as Viv knew to her cost, made us court the demons of madness more than most things. But none of this mattered. Walter must be struggling, otherwise he wouldn't have called.

She cut the price ticket off a light tweed jacket and shrugged into it, pulled down her shirt cuffs while staring at her image in the mirror. Once she'd ruffled her silky dark hair and pinched her cheeks she was ready to go. Walter would have to wait.

Viv pulled up her collar, modest protection against the chill in the air, and trotted up a double flight of stone steps that led from the West Bow onto Edinburgh's medieval High Street. For those in the know the Old Town's endless dark, damp nooks and crannies served as handy short cuts: as well as for clandestine activities. Viv skipped to avoid a paper cup but managed to kick its remains over the spilt contents of a brown paper bag. Its ubiquitous M made Viv smile, thinking how much better off the purchaser was for not finishing it.

She bounded down the Playfair Steps, struck by how often they'd had their name changed. Originally known as The Mound Steps they were, bizarrely, for a short while in the nineteen seventies, named John Knox Way. Their stone was worn by thousands of feet trampling the route to and from Edinburgh's Old Town. Viv jogged across Princes Street, up onto George Street, before beginning the steep descent of Dundas Street, reaching the Dragon Bar in a little more than ten minutes.

Margo was popular, so it would be chock-a-block. Sure enough, when Viv pushed the door she encountered wall-to-wall bodies. As Viv squeezed inside, anonymous women apologised with, 'Sorry, doll!' Her response, 'No problem,' superfluous. She couldn't make up her mind what was worse, the din of unfamiliar music, or the constant jostling by women who had already had too much to drink.

The invitation to Margo's thirtieth had been expected but when it arrived Viv was overwhelmed with work and replied to say she'd try to make it but couldn't promise. She'd received an email straight back pleading with her to go, and sensing Margo's urgency, replied in the affirmative. That morning's call had piqued Viv's interest. So there she was, already hoarse with shouting banalities, embarrassed at dancing to music she didn't know, with women she'd never met and probably never would again. Besides she'd had enough indiscretion for one week.

Viv spotted Lindy, Margo's long-term partner, looking ill at ease. Viv raised her glass above the shoulders of the crowd, and with cider dripping inside her cuff, made her way to where Lindy was self consciously nodding her head to a beat too erratic to be mimicked. They hugged and Viv, in a raised voice, said, 'Hi Lind, how you doing? It didn't cross Margo's mind to have a quiet dinner for a few friends then?'

Lindy shook her head with a gleam in her eye, 'Not a chance.'

'Not aging gracefully yet.' The words may have gone unheard but their sentiment was understood. They'd laughed and Lindy ran her free hand through her dark shoulder length hair, a habit which she repeated so regularly Viv marvelled that it never looked lank.

'She's fine, Viv . . . considering.' Lindy nodded towards the tiny dance floor where Margo was bopping with an unenthusiastic baby lezzie half her age and wearing enough ironmongery on her face to impress a smithy.

Viv laughed, 'She certainly looks happy.'

'Yeah, but you won't wake up to what I will tomorrow. Has she spoken to you yet?'

'Only at a distance to say, "Hi". Nothing earth shattering. I expect she'll get round to it when she's done with Bambi.' Viv nodded toward the dance floor.

They smiled knowingly as the doe-eyed dancing partner looked around, eager to escape. Margo at thirty was probably the oldest woman at the party, but had energy to equal them all. When Viv, Lindy and Margo met through the OTC at university, the couple were already an item as comfy as an old pair of slippers.

The music faded to a slow track and Margo made a deep bow to Bambi who shot off before Margo regained her full height. Viv nudged Lindy as Margo, wearing denims, a white shirt, and outrageous lilac cowboy boots with diamante studs across the front that probably cost more than any outfit there, jostled her way through all her chums to reach them. A corporate lawyer by day, Margo had made partner before she was twenty-eight. A faithful civil unionist by night, she could single-handedly support Edinburgh's pink economy if she had to.

'Hey, Viv. Great to see you.'

'You too, Marg. What was with all that metal work?' Viv gestured to her own face, then continued shouting. 'God, remember at uni when we did that sit-in and chained each other to those railings? I was totally freaked out by the noise the cuffs made when I tried to move.' She shuddered. 'Was worse than chalk scratching down a blackboard. Eeek!' She gritted her teeth and shuddered again emphatically as Margo and Lindy tried to contain their mirth.

Margo, no longer a rebel, with her townhouse in Stockbridge and a cottage by the sea in Aberlady, wore her lefty past very lightly. She gathered Viv up in a tight hug and, after accepting birthday wishes, loudly whispered in her ear, 'Outside.'

She linked arms with Lindy and Viv, guiding them towards the exit. They squeezed along a passage with doors off to the loos, which, like the rest of the basement, were painted midnight blue. Bright halogen lights shaped like stars and recessed into the ceiling illuminated their passage. Viv pushed down the bar of the emergency exit, which took them out onto a flag-stoned area a dozen steps below street level.

They each acknowledged with relief the quiet, cool night air. Viv, like a frog in a well, looked up to the entrance where Debs, the owner of the pub, spotted the trio, broke her conversation with a couple of blokes on their way out, and leaned over the railings. 'Hi, Viv. Where have you been hiding?' Viv had been here a few times with Dawn, but had also done some work for Deb's father, a well-known Edinburgh business man whose hairdressing salons had opened in the days when precision cutting wasn't in vogue, and setting hair in rollers covered a multitude of sins. He'd called Viv up and asked her to bring his staff up to date. Viv had been happy to oblige.

Viv was fond of Debs, whose consistent good humour was a God-sent management asset. She made time for everyone. Her beautiful chubby face, with its clear skin and cherubic smile, helped maintain an atmosphere of fun. Viv had never seen trouble in The Dragon, which may also have had a little to do with Deb's partner Karen, who was as chiselled as Deb was cherubic, and whom Viv avoided at any cost.

Viv took the stairs up to the street and was enveloped in a soft fleshy hug.

'You're looking well, Debs.' Then she stood back to take a proper look at her.

'You're not looking so bad yourself. Business isn't treating me too badly. You've been a stranger though. We're trying to organise a women's quiz night. You're brainy, you could come to that.'

'Sounds like a plan. Nice to see you.' Viv kissed Debs on the cheek and headed back down to Lindy and Margo.

Margo, keeping her voice low, said, 'Thanks a lot for pitching up, Viv. Lindy and I were hoping you'd be able to help us.'

'Well I hope I'm your woman. What's up?'

'That's the problem, Viv. We're not sure. And . . . ' She looked at Lindy. 'In fact we're not sure there is a problem. It's only a gut feeling. We were in the pub upstairs last Sunday, a women-only night, and one of the young ones, who we've seen a couple of times, and Lind has spoken to briefly in the loo, was dragged out by a guy claiming to be her brother.'

Viv raised her eyebrows and shook her head in a gesture that screamed she wouldn't get involved in a family feud.

Lindy cut in. 'Wait, Viv, hear her out.'

'Well the woman, girl really, has a Scottish accent and the chap sounded . . . How can I say this without you jumping down my throat for being racist or whatever? He was definitely not Scottish, spoke . . . sounded like a made-up language. You know the kind of thing you did at school . . . but not a hint of Scottish.'

Viv drew in a breath. 'You getting to the point?'

'Yes. It's the second time in the last couple of weeks that a bloke has turned up at the women's night and taken a girl away.'

Viv scratched her head, 'But "taken away" is different from "dragged out". Which was it? And what's happened to sisterhood, didn't anyone try to stop them?'

'That's the thing. Neither of the girls really made an attempt to resist. Just looked petulant and went without a fight. Lindy stepped in front of the girl last Sunday when she was being led out, but she just brushed Lindy aside. Neither of them has been seen since.'

'And the time frame is only what? A week? Ten days?'

'Yeah . . . But they both came every week and the girl from last week has a girlfriend who is distraught and too scared to tell anyone because . . . '

Viv let go of a deep breath and rubbed her face. 'Oh God. Let me guess. She's not "out"?'

'You got it.'

Viv took another deep breath and slowly let it go. 'And what d'you think I can do?'

They glanced at each other and Margo said, 'No idea. But don't you think it's weird? We'd hate to do nothing if something is going on.'

Viv nodded. 'Yep. Have you seen the girlfriend recently?'

'Yeah, I was just dancing with her.' Margo turned and gestured inside. 'We could go back and see if she's still there.' The three went back in and scanned the cramped dance floor but there was no sign of her there or at the bar. Margo indicated with her thumb that she'd check the loos, but returned shaking her head.

'Look, okay, I'll make a few enquiries. Any chance that you could get me the partner's email? I'm guessing she won't want anyone poking about her home.'

Margo dropped her shoulders. 'I'm sure I can get hold of her email and send it to you. She sings in a group, and a couple of the other members are here.'

Viv's vision of a head-banging racket must have registered on her face because Lindy cut in again, 'It's an *a cappella* group, not what you'd imagine.'

Once Margo had what she wanted from Viv, she was happy to be led back onto the dance floor, leaving Viv and Lindy shaking their heads in amazement. Viv took this as her cue to head home. She drained her glass, hugged Lindy, then made her way through the throng towards the door that led upstairs to another bar in the hope that she'd bump into Bambi. No luck.

Chapter Three

Saturday morning. Viv had a couple of hair clients to see. But before heading out she checked her inbox. She frowned as he read a message from Oppenheimer1, aka the guy with the almond eyes, thanking her for the other night. She wasn't frowning because it hadn't been pleasant, but because it was way too easy to get hold of anyone these days. Viv specifically withheld her contact details.

She rang Walter. 'Hi Walter, I got your message and guess we should meet.'

'Okay.'

'How about we have breakfast tomorrow?'

'Sure, Viv. Where and when?'

'How about the little French bistro in the Grassmarket? At eleven or eleven thirty?'

'Eleven it is.'

Viv stared at the receiver. He'd never been chatty, but this was economical even for him.

She perched on the sill and glanced over to Greyfriars graveyard, her window on the weather. On more than one moonlit night she'd fancied she'd seen grey hooded monks roam those medieval grounds, but by morning she'd realised that drink had influenced her sightings. After the Reformation the land had been gifted to the city by Mary, Queen of Scots, as a burial ground for the souls of her subjects, which prevented it passing into the hands of the ungodly. To use it simply as a gauge for the weather seemed disrespectfully pedestrian.

Viv rubbed both hands over her face and considered ringing Sal, but was easily distracted again by the silver birches bending and swaying along the boundary of the churchyard, a sign that it was a day to wrap up. She showered and dressed quickly then grabbed a slice of toast to eat on her way to the car. Her clients, Louise and her sister Emma, were civil servants who were always vague about the work they did. Consequently Viv guessed they must be in tax. She'd never met anyone who had owned up to working for the Revenue. They both had fabulous thick, dark, glossy Catholic hair and were committed to doing Viv's work justice. She'd suggested new looks for them both many times, but they'd said, 'If it ain't broke, why fix it?'

While she cut their hair they spent a good-natured hour and a half discussing books and chatting, during which she was entertained by their animated descriptions of some attendees at a new evening class they'd signed up for on nineteenth-century literature at Edinburgh University. Viv had once stood in for a tutor who was sick and she'd spent most of her evening fielding comments, never questions, by Edinburgh's worthy intelligensia: she could imagine exactly what the sisters meant. So passionate were they about keeping their little grey cells in good order that they attended a different class each semester, which meant their conversation had a different flavour every time Viv saw them.

Viv had heard, although they'd never said, that they were from a family of devout Apostolic Catholics, devastated by the deconsecration of Mansfield church; a building known more for its frescoes by Phoebe Anna Traquair than for apostolic religion. Viv, out for a run one Sunday morning, spotted the sisters, wearing fine hats, on their way into St Mark's in Market Street – a high Piskie establishment. Religion rarely came up in their conversations. Their hair appointment was always on a Saturday at ten o'clock and followed their pilates class. Afterwards, come rain or shine, they had lunch in one of the city's many museums or gallery cafes. Their home was immaculate, a huge ground floor flat overlooking Bruntsfield Links, full of family heirlooms. Photographs of their father in uniform, and one of a brother in vestments, were proudly displayed. Dust never deconsecrated any of the dark wood surfaces, and yet Viv didn't feel she had to tiptoe round.

Neither had married, and although the subject had come up on a couple of occasions they never showed any sign of regret or of being attracted to women, and they'd never questioned Viv's proclivities. This particular day they were off to the museum in Chamber Street, after its multi-million pound make-over. Viv adored them, and at times envied the steady rhythm of their lives. Had they been born to a previous generation she could have imagined them taking walking trips in the Tyrol wearing stout tweeds with brogues, not knowing what the word 'casual' meant.

Once she'd finished with the sisters Viv drove home, uplifted. She unfolded herself from the car and slipped onto Victoria Street, teeming with Saturday shoppers in search of eccentricities – from whisky to Willow pattern and everything in between. Viv returned the salute of Pierre's chef, who stood at the top of the hill leaning on the door jamb having a roll-up. His black-and-white checkered trousers were hemmed in by a long white apron too tight to flap in the wind; and his grey complexion and tousled hair were a sign of a much-needed break, and a blast of fresh air. The shop next to Pierre's was only open when the rather smelly, bearded, and always kilted owner could be bothered to get out of bed. It was never worth visiting in the mornings, and even in the afternoons there was no guarantee that he'd show up. Boxes brimming with books on makeshift shelves now lined the pavement – the owner had braved the spring noon time, perhaps turned over a new leaf, but more likely run out of cash to purchase more books. He didn't advertise as a rare book dealer but Viv had been in the shop when there'd been serious negotiation going on for a tome that never saw the light above the counter.

As she checked the window of the new tea emporium, her eye was caught by a lithe figure in bright red tartan trews to her left. The shop next door had been empty for weeks. Windowlene smeared across its plate glass frontage had now been cleared, and inside Viv spotted a woman with red braces that matched her lipstick. Dark framed glasses teetering low on the bridge of her nose lent her an air of self-conscious intellectualism. She fiddled with a new display. It took Viv a few minutes to realise that the woman was smiling at her, so, red faced, she pretended to be interested in a piece of pottery in the display. The woman beckoned her in, and Viv looked over her shoulder to check that there wasn't someone else behind before turning the brass handle and entering the shop. An old-fashioned bell tinkled as she pushed the door to. Viv shivered: it was chillier inside than out, and the noxious smell of some poison used to restore old furniture hung in the air.

'Hi, can I interest you in the Clarice Cliff? That is what you were looking at, wasn't it?'

Viv looked around into the display. 'No, actually I was looking at the Susie Cooper plate.'

'Ah, you look like a woman who knows her Susie from her Clarice.'

Viv flushed. The woman began to sing, unashamedly, to an Annie Lennox track playing on a CD, trying but failing to reach the same sort of heights that Annie did without effort. Viv couldn't help smiling as the joy on the woman's not unattractive face conveyed itself. Unwittingly Viv pulled the collar of her jacket close to her neck, and said, 'I have a magpie collection of thirties' tea sets. That plate is one I don't have.'

The woman returned to the window and retrieved the plate before handing it to Viv, who grasped it as if it were the crown jewels.

'It's a good piece. It's getting harder and harder to find things that haven't been chipped. There's a whole generation out there who don't see this stuff as "valuable".' She made inverted commas round the word.

Viv turned the plate over and spotted the unmistakable mark of Susie Cooper. 'I'll take it. And while I'm here I'll look at the Clarice Cliff as well.'

The Cliff salt and pepper set was one that Viv already had, but she couldn't resist. 'Okay, I'll take them both.' This wasn't Viv's normal way of purchasing Deco – she usually took pleasure in haggling. The woman noticed her slight hesitation, 'I'll give you ten per cent off since you're my first customer.'

Viv was about to argue but realised that it was part of the deal. 'Thanks, that's generous. I had no idea I'd be your first customer.'

'Yes. Just brought the stock in this week and had one or two pieces that needed cleaning up.' She pointed to a wooden staircase leading down into a basement. 'Repairs happen down there, in the dungeon. So if you need anything rescued I'm your woman.'

Viv lifted her purchases, now carefully wrapped in tissue paper, and handed over the cash. 'What days will you open? Some of the guys in the street only open at the weekends and then only if it's not raining or . . . '

'No, I'll be here Tuesday to Saturday ten 'til four, Sundays I go to fairs or the Barras to get stock, and won't get in until nearer twelve thirty.' Her pale blue-grey eyes looked directly at Viv. 'Come and have a coffee sometime. I can see myself getting bored during the week and it'd be nice to chat about china . . . Oh, and I promise to have the heater on.'

Viv, although surprised, grinned. 'Yeah, okay.' The tinkle of the bell as she left had a reassuring effect, as if something of her childhood had been recovered. Although desperate to look back she was too nervous, and when she eventually stabbed the key into her stair door she grinned all the way up to her top flat.

The Annie Lennox tune had attached itself to her head like an ear-worm, and she hummed as she unwrapped her new acquisitions. She gently placed them alongside her other prizes on the top half of a Victorian dresser which, although parted from its bottom half, had been screwed to the wall above a bookcase. It had been a while since she'd been enthusiastic for anything other than work, and the flutter in her heart should have been as alarming as the flutter of two nights previously.

Chapter Four

The light blinking on the answering machine gave her a reality check. The first voice belonged to Mac, but the next was her sister's. This immediately punctured Viv's high spirit. As she felt her energy slip she made a conscious effort to recall the open face of the woman in the shop, singing without a care, and wished that she'd asked her name. Lennox suited her, despite the fact that she was nowhere near those top notes: at least she gave them her best shot. Viv grinned again and her belly gently contracted at the idea of finding an excuse to have that coffee. Then she warned herself off. She dialled Mac and left a message. Then before she talked herself out of it she rang her sister.

Manda picked up, 'Did you get my message?' Always keen to state the obvious.

Viv, never known to ring Manda without a prompt, bit the inside of her cheek and raised her eyebrows. 'Yep. Got it. About Mum, is it?'

'Yes.' Manda hissed like the Disney version of Kipling's Kaa.

Viv visualised her sister's eyes spiralling. 'I'm going to Mum's tomorrow . . .'

She was interrupted. 'Not before time. She says you haven't been for weeks.'

'She says the same to me about you. When are you going to get the hang of that? She doesn't remember when either of us, or anyone else for that matter, has been in to see her.'

'You always make her sound worse than she is.'

This was a tired argument and not worth getting involved in again. So Viv buttoned her lip. Manda wanted their mum to be more able, and to improve. Viv had done her homework and knew that was never going to happen, as much as she'd love to think there might be a cure round the corner. She reflected that her mum was happier now than she'd ever been.

'Well, there's never any evidence that you've visited.'

Viv lost it. 'What! Because I don't leave garage flowers, or cheap boxes of chocolate brazils? Even you must notice she's had her hair cut!'

Manda stuttered. 'Dot said that they'd had a hairdresser in to do their hair and nails.'

'You think what you like, Mand. I'm doing my bit whatever you care to imagine. Now I've got work to do.'

True to form there was an explosion. 'What? You think I'm sitting here on my . . .'

Viv interrupted. 'We've been here before, Mand. Speak later.'

Manda slammed the receiver down.

'Phew!'

Viv banged her knee against the desk and woke up the laptop. There were a couple of unread emails. The first from Margo, with the email address of Bambi from last night; the other from a client about a future appointment. Viv flicked through her diary and sent a quick reply giving options for dates. Sitting down she drew in the chair and began to scribble a few questions on a pad before rephrasing them in an email to Beccs1 alias Bambi.

What Viv needed to know was who had gone missing; where and when she was last seen; and if there could be any explanations to account for her not being around. Viv had worked on missing people before and, once recently a pissed-off teenager had gone on a 'trip' because he'd fallen out with his father. He was gone for four days before he decided that home comforts weren't so bad after all. Viv wanted to cover as many bases as she could before getting anyone else involved. With the email winging its way she checked the Dragon's web pages. Viv grimaced. Their photographs, advertising the 'women only' nights, could attract more than the odd lusty lesbian.

She took a note of the contact details, and switched her laptop off and then on again, cursing that she hadn't checked the Lothian and Borders missing persons website. The idea of two young women going missing and their families not reporting it was pretty unlikely. Until she had names for them her enquiries were a waste of time, but she wondered if the dates that Margo mentioned might match any girl on the site. There were far more missing people than she had imagined – that'd keep L&B busy.

As she scrolled through endless grainy photographs of men and women who hadn't turned up at places where they should have, she could feel herself being drawn to look for all of them. How many lives would be in limbo because their mother, father, brother, sister, son, daughter, friend, partner or colleague had not been found? Some of them mustn't want to be found, but still.

Dawn had had a habit of arranging to meet Viv then not showing up. The first couple of times it happened Viv had been anxious, but she soon got the hang of Dawn's unreliability. It was sad that some of the faces smiling back at her might no longer be around. Mostly when you're being photographed you're trying to look your best. Viv's eye was caught by one young girl, but only because of her piercings. The date that she went missing didn't tally with dates Margo had given her. Viv berated herself for stereotyping, until she spotted a stunning young woman whose eyes and smile jumped off the screen. Her dates did add up. The information stated that she was a student who had gone missing from a city centre pub in Edinburgh, no mention of which one, or what kind of pub. Viv decided to give the 'confidential line' a call. 'Hello, I was wondering if any more information had come up for Gwyneth Stott.'

After a few clicks, and much sighing on the other end, the officer replied, 'Not much. A few alleged sightings that we're still following up.'

'How come this hasn't made it to the TV news? It's been ten days since she was reported missing.'

'Family.'

'Family what?'

'They're frightened.'

'But surely they want to do everything they can to find her.'

The officer sighed again. 'Yes, they do. But they don't want a media circus.'

'Are they famous or fabulously wealthy?'

'I couldn't say.'

Viv shook her head and with more than a touch of sarcasm said, 'No. I suppose not.' Then, echoing his sigh, she ended the call.

She Googled Gwyneth Stott. One hit on Facebook but not the one she was looking for. Unusual. She tried Gwyn Stott and found a photograph of the smiley, bright-eyed young woman. No postings for ten days. Not good in times of social network addiction. She checked her own email for a reply from Beccs1 but there was nothing.

Time to eat. The fridge offered up a small bowl of elderly mashed potato hiding beneath a layer of cling film, and a tin of tuna. Within ten minutes Viv was sitting cross-legged on the couch tucking into a poor rendition of fishcakes with a dollop of organic tomato ketchup – better than starving. She pressed the remote and the TV flickered into life. She surfed until she found a Scottish news update. Politics, politics and more politics. There couldn't be much happening in the world. On the 'breaking news' at the bottom of the screen she read that the body of a young woman had been recovered from the Union canal outside Edinburgh. No name – too early for details. Mac might know.

She dialled his number and he answered with distinctive sounds of a pub in the background. 'Hi, it's Viv. Where are you? Or rather, can you talk?'

'Talk to you any time, honey . . . I'm in the pub. After match post mortem.'

Viv looked at her receiver. He must have had a beer or two, or be putting on an act for the benefit of his mates. He'd never call her 'honey'. Mac occasionally played for the police football team – and she remembered it was one of his training nights. 'Look, I'll call you later.'

'Sure. Sure.' The line went dead. It wasn't like him to cut her off either. Maybe he was drunk. She flicked through the channels again, and catching sight of an episode of *QI*, stood for a second before quickly switching off. Too more-ish and she had to work. Just as she was getting things ready for the night ahead her phone rang. It was Mac with traffic noise in the background.

'Hi, Viv. Sorry about that. I'm actually working on something, so had to act like a dork to keep my cover. What are you after?'

'No. No. It was just that I saw something on the news about a body found in the Union canal. I guess you won't have heard about it yet?'

'No. I haven't been in the office. I actually had to play today.' There was suddenly more shouting and high jinks in the background and Mac, again using a cocky tone said, 'Listen, I can't speak now. I'll ring you later.'

'No, don't. I'll ring you.' But he'd already cut the call.

Viv wondered what he could be working on if it involved being forced to go to the after match booze–up. Internal trouble? Interesting. A reply from Beccs1 entered her in-box. Viv read a long, rambling, fearful account of the night of the 'abduction'. The girlfriend's name was Tessa Grant and Beccs1 didn't know if Tess's parents knew that she'd gone missing. It was term time and Tess, a geology student, was meant to be doing 'fieldwork on Arran' but had skipped it, so they wouldn't be expecting her to be in contact. Beccs1 hadn't heard anything since the night at the Dragon and was terrified for her girlfriend's safety but only marginally more so than that people could discover that she was having a relationship with a woman.

Viv, astonished at this still being the case in the twenty-first century, shouted at the screen, 'For Christ sake! She could be . . .' All manner of hateful things floated through Viv's mind so she fired an email back asking if they could meet. 'Yes,' came the reply. Relieved, Viv sent another email suggesting a time and place. The coffee shop in Victoria Street just opposite the flat was as good a place as any, and served food until nine pm. It was bound to be busy on a Saturday night because it was a BYOB establishment. They offered her a table at seven thirty but needed it back by eight. She took it. She and Beccs1 could move on if necessary.

She flicked the TV back on. The news channel now had a team at the scene on the canal, and a female reporter yelled a piece to camera above the noise of a generator, which was providing enough light to cover Tynecastle stadium. They didn't have much information other than that the body was of a female in her late teens or early twenties. The reporter didn't look much older than that herself as she swiped at a strand of hair that had blown onto her lipstick. She pointed earnestly at an area on the canal as if the body was still there, but it wasn't. The site looked grisly nonetheless. Brambles along the water's edge entangled all sorts of rubbish, making the water inaccessible. The black undergrowth was dotted with polystyrene cartons, and plastic bottles bobbed benignly on the water's surface. Viv shook her head at the sight of an incident tent. A total waste of time given that the tow path was a well-trodden dog walker's, jogger's and cyclist's route from the west into the centre of Edinburgh. It would take months to eliminate that many tread-marks.

Viv recognised the area as near the site of the old paintball club that used to be on Slateford Road, and wondered about taking a look. It was hard for a reporter or police constable to give nothing away if she was actually at the scene.

With a quick glance at the clock she decided, if she got going, she could get there and be back in time to see Bambi. She grabbed her rucksack, mobile, keys and a warm jacket, locked up and took the stairs at her usual pace.

The car was parked at the west end of the Grassmarket and she had to dodge and duck to avoid high-spirited Saturday night revellers. It took ten minutes to reach the new flats that had replaced the paintball centre, and another four or five to jog back along the towpath to where the police and bright lights were. The young female reporter hovered beside a redundant cameraman, stamping her feet and drawing on a cigarette as if it was life support. Viv felt a pang of pity that they had so much hanging around to do – couldn't afford to let the opposition get more than they did. The incident tent and blue taped cordon of a suspicious death were a magnet for the nosey parkers, of whom she was one among many. There were a million places that a girl could commit suicide. The Union canal wouldn't have been Viv's first choice.

Viv, with notebook in hand, sidled up to the reporter and smiled, 'Bet you've got better things to do on a Saturday night.' The woman looked at Viv with such disdain that Viv checked back over her shoulder. Viv knew a couple of reporters who belonged to Edinburgh's TV elite, and said, 'This is the kind of thing they usually give Gavin, he's always moaning about folk dying and inconveniencing him when he's planned a night in the boozer.' The reporter thawed slightly but Viv realised she had a long way to go if she was going to get anything useful from her.

Then she spotted a police constable she'd met when working on a case with DI Sandra Nicholson, known to Viv as Red because of her long curly red hair. She couldn't remember the guy's name but approached him with stealth over the muddy path, 'Hi, mate, Sandra's not covering this, is she?'

Recognition slowly crossed his face, 'Oh, aye, she is. She's just gone to get . . .' he looked around him, ' actually, to have a pee and find a fish supper.'

Viv smiled, 'A girl's got to . . . eat.'

She watched the reporter's interest grow as she chatted to the PC.

The PC clapped his hands against his upper arms to keep warm, 'Aye, she can fairly pack it away. I think she's got hollow legs.' He laughed, warming to his own humour.

Just as Viv was about to ask him what was happening she heard a familiar voice shout, 'Doc!' She turned to see Red on the other side of the canal, with a handful of Scottish nutrition wrapped in brown paper.

Through a mouthful, Red shouted again, 'Wait there!' And Viv watched as the tall athletic figure, dressed head to toe in black, jogged along the other side of the canal and over a pedestrian bridge. The reporter, now beside herself, smiled at Viv as if she was her best pal. Red offered Viv a chip, took out a brown paper wrapping and handed it to the PC. He beamed, opening it and finding a chip roll.

In her lispy voice Red said, 'Well, Doc, I didn't expect to see you here. You telling me you've got nothing in the diary on a Saturday night? They're usually clambering over each other to get to you.' She winked and punched Viv playfully on the shoulder.

'As it happens I do have something else to do but I thought I'd check this one out. What's the scoop?'

'Been watchin' too much American TV if you think all you have to do is ask the officer in charge and she'll give you tomorrow's headlines.'

'Come on, Red. It's already been out to four million viewers. It's not like an exclusive, and besides I'm not after a story.'

'Aye, sure, Doc . . . but to be honest' – these last words alerted Viv to the flannel that was bound to come next – 'we don't know anything until the post mortem report comes back. The only thing I can say is that she wasn't in the water for long. And she's definitely had a bang on the head. With what I've no idea. That do you?'

'Meagre pickings, Red, but better than nothing. If I told you that I've got a tickle on a missing person, although she's not been reported, what would you say?'

Red screwed up her eyes. 'I'd say . . . ' With a well licked finger she pointed at Viv then to herself, 'We need to have a proper talk. Here or back at HQ?'

'I've got to be somewhere at seven thirty but if I get that wrapped up quickly I'll give you a ring.'

'You'll give me a ring anyway, Doc. Otherwise you might be withholding information in a murder enquiry.'

Viv turned to walk away, 'I'll ring you, Red. No worries. And by the way, go easy on the "Doc" malarkey?'

Red narrowed her large green eyes. 'You know what I know about you, Doc?'

Viv stopped. 'No, surprise me.'

'I know that you were top of your forensic psych class two years on the trot.'

Viv grinned. 'Don't you go believing all the stories you hear.'

'Good source, Doc.' She tapped the side of her slender freckled nose.

Viv laughed. 'And your point is?' She held out her hands.

The reporter was eyeing their encounter with interest.

It was Red's turn to grin. 'No point, just sayin'.'

Viv shook her head and threw a shrug in the direction of the reporter as she retraced her steps along the towpath.

'Shit.' The car was blocked in. She tooted her horn and blasphemed until a beer belly attached to short legs and a thick neck waddled out and yelled, 'Hud yer horses, missus. I'm no deif.'

Viv, knowing it was best to say nothing, couldn't stop herself, 'But not as sharp as you could be.'

'What wis that?'

She started up the engine, and he decided she wasn't worth pursuing but indicated with his middle finger what he thought of her. It was a long shot that the woman they'd dragged from the canal was the woman from the Dragon, but better pursuing a long shot than nothing at all.

Chapter Five

Viv whipped into a parking space at the Castle end of the Grassmarket and jogged back towards the West Bow – this time sticking to the cobbled road and avoiding the high jinks of crowds of drunks staggering along the pavement. As she passed Mo's she read a billboard with a glitzy news headline that reminded her of Thurza. She smiled, wondering how the event had gone.

When she reached the café she saw its once shabby chic appeal had become simply shabby, although the smell of coffee was still impressive. There was no sign of Bambi. The waitress recognised Viv and smiled apologetically before offering her a grubby laminated menu and a table for two that hadn't been cleared, by a window streaming with condensation. Viv shrugged out of her jacket and slipped it over the back of her unsteady wooden seat, then ordered an espresso. While she waited, she checked her phone for messages. If she'd been sensible she'd have given Bambi her number. With only fifteen minutes left before she had to relinquish the table, the door opened, and bashed against the chair occupied by a grumpy red-bearded bloke whose tut-tutting was clearly audible. The girl, rosy faced and flustered, moved directly towards Viv, all the while checking behind her.

Her first words were, 'I'm sure someone is following me.' She unwrapped her scarf and laid it on top of the food remains still lying on the table.

Viv wondered how the girl knew who she was. Bambi took out a huge, dark blue, spotted handkerchief and blew her nose. Viv winced, imagining the pain with so many studs to negotiate. The girl didn't seem to notice and stuffed the hanky back into the pocket of her oversized cargo pants. She didn't remove her equally oversized leather biker's jacket but scraped the chair opposite Viv out from beneath the table.

Viv stretched out her hand, 'Hi, I'm Viv.'

The girl, taken aback, returned a tentative shake, and in a surprisingly cultivated Edinburgh accent replied, 'I'm Rebecca. Rebecca Younger. Everyone calls me Beccs, apart from my family that is.'

'Would you like a coffee or tea or something?' Viv asked as she beckoned the waitress, who looked as anxious to serve them as Viv was to be served.

'Camomile tea, if you have it.'

The waitress waited, 'Is that everything?'

Viv and Rebecca both nodded and in unison replied. 'Yes, thanks.'

Viv glanced towards the door and back to Rebecca, 'Now why would someone be following you?'

'Oh I don't know, but since Tess went . . . was taken, I've been on edge all the time. It's probably my over active imagination.' She shrugged her slim shoulders, causing the leather jacket to move up like a tortoise's shell. 'Margo said I could trust you. That you'll do everything to find Tess.'

Viv held up her hand. 'Wait. Margo is hoping that we will find her unscathed, and the longer she's . . . at large the less likely that is. I'm sure you were hoping that the police wouldn't have to be involved, but just think how unrealistic that is. She's made no contact for . . . how long has it been?'

The girl blinked and dropped her head as silent tears began spilling down her face. She rubbed her hands up and down her cheeks while Viv barely contained her desire to scream, 'Be careful!'

When Rebecca raised her head and met Viv's eyes, she said, 'My dad's a politician.'

Viv nodded, recalling one politician called Younger. 'And he doesn't know about your sexual preferences?'

'No. He doesn't. But actually, I don't care now, we've got to find Tess.'

Viv nodded, guessing that Rebecca cared a whole lot about both Tess, and whether her family found out. 'I didn't say it was impossible but a week is a long time, unless she's with friends or something.' She tailed off. Then, realising how feeble she sounded, Viv continued in a low voice, 'I think we'll find it's the "or something".'

The tea arrived in a chunky hand-thrown pottery mug and Viv begged a top-up for her coffee. She started again. 'Okay. Take me through the days before Tess went missing. Was she behaving normally? Did she mention any odd phone calls or emails? Anything that was out of the ordinary?'

'You'd have to know Tess. There's not much that's ordinary about her. She's not a wild child exactly, but she rarely does anything by the book. Hates authority, but that's nothing unusual for a student. Not that keen on men obviously. Didn't talk much about her home life. I always get the sense that there's something she's not telling. But that could be because I'm doing psychology and think everyone has cupboards full of skeletons.'

Viv was tempted to say, 'Projection or what?' but held her tongue.

Rebecca continued, 'She's amazingly bright, got firsts in everything. She speaks a couple of languages, although geology is her passion. Her family live in Aberdeenshire: her dad's in oil and her mum's a teacher. I've only ever met them once and obviously I was just Tess's "friend".'

'Why "obviously"? Don't you think they'd find it odd not to meet Tess's flatmates? I mean to emphasize that you were friends would surely have been overstating the obvious.'

'Suppose.' She looked unconvinced. 'I've not heard good things about her brother, though I can't imagine it would have been him that she left the pub with. It all happened really quickly. She can't stand him and she'd never have gone quietly if it had been him. I'd gone to the loo, got chatting to someone, and when I came back she was gone. I ran out onto the street but couldn't see anything. The flat was empty when I got back. Two friends came with me and tried to calm me down but I was mad at myself for leaving her for so long.'

'But you couldn't have known this was going to happen.' Viv caught an odd look crossing her face, 'Could you?'

Silence. Rebecca shook her head and her big doe eyes filled up again.

Viv noticed the waitress getting fidgety. 'Look, drink up. We'll have to give up the table.'

The girl looked confused.

'They only had a table free for half an hour. We can go across to the pub and find a seat there.'

The Bow Bar was packed with people who love real ale and finding a seat wasn't easy, but a couple of stools at the back had coats on them and Viv asked if it was okay to shift them. It was, and they perched at the edge of a beer soaked table, staring into a sea of groins belonging to punters whose chatter was so loud, at times raucous, that Viv couldn't hear herself think. She began to shout a question but shook her head and gestured towards the door with her thumb. Without ordering a drink, they made their way back through the throng and out into the cold night air. Viv looked up and down Victoria Street for inspiration. 'Everywhere will be busy.' The idea of taking Rebecca upstairs to the flat did cross her mind but only briefly before she suggested, 'How about I just work with what you've given me?'

'But I thought I could help.'

'You have. By the way, I know this is self-evident but have you tried her mobile?'

'I've left so many messages that Orange say she has to delete some before they'll accept any more.'

'Can you give me the number?'

A slight hesitation before Rebecca reached into a deep side pocket in her trouser leg, pulled out her phone and searched. She read the number and Viv keyed it into her own phone. It struck Viv that with a bit of effort she could find the location of the last use of the phone, but all she said was, 'You've given me enough of Tess's details to make a start. Leave it with me. I'll keep you posted if I find anything, and you do the same.'

Rebecca looked doubtful but nodded her agreement. 'Right. See you.'

Viv watched as the hunched-up figure walked across the road and disappeared up the stone steps that led to the Upper Bow and the High Street. There was no sign of anyone following her but some instinct made Viv go after her. As Rebecca reached Milne's Court, on the other side of the High Street, she stopped, took out her phone and spoke to someone for a minute or so, her body language in complete contrast to five minutes before when she was with Viv. Fascinated at the change, Viv hovered in a shop doorway until Rebecca continued on her way through the close towards the top of the Playfair steps. Leading to Princes Street.

Chapter Six

Viv let herself into the flat, closed the door and leant on it, feeling uneasy about 'Beccs' and wondering where to start her enquiry. The university website was her first port of call. She typed in Tessa Grant. Only one thing came up. She had won the first year geology prize. Viv cursed then emailed Beccs. She hadn't got a photograph of Tess and there was biff all she could do without one. She checked her mobile and listened to a message from Mac. 'I said I'd ring you, but I'm now going to be busy for the rest of the night. I'll try you in the morning.'

She flicked the TV on and scanned for local news. Nothing could compete with 'Strictly' unless the world was ending, and even then Viv imagined the news channel being interrupted with updates about competitors. She found the BBC's Scottish news website running the same piece on the canal, but no update.

She rang Red. 'Hi Red, you still want to meet? I could do with picking your brain.'

'Sure, Doc. Like there's anything in my brain that's worth picking.'

'I didn't say I was looking for superior info.'

They both laughed. Red was a DI who'd been fast-tracked for good reason but even so Viv's qualifications were always a source of wit or wonder and Red was not the only person who just couldn't get the hang of Viv being a hairdresser, with a PhD, who wrote the occasional column. The writing bit should be less problematical than the other two: anyone could be inquisitive.

'What have you got, Doc, that I can use? I'm guessing it must have something to do with that young woman otherwise you wouldn't have shown up at the canal. Am I right?'

'Yep. So how about a coffee or . . . '

'No can do, I'm not coming off shift anytime soon . . . although you could always come to HQ. Great coffee here.'

'Since when?'

'Since we clubbed together for a supersonic Gaggia, that's when.'

This was all the incentive Viv needed. 'Okay, I'll head down now. Alert them at the desk, will you?'

Before she set out she took a quick look at her inbox again. There was a reply from Beccs, sent from her phone, with a photograph attached: a fantastic, clear picture of Rebecca and a girl who must be Tess, mucking about in front of the camera. Beccs, in days before piercings, looked too young to be out alone, with her dark blonde hair, full lips and a twinkle in those huge brown eyes. Tess was a fresh-faced, blue-eyed blonde clinging round Beccs's neck. They were both grinning for, or at, the photographer. Joyful times couldn't have been that long ago. Viv copied the photograph to a memory stick and headed back out onto the West Bow.

It took her twenty minutes to drive to Fettes, Edinburgh West's police headquarters. The guy at the desk asked her to sign in and handed her a visitor's card on a ribbon, which she slipped over her head. Viv hovered while he rang Red. Apart from new carpets and a lick of paint, the place hadn't changed all that much since her dad had brought her here as a child. Two minutes later a door on the far right of the foyer opened and Red sauntered towards Viv, pointing to some new comfy chairs set on either side of a low table by the window. They were almost equal in height although Red was broader and seemed to take up a disproportionate amount of space on her seat.

'What about my coffee?'

Red, in a hushed tone, said, 'You'll get it in a minute. Sal's in the incident room at the moment so I can't sneak you through until she's gone.'

Viv's panic began to rise. Sal wasn't supposed to be back for the weekend.

She was in no position to explain to Sal her lack of communication. But she heard herself stutter, 'Why would she object?'

Red snorted. 'What, as to the small matter of me bringing a hack into the hub of an unsolved case?' She tapped her chin. 'Now, let me see.'

Viv ran her hands over her face and through her hair, and winced at the memory of Rebecca doing a similar thing earlier. A look of distaste must have registered on her face because Red looked questioningly at her, 'What's with the face?'

'Oh nothing . . . but listen, I have a problem. Friends have asked me to look for a missing person. Which in itself wouldn't cause me a dilemma. I'd just go about my unscrupulous digging and expose whatever I find, but the girlfriend of the missing girl is the daughter of a politician, and she's terrified of being outed. Now, I know that when I start snooping there's bound to be all sorts of stuff that surfaces, but will I be able to use it? No is the answer because my good friend Margo has sworn me to secrecy.'

'So, why bother, Viv? You could just give me the details and we'll take a look.'

This was exactly what Viv was hoping for and she grinned at Red. 'Would you do that for me?'

'Oi! Stop taking the piss or I'll retract my offer. What have you got so far?'

'Not much. Two women allegedly missing. Each one from a different night at the Dragon. The first I know nothing about, but the second, more recent, is known to these friends of mine and they're worried about her. She's a geology student at Edinburgh University called Tessa Grant, apparently from Aberdeen. Her dad works in oil and her mum is a teacher. Tess lives in a flat with three other females, all students, one of them her girlfriend – Rebecca Younger.' Viv raised her eyebrows.

Red grinned. 'Don't tell me, daughter of Malcolm Younger MP?'

'You got it. And he doesn't know that his daughter is . . . '

'Gay. God, Viv. It's unbelievable how many youngsters are too scared of their parents to tell them who they are. Anyway, we've got the young woman from the canal, who doesn't seem to have been reported missing, and all we have is a tiny floral tattoo and some old scar tissue where she was bludgeoned, so far, to identify her. She's in her early twenties, twenty-five at most. Stomach contents show no sign of alcohol, only white bread and processed cheese. But listen, your girl has now been reported, if not officially, at least to you.'

Viv wondered what the chances were of getting to see a photograph of the girl from the canal, and as if Red had read her mind she said, 'I'll let you have a peek when Sal goes.' Then suddenly, 'No, wait.' She took out her phone, 'I forgot I had these emailed to me so you can have a quick look here.' She scrolled through her emails then handed Viv her phone. The poor girl in the photograph, although barely identifiable, had reddish pink hair and so wasn't Tess. Red noted the relief on Viv's face. 'It ain't your girl then?'

'No. No, it's not her. But what a mess. That can't be death by natural causes.'

'We think not but it'll be a long haul to find out who she is and why this happened to her. Suzanne McDermid is the pathologist. She's thorough and won't be rushed, so I'm not expecting anything on paper anytime soon.'

Viv hadn't met McDermid, but had covered work that she'd been involved in. She'd heard detectives call her a ball-breaker, which usually meant she was intimidatingly good at her job.

Viv took out her memory stick and held it up. 'Anywhere I can show you a picture on this?'

Red nibbled on her lip for a moment, then said, 'Through here.' She put her security card up against a pad and the door released. They walked along a wide, brightly lit corridor with carpet on the floor. It smelled like any other office. If criminals had access here the floors would be tiled and the walls painted institutional grey: the colour which least excites the excitable. Viv smiled at the notion of some bloke off his face on some unmentionable chemical cocktail being influenced by some bureaucrat's choice of paint.

They entered a room with windows almost floor to ceiling along one wall, overlooking the car park. Red sat, and rode a chair on casters across the room to a desk that already had a chair beside it. 'Grab that seat and we'll boot up.' When the image appeared Viv spotted a couple of details in the photograph that she hadn't noticed earlier. She zoomed in a couple of times and confirmed that Tess sported a small tattoo on her upper arm. A floral motif.

Red, screwed-up her eyes, 'Hey, Doc, I know you hate coincidences but that there tattoo is looking a lot like the one on the princess from the canal.'

They looked at one another bemused. Then Viv asked, 'So, what's next? Can we run this picture through your system to see if there are any matches? It would be really useful if my young Tess has had cause to be involved with the law.'

Red scratched her head, loosening a few rich red curls, and drew in a huge breath, releasing it emphatically. 'I'd love to do that, Doc. But I can't unless she's been officially reported missing.'

Viv raised her eyebrows. 'And being a very clever officer you're about to tell me that you know some way round such an inconvenience?'

'No, I'm not. Every single time a computer is switched on, each action is logged and I'm not taking the rap for running a long and expensive programme for . . . '

'The coincidence of two similar tattoos on two girls, one dead and the other . . . who knows where? Come on, Red, you can do it.'

Red fidgeted. Then said, 'Leave it with me. I can't do it at the moment. There are too many people in the incident room.' She copied the photograph of Tess onto her phone and as she did asked, 'How come you're involved in this, Viv, and why didn't Margo Mackintosh just come to us?'

Viv shrugged. 'No idea. I'm just helping out a friend.'

Red shook her head. 'Why do I find that difficult to believe?'

'Margo's a good friend.'

Red was obviously impressed. 'She'd have to be. Hope she's paying you well. Saturday night . . . double time at least.'

Viv shook her own head. 'See you guys on PAYE, you're always trying to screw the last ha'penny out of the system. You should try being self-employed for a while. Whether I get paid or not is none of your concern.'

'Must be love, Doc. Nobody works for nowt.'

Viv laughed. 'Red. I didn't say I was working for nowt or otherwise, so save your breath . . . to cool your porridge.'

'That you offering to make me porridge?'

Viv sniggered again. 'You're a total lost cause. I'll phone you tomorrow for an update.'

Red got to her feet and they wandered back to reception where Red rubbed Viv's shoulder. 'I'll do what I can.'

'Thanks . . . By the way if I die of caffeine deprivation it'll be your fault.'

Red began to reoffer but Viv just waved her hand and walked toward the exit.

As Viv approached her car, a familiar voice shouted, 'Viv!' It was Mac. 'What are you doing here?'

Cautious not to give too much away, 'I was just in to see Sandra . . . '

He looked doubtful.

She stressed. 'I'm here by invitation!'

'Yeah sure, Viv. It's Saturday night.'

She shook her head again. 'What *is* it with you guys, and your obsession with Saturday night? Am I missing some kind of sacred ritual thing or what?'

He turned round and emphatically parted the hair at the back of his head. 'You seeing a zip or buttons or what?'

She conceded, 'Okay. I'm looking for someone and Sandra has a case . . . the girl found in the canal and . . . '

He interrupted, which was unusual for him. 'And you thought it might be your girl, and wheedled a way in to sweet talk DI Nicholson into sharing confidential information with you.'

'It wasn't like that.'

'Sure.' He gestured with his head for her to go back inside. Viv hesitated, weighing up the possibilities, but decided co-operation was best. He held the door and she brushed against him as they tucked themselves into the space between the sitting area and the door. Gone were the days when he'd have been reeking of smoke after a pint in the pub; now a fresh lemony smell hung in the air between them, which reminded her he'd had a post match shower.

'How was your game?'

Mac wasn't daft and didn't bite, but grinned and raised one eyebrow. 'Fine, thanks. Want to fill me in on your missing person?'

Viv identified the command veiled as a question, and conceded. 'I've told Sandra everything that I know.' This was a white lie, but since her enquiries were all supposed to be unofficial, she didn't want to give everything away too soon. There was always a chance that it would all turn out to be a big mistake. Tess could have taken herself off somewhere for a break. But unconvinced by her own rhetoric she said, 'Okay, here's what I've got: a women-only night at the Dragon, a young woman escorted outside by a bloke, possibly her brother, and hasn't been seen since. Friends of mine are worried and asked me to help. When I heard the piece about the girl turning up in the canal, naturally I thought it worth a look and discovered Red.' Seeing his confusion she continued. 'DI Nicholson was heading the case. She hasn't told me anything about it, but at least I know that the body from the canal is not the girl I'm looking for. Is that okay for you?'

'No, it is not. Why hasn't she been reported missing?'

Viv ruffled her fringe. 'I don't know. She's a student at Edinburgh. It's the middle of term. Her parents may not even know that she's not around. I didn't ever contact my mum from one week's end to the next, so that's nothing unusual.'

Mac nodded. 'But if someone's worried, then the circumstances must have been odd. Who wants you to look at this?'

Viv nibbled the inside of her cheek. 'Margo Mackintosh.' This had exactly the effect that she guessed it would and he nodded with his head on the side.

'Well with a legal nose like hers twitching there's more than an outside chance that something dodgy happened. Describe to me exactly what Ms Mackintosh saw.'

Viv went over what she'd been told by Margo, Lindy and Rebecca. Mac's only response was, 'So much for feminism.'

Viv snorted. 'Oh, don't be fooled into thinking that lesbianism has anything to do with feminism. Lesbians can be as misogynistic as the next bloke. It's a sad fact that some are much worse. My friend Lindy did try to stop the guy from taking her but the girl didn't want help. This makes me think that she must have known him and had some kind of relationship with him. Margo and Lindy said that he spoke with an accent that wasn't Scottish. How they could tell this with the racket in there is anyone's guess. The girl's parents live in Aberdeen but no one has mentioned that she speaks with an Aberdeenshire accent, although they did say Scottish, definitely Scottish.' It crossed Viv's mind that perhaps the 'foreign accent' was the Doric, an easy mistake for a lowlander to make.

Mac was a good listener and when he was sure she'd finished he said, 'If you can get a photograph of her, we'll run it through the system.'

Viv smiled, and he nodded knowingly. 'I see. That's already been done?'

'Not quite. But Red says she'll do it if she gets a chance.'

He ran his hands through his hair. 'You never get bored doing this kind of stuff?'

'You forget, I've got other strings to my bow, which means I never get bored.' She stood to leave. 'Besides, boredom is an activity of anticipation.' She watched as he ran this round his head.

'Not bad for this time . . .' and in unison, 'on a Saturday night.'

They laughed and she asked, 'Can I go now? I've got work to do.'

He eyeballed her. 'Sure . . . We must get a coffee sometime.'

She smiled back over her shoulder as she headed out the door. Viv and Mac almost had a history. He said that she blew it, but she said it was his call. Whoever it was, it never got further than the starting blocks. But there was no animosity between them, and Viv had become as useful to him as he was to her.

Chapter Seven

Once back in the flat Viv wrote a to-do list then got to work online. She emailed Rebecca to ask for any information she could get her hands on about Tess's family, photographs, address, also any details on the other two flatmates. The more information she gathered about everyone involved the better, and she soon found herself engrossed in web pages about a man she believed was Tess's dad. This was probably not her most practical use of time because she got hooked on reports of a battle he'd been involved in to do with the size of pipes used in the North Sea – not information that was likely to find his daughter. Nonetheless, the news reports went on and on about his company, who produced and supplied the original pipes, and another company who were trying to muscle in with a new product, which was different and cheaper. Inevitably there was tuppenceworth thrown into the mix by an MP who only marginally managed to veil threats of cutting government funding.

Slowly she scrolled through the newspaper articles on Andrew Grant, a marine engineer for Off-Carne, a company based in Stonehaven, which reminded her of a journey she had taken through the Mearns and Aberdeenshire to visit Dunnottar Castle, with Katherine, a nurse who'd turned out to be more unhinged that even Viv could have coped with. Aberdeenshire wasn't short on castles, but Dunnottar had the most spectacular setting ever. Maybe she'd use this enquiry as an excuse to revisit.

Eventually she came across an odd article – a report by an Andrew Grant who, it seemed, was the treasurer for some church group called 'The Eastern Brethren'. Viv had never heard of them and did a separate search on them to find out more. It turned out that they were founded in 1915 in Pennsylvania. 'What's it doing in Aberdeenshire?' She went back to the report. It seemed as though there was in-fighting to do with missing funds and Andrew Grant had resigned. The article was dated four years ago. There are more than a few Andrew Grants in Aberdeenshire so she'd have to wait for a photograph to compare with those fuzzy images she'd seen online.

Her email pinged and she read what Beccs had written in her reply. 'I think it might be better if you come here and take a look. I don't feel good about going through her things.'

Viv checked the clock, ten thirty, and decided that now was as good a time as any to check it out. Within half an hour she was ringing the buzzer of a flat in Broughton Place. Beccs answered with, 'Top floor.' Viv checked out the lists of names on all the doors – a student ghetto or just big families? She knew where she'd put her money. Beccs was waiting on the landing and showed her into a long wide hallway where their footsteps echoed on broad wooden boards.

Viv breathed in a whiff of healthy vegetarian food that lingered in the air, and swept her eyes round the ornate cornicing. 'Big flat! Which is Tess's room?'

'In here.' Beccs pushed open a door onto a huge room with three tall windows at one end. A king-sized bed with a black and white duvet cover and bright red cushions occupied half of one wall. One side of the bed was crumpled. Mahogany bedside cabinets sat on each side with different alarm clocks on top. Very domestic.

Viv nodded. 'Nice space. You both sleep in here?'

She wandered across to the window, drew back the voile and stared down at the street below. The room remained silent. So she glanced back at Beccs who threw her a filthy look. Viv raised her eyebrows in another question but it also remained unanswered. Viv shook her head. 'I'm not asking for my own sake, Rebecca.'

The smell of French lavender oil edged its way into Viv's consciousness and she spotted an aromatherapy vase with sticks poking out of it sitting on a chest of drawers. Shelves, with books stored alphabetically, stretched along one wall. Hanging above those was a row of geological maps in fine black frames. Clean and tidy for a geology student. Viv had expected rucksacks, boots and endless waterproofs, but everything was clean and neat. She swung open the door of a highly polished mahogany wardrobe. Immaculate.

'Tess always this tidy?' Beccs's body language couldn't have been more defensive. Arms crossed high on her chest. Viv continued. 'I can see why you might be intimidated by this place. Where is her computer?'

Beccs pointed to a door at the far right hand corner of the room. The sort of door that in most Edinburgh flats would lead to nothing more than a press, but when Viv opened it there was a box-room big enough to hold a desk, chair and two filing cabinets, again unusually neat. A laptop sat closed, looking forlorn on a large, Victorian, leather topped desk. If Tess had taken off of her own accord she'd surely have taken her laptop.

'Beccs, it might be worth me taking a look at her correspondence. Emails, letters, anything that's lying around.'

It was all too tidy, which in itself said plenty. 'How about you go and make us some herbal tea and I'll get to work.' Viv was not prepared to have Beccs drawing in breath with every file she opened. Beccs hesitated but went. The laptop hadn't been switched off, and leapt into life when Viv lifted the lid. She knew a few tricks where accessing material was concerned, but she didn't have to try because Tess's email account had been left open. There were dozens that had been unopened. Viv drew in her breath and released it really slowly – this could take a while. She removed her jacket and set to work. Beccs arrived with a steaming mug but didn't ask anything and retreated to another room. Viv, relieved by this, carried on methodically until she remembered the tea. She stretched and sat back and distractedly reached out for the mug.

The flat was warm and homely. The desk, although tidy, had trinkets. One unusual piece of kit with multi-coloured feathers dangling from it looked like a wire mesh upside down cloche cap. Viv guessed it was some kind of new-agey dream catcher. A Zen garden set with miniature implements, rocks and sand, sat at the back edge of the desk. Viv's hand hovered over the tiny rake but she resisted temptation. She gently ran her fingers over the surface of a note pad: no indentations to speak of, but she rummaged about inside the top drawer and found a long wooden box with an oriental motif carved into the top. She slid the top along and exposed pens and pencils. 'Good girl, Tess.' she whispered. Then with a sheet of A4 she rubbed the top of the pad. Viv grinned as a significant part of a number became visible. She folded the A4, stuck it in her pocket, and continued checking inside the desk drawers. They were all in order: the girl's correspondence was filed alphabetically. Under 'Personal' she found letters to Tessa Grant at an Aberdeenshire address, which had been scored through and replaced by the Broughton Place address. She glanced through three or four with the same writing then found one in a different hand, 'not known at this address' written. This had also been scored out and the Edinburgh address scribbled in. Odd.

She wrote down the Aberdeenshire address and turned her attention to the emails. The unanswered messages were not of much interest. Mainly chums seeking meetings and wondering where she was. Those prior to the date of abduction, if this was what it was, were of more interest. Beccs returned and quietly perched on the edge of the desk. 'You've obviously done this kind of thing before?'

Without lifting her head Viv replied, 'Yeah. More times than I can remember. Human beings are as alike as they are different.'

'That sounds cryptic.'

'Not really. Most of us have patterns. Not so that we'd recognise them, but patterns nonetheless. For instance I can see from the timing of her emails that Tess gets up early – well seven thirty – checks her emails and then there are a few minutes before she answers them. I guess she goes for a shower or makes herself a cup of tea.'

'I don't always feel her getting out of bed, but yeah she does have a habit . . . So do I, come to think of it. I check my emails when she comes in here. I don't get out of bed, though.'

Viv looked up. 'You're doing psychology, aren't you? Did you notice anything different going on in the weeks before she went?' She had been going to say 'missing'. Beccs directed her huge brown eyes towards the ceiling while poking her tongue around her teeth. Viv caught a glimpse of a stud on the middle of her tongue and grimaced. For most of us the tiniest grain of foreign matter in the mouth feels like a boulder, and Viv was sure an immobile lump of metal in her own mouth would make her gag.

Beccs looked back at her. 'We were not getting on too well with one of the flatmates. She and Tess were having a "quiet period".'

'What did that mean? They just weren't speaking, or what?'

'Yeah. They'd agreed to only speak when necessary. Like if there was a phone call or something.'

'But what caused it?'

Beccs shook her head and shrugged. 'Tess was telling us a story about their school days. They were at the same secondary school, and Paula said that Tess had got the story wrong, that the event had been quite different and that Tess was embellishing it to get attention.'

'And did it seem like that to you?'

'Not at the time, but now it does. Tess is funny and it sounded like a funny situation.'

'What was the story?'

'Nothing, really. Just this preacher guy had turned up at the school and they had to sing songs. Tess was doing all the hand actions to the songs and that's when Paula got pissed off. She said it hadn't been like that. But Tess argued that it was. Paula went off in a strop and when I saw them together again they had agreed not to talk about school. But that seemed to spill over into everything.'

'The atmosphere can't have been much fun.'

'We're all doing different courses. Our paths don't cross that often. Paula and Leanne are doing biomedical science and have labs every day. They spend a lot of nights in the library. I do my studying here and Tess tends to work here as well. But listen, you don't think that Tess falling out with Paula could have anything to do with Tess's disappearance?'

'Stranger things have happened. But let's wait to see if anything comes up in her emails.' Viv turned to the laptop and after sorting through more dross about *a cappella* singing and field trips to Arran she spotted a conversation, which took place over twenty-nine emails. The first, sent by 'RTG', said, 'You will return to us. I know you. You can't survive without us.'

Tess's reply was brief. 'You think?'

The response. 'You forget, we are watching you, we can see that you are failing.'

Her reply. 'Good for you. I'd get a life if I were you, Si.'

The reply. 'I have my life in God. You will return to us.'

The article, with the report by her dad, now made more sense. Viv turned to speak to Beccs but she'd gone. 'Rebecca!' Viv found her staring out of the kitchen window with earphones in. Viv tapped her on the shoulder then had to jump free of the elbow, which just missed her solar plexus.

Beccs ripped the earphones out. 'What the fu . . . You gave me the fright of my life!'

This struck Viv as a serious over-reaction, given that she was the only other person in the flat, and here by invitation.

Beccs now said sheepishly, 'Sorry. Sorry, that was over the top. I told you I've been feeling spooked since she was taken.'

'I found a few emails which make me think Tess has been involved in some kind of religious group. You know anything about that?'

Beccs hesitated. 'No, just the school story made me think that maybe her family are religious. She didn't talk about it. In fact, she didn't talk about them much if she could avoid it.'

The kitchen was well equipped and also too tidy. No dirty plates or mugs lying around. A refectory table with eight chairs round it, none of which matched. A wooden carousel with jars of peanut butter and jams on it. Two candlesticks like dragon's heads with multi-coloured candles protruding from their upturned mouths sat neatly and equally spaced on the table. It was not like any student flat that Viv had ever lived in. Even the wooden floor looked clean. A six-burner cooker with a giant shiny hood stood against the wall. The only evidence of its recent use was the smell of Cranks in the air.

'Look. Those emails. You want to check them out?'

Beccs shrugged. 'I'll take a look.'

They returned to Tess's study. Beccs took the chair this time and Viv perched on the desk. It took a good few minutes for Beccs to read them all and when she looked up her eyes were brimming. 'How can this be? Like, how could she not have told me about this? He sounds like a serious nut case.'

'Maybe she's scared to talk about it. Maybe Paula knew about this. Where is Paula?'

'I think they've gone to a potluck supper. She and Leanne were cooking earlier. It looked as if they were going to feed the five thousand.' The irony struck her. 'Sorry. I didn't mean to . . . '

'So that's why this place smells so homely?'

Beccs nodded.

'I know this isn't a polite question, but are Paula and Leanne an item?'

Beccs snorted. 'God, no . . . Paula has sworn to celibacy. But Leanne, I'm not sure. I'd guess that they wouldn't have chosen to live with us if they weren't sympathetic. Neither of them have lovers but . . . ' She stalled and Viv prompted. 'But what?'

Beccs stood and left the room, returning with a collage of photographs showing the four flatmates larking around.

'Who is who?' Although Viv recognised Beccs and Tess they looked nothing like the carefree girls from the earlier photograph that Beccs emailed.

Beccs pointed to a black-haired, pale-skinned girl, who was wearing as much face make-up as Siouxsie wore thirty years ago. 'That's Paula.' Then, pointing to another Goth, said, 'That's Leanne.' She also had dark hair and was well made-up, but at least her eyes were visible. Both girls were heavily built and looked as if they were having a whale of a time. Viv was aware that people didn't put on that kind of anarchist's armour if they were really having fun. The over-tidiness of the flat could be an indication that there was something underlying their joviality.

Viv turned from the photographs and wandered to the kitchen window. It looked out onto a green with lots of pots and wooden carvings. 'Who does the flat belong to?'

Beccs had joined her, and said, 'Tess's dad.'

'Don't suppose I could have a look at the other rooms?'

'No way!'

Viv, getting bored with her lightly lightly approach swung round. 'For fuck sake! You want me to find Tess or not?'

Rebecca, startled, reluctantly pushed open a door onto another huge room and Viv glanced in. A double bed adorned with white damask bed linen convinced her that student standards had definitely leapt up a notch or two. A huge desk sat with an empty space where a laptop should have been.

'Whose room is this?'

'Leanne's.'

'I'm guessing she takes her laptop with her?'

Beccs shrugged and quickly pulled the door closed again. 'Over here.'

Same thing. Beccs pushed open a door onto a room only slightly smaller but still with a double bed and a big desk in it. No laptop there either. Viv couldn't believe how domestic it all looked. It was as if they had someone clean for them. 'You don't have a cleaner, do you?'

Beccs crossed her arms across her chest. 'What if we do? Gives her pocket money.'

Viv felt like swiping her round the head for condescension. But she didn't have to - the look on her face was loud and clear.

'Come.' Beccs beckoned toward the final room. It was neat enough but didn't have the tightly controlled quality that Tess's had.

'Does Tess ever sleep in here?' It was also a large room with windows out to the back, north facing, much darker than Tess's, but still it had a healthy, youthful, restlessness, about it.

'Not any more. When we first moved in she was fine in here. But she gets SAD and needs full light. I know how she feels, and anyway I love her room, although I don't work in there.' Beccs's desk had the usual stuff of study on it: piles of books with coloured tabs stuck to pages of interest, endless sheets of A4 both printed and hand written. Viv smiled at a nodding doll of Freud. 'What do the others think of your Freud?'

'They think I'm a traitor. We're not even taught about Freud. Psychology without Freud – how bad is that? I'm fascinated by his stuff.' She looked at Viv, waiting to see what camp she'd fall into.

In Viv's experience there was no middle ground with Freud. People either loved him or hated him. She had had to justify her own passion for his work many times, and smiled recalling when Jung, accused of anti-Semitism, had fallen from grace, and Freud had made a come back. 'I'm with you on Freud. People are too fond of bashing him up without really knowing his theories. We all make mistakes, but if you're famous that's not allowed. Worth remembering that, if you were thinking about it.'

Beccs gave the slightest smile. 'No thanks, it's bad enough having parents in the public eye.'

Viv had lost sight of this. 'Yeah. I guess that's not much fun. But what's your mum like?' She hadn't heard much about Mrs Malcolm Younger, which was odd given her husband's high media presence.

'Mum's a psychiatrist, Betty Bates. You've probably heard of her.'

Viv had, and tried to disguise her surprise with a cough. She'd never have put Prof. Bates, as Viv knew her, together with Malcolm Younger.

Beccs continued. '"Too busy" is her war cry. She doesn't get involved in his life . . . unless absolutely necessary. I mean she does, but she hates it. She can see it for what it is.' The vehemence in her voice betrayed her, and the look of distaste that crossed her face was unequivocal.

'And what's that?'

'Well, he's obviously working out some kind of power struggle.' But then, as if she'd crossed her own line, she turned and stepped toward the bedroom door. Meanwhile Viv had crouched down to look at a series of books on the bottom of her bookshelf. 'A fan of Buffy, then?'

'Used to be. Brought them with me from home. Should really give them to charity. I don't imagine ever rereading them.'

The rest of the shelves had a typical selection of student angst and course 'must haves'. Psychology at Edinburgh was known as 'rats and stats', and the titles here didn't do anything to persuade Viv that it had changed since she'd been there.

She reached for her pocket as her phone vibrated. She didn't answer it but checked the number. It was Mac. Although she would probably have to come back, she had enough leads to be getting on with. Nothing she couldn't do in the comfort of her own flat. 'Okay. D'you think you could pass on my email address to the girls? I'd like to speak to them as well.' Rebecca nodded as Viv continued, 'I think we're done here. If anything comes to mind that would help, let me know.'

'I know that they are both going home for the holidays. So if I don't see them I'll send them an email.'

When Viv turned onto Broughton Street the crowds reminded her that it was the busiest night of the week. She shivered seeing young men dressed in skimpy tee-shirts and skinny jeans, the absence of girls in platforms with exposed abdomens was a stark reminder that she was in the gay ghetto. She pulled her own collar up against the chill. Keen to get home, Viv tucked in her chin and marched up the slight rise before taking a right turn onto Albany Street where the noise of chattering high spirits tailed off. An east wind bit into her cheeks so she broke into a jog and within twenty minutes she was home, where the first thing she did was strip off and step into a hot shower. She pulled on brushed cotton tartan PJs before relieving the fridge of the ingredients for hot buttered toast. Her first bite made her groan, as she realised how tetchy lack of food had made her. She wiped her hands on a sheet of kitchen paper then set to work on the net. She hadn't been at it long when her mobile vibrated. It was Mac again, and this time she answered, between mouthfuls. 'Hi, Mac, sorry I forgot to ring you back.'

'No probs, Viv. Sorry to ring so late but something you said earlier has got me thinking. When you said I'd confused feminism with lesbianism, it switched a couple of lights on in my otherwise blacked-out head. I've been working on an internal thing . . . ' He hesitated, as if deciding whether to tell her or not, then continued, 'Say, hypothetically, a female officer is caught with porn on her computer?'

Viv was glad that he couldn't see her eyebrows reaching for her hairline.

'From the outset my gut tells me it's nothing to do with her. So I look at her male partner, a guy who has always been pretty straight and I don't just mean sexually. I think, he could have done it, but he's a career cop hoping for a transfer to Strathclyde and I can't imagine him sullying his reputation before the next board. Then you said that thing about lesbians and feminism. Did you mean that they don't care about each other just because they share their sexual orientation?'

'Kind of. But Mac there's no way it's safe to assume anything.' She put her hand up as if he could see her and was about to butt in. 'No wait, lesbians come from all walks of life, and, trust me, they're as selective about who they spend time with as anyone else. It's dangerous to think that because we like women, we like all women any more than you would. You hets have a lot of evolving to do before you catch us up.' She imagined his tall taut frame sitting at his desk running his hands over his shaven face and dark hair. 'So why are you asking me about this?'

'Well, what if I have another female who is pissed off? Who's been passed over for promotion?'

'Whoa! Mac, that's already too much speculating for my liking. You've got a woman's computer with porn on it, and a woman, or possibly a man, with a grudge. Surely all you have to do is find out who has been tampering with the computer? Someone could have her password. Take a closer look at the pattern of use by the accused. You'll soon see discrepancies. We are creatures of habit – trust me I'm a doctor.' She snorted then cringed at how crass she sounded.

'Ha bloody ha. I do trust you but this is a hypothetical conversation and also confidential.'

'I assumed that when you said it was internal.'

'But listen, Viv, this male partner, apparently he's been coming on to her and she's told him to back off in no uncertain terms. But I don't think his pride was so hurt that he'd set her up for dismissal. Whereas this other female is a nasty piece of work and I could see her doing something like this. '

'You of all people should remember, "Deduction Watson. Deduction."' She heard him blow out a breath.

'I'm thinking of two words right now. One begins with F and I'm guessing you'll know the other.'

Viv laughed. 'Okay. Okay. Presumably you've checked for prints, DNA etc.'

'Sure. Forensics have been over it and they've found a tiny amount of DNA at the edge of the mouse but nothing on the keyboard.'

'Which tells its own story. Who has a computer without prints on it. Get them to go over it again. There's no way it's completely clean.'

'I've already thought of that. Anyway enough of this, d'you fancy brunch tomorrow?'

'No can do, already got a date.'

'Who's the lucky . . . ?'

'Man actually.'

'Ooh, good for you.'

She sensed disappointment behind his sarcasm. And began to justify. 'It's work. Let me know if you need anything creative done with that computer.'

She laughed again but she heard him draw in breath. 'Sure Viv, and jeopardise the whole case? Not a chance.'

'Your call.'

They disconnected.

Viv took out a huge sheet of paper and knelt on the floor with a set of coloured pencils. When in doubt, she mind mapped. She jotted down all the information she had about Tess, and from the overview wondered what it was she wasn't seeing. Who was the bloke that took Tess away? Brother, uncle, father, lover, old friend, new acquaintance, hired hand, fellow geology student, stranger? From Margo's description it didn't sound like a total stranger, otherwise Tess would surely have put up a fight. Her laptop pinged with an incoming message.

It was from Red. 'Not a mention of Tess Grant anywhere in the system. Not even a single traffic offence. On another note, the tattoo on my canal girl is of a rose.'

Viv sent Red a thank-you in reply. Then she stretched, yawned and rubbed her eyes, thinking perhaps it was time to call it a day, but not without one last peak at the TV news, which showed no developments. She filled the kettle in preparation for her hot water bottle.

Chapter Eight

Sunday. Viv woke early, energised. She pulled back her bedroom curtains to a bright day. High broken cloud, with the odd sliver of blue lurking behind, made her hopeful. She donned jogging pants and a sweatshirt, checked that she had enough shampoo in her kit bag, and headed out to the local swimming pool. A five minute jog took her to the entrance of the Victorian building where a notice, which she read aloud, said, '*Closed until further notice. Please accept our . . .*'

'Shit!'

She decided to go back and dump her kit before running round Arthur's Seat. Swimming was what she relished, although with recent scares about the toxic brew in public pools when urine is mixed with chlorine, she wasn't keen to swim at the end of a day or in the school holidays. But this morning she had been in the mood to risk being submerged for half an hour and now it wasn't to be.

Her kit slung inside the door of the flat, she bolted downstairs for the second time. After a few paltry stretches she was off down the Cowgate and into the Queen's Park. It was cold with a light breeze, no rain – perfect running weather. By the time she began to climb the Radical Road to Dunsapie Loch she was really into a rhythm.

A couple of terrifying panic attacks had been her motivation for taking up jogging. Her over-active adrenaline got caught up doing what it was meant to do, and her breath didn't get the chance to remain shallow. From the south side of the loch she could see for miles over to the east, beyond Cockenzie's disused power station, to the Bass Rock, and to the west a panorama that took in the Pentland Hills. She stopped, placed her hands on her hips and soaked up the intermittent sun. There weren't many people about, just a walker striding at a good pace with his collie on an extending lead, and a couple sitting in their VW Polo reading the Sunday papers. They reminded her of her own parents, Sundays in her early childhood when her dad dragged her and Mand along the prom at Portobello, while their mum sat in the car and read the *Sunday Mail* and *Sunday Post*. Whatever the weather Viv and Mand had had to march out, with no complaints. Now she loved being in the open air. Besides, once she was outdoors the weather didn't matter. She picked up her pace and headed back down towards Holyrood Palace, one of the Queen's Scottish residences. Viv grinned at the drama of the landscape and commended herself for choosing to live in the West Bow with all this beauty on her doorstep.

As she rounded the bend at the bottom of the Bow she spotted the woman who owned the antique shop unloading her car. She felt colour rising up her neck but justified it after her forty-minute run. The woman's head was stuck well beneath the boot lid and she didn't see Viv approaching. She was struggling with a cabinet that was jammed beneath the shelf of the old Volvo.

'Hi there, can I give you a hand?' Viv wiped her face on the bottom of her t-shirt, exposing her taut mid-rift but dropping the fabric just before the woman turned round.

The woman pulled her head out. 'Great timing! If you could hold the shelf up I'll be able to lever this thing out. Thanks.'

Viv pushed the shelf up but the woman was staring at her. Viv wiped her nose and mouth on her sleeve wondering if there was something there that shouldn't be.

But the woman just smiled. 'I was hoping I'd see you again.' Then she edged what turned out to be a nineteen-thirties radiogram onto a blanket that was lying on the pavement. Once the piece was safely lowered to the ground she looked up at Viv. 'Thank you. I just got lucky with this at the Barras this morning and wanted to drop it off before heading out to another fair.'

'It looks great. Does it work?'

'Well it did when I left Glasgow, but I've been swearing at it for about half an hour so it might have become stroppy.' She gently stroked the walnut surface and said, 'I didn't mean it, honest.'

Viv winced at the anthropomorphism. 'I'll give you a hand in with it if you like.'

'I like,' beamed the woman.

Between them they walked it across the blanket on the pavement and then with a heave they lifted it up the step and into the shop. The woman was wearing thick wool Edwardian jodhpurs, over-sized enough to require braces, a pale grey striped shirt and a thin black ribbon tied in a bow at the collar. The outfit reminded Viv of the young Coco Chanel; all she needed to complete the ensemble was a hacking jacket nipped in at the waist.

'That's such a great help. I'd offer you that coffee but I have to get up to Aberdeen before twelve.' She glanced at a huge watch that was strapped over her shirt sleeve.

Viv blurted out, 'I was thinking about going to Aberdeen today.'

The woman smiled at her. 'Were you thinking about changing first?'

Viv glanced down at her joggers. 'Yes, sure.'

'I've got about five maybe ten minutes before I have to be on the road. If you can do it we could go together.'

'I can do that.'

Before Viv knew what she was doing she had belted upstairs, leapt into the shower and was thinking up an excuse to give Walter. And ten minutes later she was closing the outside door and checking right and left before skipping across the road to where the woman was waiting by the Volvo.

'This is mad. I don't even know where about in Aberdeen you're heading.'

The woman stuck out her hand. 'Gabriella. The name's Gabriella.'

Viv shook the proffered rough hand. 'Viv. It's Viv.'

'It's a start. Now we're going to be confined together for the next three hours.' She looked startled, as if she'd only just realised the consequence of her rash behaviour, but jumped into the driver's seat and in one scoop cleared a load of papers and wrappers off the passenger side into the foot-well. 'You'll have to excuse the mess. This has been my office for too long. Never had a cleaner.'

She fired Viv a fabulous white toothy smile, then started up. The Volvo was a battered old thing. If they made it to Aberdeen in one piece they'd be lucky. But Viv fastened her seatbelt, feeling like the cat that got the cream and, with a hamster in her belly, they were off.

Viv wasn't usually known for spontaneity, at least not where relationships were concerned, yet there she was sitting next to a complete stranger on a journey that was just an excuse to spend time in her company. She remembered Walter and scrabbled about in her pocket for her phone. 'D'you mind?' She held up the phone and Gabriella nodded. 'Sure. Go ahead.'

Viv pressed in his number. 'Yes!' She exclaimed when it was his answering service.

She looked at Gabriella who said. 'Voicemail?'

Viv felt her face stretching with a smile. 'Absolutely. Some days there is a God' She put one finger in her ear and spoke to his machine. 'Hi Walter, it's Viv. Something's come up.' She looked at Gabriella, who was holding back a snigger. 'And I'll have to cancel this morning. Can I ring you tonight and we'll reschedule?' She closed the phone, grinning but too nervous to look at her companion. Then she did, and they almost wept with laughter. Good start.

With the heater on full power they sailed warmly and effortlessly over the Forth Road Bridge. Viv recalled her visits to Dunfermline to see Walter: once, twice, sometimes three nights a week in the hard times. She would cross this body of water, a signal that the therapy had already begun, like journeying into an altered state, to be met by Walter, a man – and that was significant – whose countenance was so peaceful and unconditional that he wouldn't break into her reverie. He was fantastic. A pang of regret found its way into Viv's conscience before Gabriella interrupted, preventing it from taking root.

'So, Viv, what are you passionate about?'

She was surprised by the question and had to think for a few moments before answering. The sky had cleared and the bright light made everything dazzle. 'I'm passionate about Scotland, specially on days like this . . . I'm not a political animal but I feel passionate that people should take responsibility for themselves. Stop blaming others for their own condition. I've a sister who has got every conceivable material necessity and she does nothing but moan. I suppose I'm passionate about gratitude and about making my own glass full to bursting. I can't stand whinging and whining in myself or in others . . . ' She sniffed. 'Says she, whinging and whining.'

She looked at Gabriella. 'What about you Gaby? What are you passionate about? By the way, it's a great question. No one has ever asked me that before. It beats "And what do you do?" That's a question to filter you into this camp or that, assessing your productivity. It's a post-Reformation question, because since then our highest value has been in doing, not being. If you ain't doing, you ain't of value.'

Gabriella looked slightly sheepish. 'It's never Gaby. And by the way I'm not sure I'm with you.'

Viv hesitated not sure whether the boo boo with her name was worth following up but decided to ignore it. 'Well stick around.'

Gabriella smiled and gestured with her hand for Viv to carry on, 'I'm not going anywhere.'

'Well . . . Before the Reformation, the good life, the life worth living, was the life of contemplation . . . When was the last time someone said they admire you for your ability to contemplate? Never, right? We don't contemplate because it isn't valued. Doing stuff is what is valued. Doesn't matter that the stuff is useless, or immoral, or at times illegal. As long as we're seen to be doing, people admire us.' Viv nodded, indicating that her rant was over.

Gabriella took a deep breath. 'Good. I like that . . . I'm passionate about Scotland too. About the landscape and what we are doing to make it ugly. Wind farms, I hate them with a passion. No, that's not quite right. I don't hate windmills. I dislike them intensely. I'm passionate about architecture and almost anything from the thirties, but you already guessed that. I like people who care about style.'

Viv glanced down at what she had thrown on in her effort to beat the ten-minute deadline. Black jeggings, riding boots, a white shirt and a tweed jacket:

not bad for unconscious co-ordination. She ran her hands through her damp hair and tried to fluff up the fringe.

Gabriella said, 'You look great.'

'And you.'

The colour rose up Viv's neck again and into her face. She instinctively covered her cheeks with her hands.

Gabriella said. 'Shy?'

Viv responded too quickly. 'No. Not usually.'

They both grinned again, then Gabriella said. 'I'm an architect to trade. But can't stand bureaucracy so only do the odd independent job now and again. Rest of the time I'm scouring the country for stock for my new venture.'

'The shop?'

'Yeah. God knows how it'll take off but Victoria Street's as good a place as I could think to sell . . . curios. I like that word. Curios.'

'Yep. "Curios" is good. I take it you're resisting calling yourself an antique dealer for a reason?'

As they chatted they passed Loch Leven with its romantic castle nestled on the island, and Viv mused on how nice it would be to visit. She'd never been, and a day like this would be perfect.

'The nineteen-thirties,' Gabriella continued, 'don't seem far enough in the past to be called antique. As my mum takes delight in saying, "My mother threw one of those out". Infuriating. But it doesn't stop her doing the same.'

'Any brothers or sisters?'

'Two brothers and a sister. I'm second eldest. The only one that isn't married.' She glanced at Viv then continued. 'And they're ever hopeful. But I'm guessing it's never going to happen. How about you?'

'There's just my mum and my sister now, and she is a . . .'

'Wait. Hold that thought. I'll have to concentrate for this next bit otherwise we'll end up in Inverness instead of Aberdeen.'

Gabriella indicated and took the slip road for Dundee and all was well. The Tay glistened and inevitably McGonagall's words 'the Tay, the Tay, the silvery Tay' ran through Viv's head. It was such a huge river, weaving its way through stunning countryside; still navigable until the early nineteenth century, but now used for little beyond recreation. Viv wondered what the chances were of Gabriella lending her the car for an hour, and wished she'd given this a bit more consideration. See-sawing between two mindsets wasn't going to make a pleasant drive and she sat back and sighed.

Gabriella said, 'What were you going to say about your sister?'

'No matter, I can't remember.' The opportunity to be a passenger was rare for Viv, who liked to keep her hands securely on the wheel. On this journey she watched the rolling green Perthshire countryside go by, and let the striking woman to her right make the decisions.

'How long will your job take? No hurry, just wondering about the time frame.'

'It would be great if I could have a couple of hours before the punters come in. Trade get first pick at noon, and the public get entry at two. It's quite a big fair, this one, and tons of dealers come from all over the north-east, so it'll definitely take me that time to get round them all. Shit! I forgot to leave a note on the door to say I'd be closed for the day.'

'How would you feel about lending me your car for an hour or so?'

'No probs. If I buy anything they'll put it to one side until you get back.'

Viv couldn't believe how easy-going this woman was. Angst must be in there somewhere. They spent time going through friends that may or may not be mutual. The process of filtering was good fun and they did have people that they both knew, some they shared a dislike of, and others who were 'darlings'. Gabriella knew Margo and Lindy, but Viv wasn't yet sure of her ground, so when Gabriella asked what her job for the day was Viv kept her details vague. 'Seeing a client.'

Gabriella didn't persist. When eventually they pulled up outside a modern hotel on the outskirts of Aberdeen, they both jumped out and nodded towards the automatic doors, understanding each other's urgency to visit the loo. They ran to the entrance and panicked at the slight delay in it opening. A short while later, after washing their hands, Gabriella shook the car keys at Viv. 'You be okay?'

'Yes. Sure. I hope I'll be back in an hour. Less if things go well.'

Gabriella raised her eyebrows in an enquiry, but Viv just got into the driver's seat and adjusted it along with the rear view mirror. Gabriella gave a tentative wave and watched until the car was out of sight. Very trusting, given they'd only just met.

Once away from the hotel Viv pulled into a bus stop and checked her emails for the Grant's address, then, using Google maps, found directions. They took her towards the centre of Aberdeen then west out into the countryside. Ten minutes later she was driving on a quiet road surrounded by farmland. It wasn't long before she spotted a stone farmhouse set back off the road, with barns and a couple of cottages within shouting distance that could be the Grants's. A rough track from the main road appeared to be the only access.

The poor old Volvo bumped and heaved over the tractor ruts. A high beech hedge protected the garden from easterly winds and a shabby lawn was home to a child's swing that looked as if it had been there a long time. No sign of fancy ornaments or neatly defined flower-beds; nothing to prevent children playing. The house itself looked pretty forlorn with its upstairs curtains drawn and no sign of life.

Viv stepped out of the car onto a gravel drive and sauntered over to a small wooden barn sitting at the left of the house. The barn door was ajar and she swung it back to expose a disused chicken shed. There were nesting boxes along the back wall and straw on the floor, but the poo on the floor was dry and not very smelly, so Viv guessed it hadn't been inhabited recently.

She walked round to what was most likely to be the house's front entrance. She pushed at a gate that obviously hadn't been in use because it took a bit of effort to lever it over tufts of couch grass. An iron doorknocker, a bit grand for these premises, produced a thudding hollow echo. A tiny stiff letterbox also took a bit of persuasion to open, but she hunkered down and managed to peek into a spacious hallway. A shaft of light fell onto the staircase exposing marks where a runner had been on the wooden treads. An empty black cast iron umbrella stand, with a mirror on the wall above it, were the only other things she could see. It looked derelict. She tried the door. Locked. She retraced her steps and found the back door. A slight gap in the lace curtains in the glass porch revealed a similar picture. The Grants had definitely moved out.

Not sure what to do next, she became aware of the sound of voices and stood on tiptoe to see beyond the garden hedge, trying to identify where they came from. Then she heard a car door slam and an engine start up. To her surprise the truck drove up the track towards her, halted, and an athletic young bloke jumped out. In a local accent he said, 'Can I help you?' He was not unfriendly, but not chummy either.

'I'm looking for Andrew Grant.'

His mouth twitched, but he didn't take his eyes off her. Viv could hold a stare, and did. He glanced at the chicken shed, causing Viv to briefly follow his gaze. 'They're not here. Gone to . . . ' He stopped himself. Then continued. 'Away. They've gone away.'

Viv tried to keep her tone light. 'Any idea where I might find them?'

'No idea. Been gone for some months now. New tenants coming next month.'

His eyes moved back towards the chicken shed. She wondered what the attraction was. She brushed an imaginary hair away from her face and nodded in the direction he came from. 'D'you think anyone else round here might know where I could find them?'

Quick as a flash he responded. 'No. No, I don't. They didn't mix.' His posture changed, his long legs parted, and he hooked his fingers into the belt loops on the back of his trousers. 'Who are you anyway?'

She looked around and this time his stare was following hers. 'Um, just a friend . . . Thanks for your help. I'll try the church.'

Now his tone became distinctly unpleasant. 'Did you hear me? They're gone.'

'Yes. But I thought . . . '

He interrupted. 'Well you thought wrong. Now . . . ' He gestured with his thumb for her to get moving.

Viv walked toward the Volvo knowing that he was watching her every move. Once in the car she mouthed, 'Well, what the hell was that about?' She drove quickly out of sight, let go of her breath, and tried to recall the route back to the hotel.

Chapter Nine

There was no sign of Gabriella at the hotel door, so Viv walked into the reception area and followed the signs for the ballroom and the Antique Fair. It was heaving with traders in the process of unwrapping stock from old newspaper and bubble-wrap. She still couldn't see Gabriella so elbowed her way through the throng of trestle tables set up in long crowded rows. She bumped and squeezed until she spotted the nape of Gabriella's neck. The dark graduated bob had been beautifully cut and Viv wondered whose scissors had been there. She was crouching next to a bookcase, inspecting beneath the shelves.

Viv, hoping not to alarm her, gently tapped her on the arm. 'Hi. How's it going?'

Gabriella straightened up and grinned the most welcoming smile. Viv's heart took a leap. She grinned back. 'You had any luck yet?'

'Yes. I'm doing pretty well.' Gabriella pointed to a pile of goods behind a trader's stall. 'That lot is for me. I'm just trying to decide if this bookcase has too much woodworm in it to be rescued. I think it'll be fine. It's a risk but no one will die.' She turned to the trader and said, 'I'll take it.' They must have already negotiated the price because Gabriella counted the notes into his hand and started to lift the case toward the other things. Viv grabbed the opposite end and together they edged the bookcase round behind a small chair with distinctive thirties' arched arms, in a rough brown and blue fabric. Gabriella nodded to the trader and pointed at her watch. 'Half an hour, while we grab something to eat?' He nodded back and Gabriella gave him the thumbs up.

In the foyer they checked the hotel menu. It looked fine and they were both too hungry to go in search of anywhere else. The restaurant was busy with families making the most of the 'eat as much as you can' carvery. Gabriella's eyes bulged as a short, bald, pastie-faced guy passed with his plate piled with meat and Yorkshire puddings. 'God, that's enough to put me off.' A sullen waitress came and showed them to a table awash with coca-cola and crumbs. They exchanged a questioning look before Gabriella said, 'Can you do this?' gesturing at the mess.

Viv shook her head. 'No. Let's find something else.' They headed back to the ballroom, collected the purchases, and once the car was loaded they drove south towards Forfar, scouring the roadside for any signs of somewhere to eat.

'Right. If I don't eat . . . like now, I'm going to start chewing off your arm.' Said Gabriella.

Viv laughed, and pulled out her phone. 'D'you mind?' she held it up. 'I'll find us somewhere to eat in Forfar.' This was easier said than done. It's not that there weren't restaurants in Forfar, but nothing seemed to open on a Sunday. They settled for a modest-looking place right beside the A90. The loos were clean, as was the table, and, unbelievably, they had a homemade vegetarian dish which Gabriella fancied. Viv was fleetingly worried that if Gabriella was a veggie, she'd be picky about all sorts of other things. Once they'd settled at a table, a jolly, homely woman took their order and as she gathered up the paper menus Viv asked Gabriella, 'So, how long have you been a vegetarian?'

'Oh, I'm not. I'm not even an aquatarian. I just liked the sound of the aubergine thing.'

'Glad that you ordered chips. I was out with a work crowd once and every single woman said no to chips until they came, then they all wanted 'just one'. So I ordered chips for ten and at the end of the meal all plates were clean.'

'Women who police what they eat get on my tits.' Gabriella put her hand up to her mouth. 'Sorry, it just slipped out.'

'Start as you mean to go on. You're right. I don't know a single woman who isn't on a diet, hasn't been on a diet, or isn't just about to start a diet.

And yes that gets on my tits too. So we've established that we've both got tits and that there are occasions when things get on them.' Viv caught Gabriella's profile as she glanced out of the window, and wondered when she had managed to renew her bright red lipstick without Viv noticing. She idly started to rearrange the condiment set on the table but Gabriella put her hand on top. Viv withdrew her hand. Then realising that Gabriella looked concerned, said, 'Sorry. It felt as if I'd been stung'

'Maybe you had.'

'I didn't mean to . . . '

'It's okay, Viv. You don't have to justify being nervous.'

The waitress approached and they both sat back to give her access to the table.

When the waitress withdrew, Gabriella said, 'So you haven't told me what it is that you spend your days doing. Is that an okay question?'

'Sure. I'm a hairdresser.' Viv's heart sank as she spotted the look of disappointment on Gabriella's face.

'Really?' She tried to recover her composure, but the pitch of her voice gave her away. 'Where do you work? And how come you were swanning about in Victoria Street on a Saturday? Isn't that a hairdresser's biggest day?'

Viv, uneasy at the need to defend herself, continued. 'I work for myself. Freelance. I travel to people's houses, and have done for years. I suppose I've managed to train my clients, well, those who can, to have their hair cut during the week. I do have some who can't do any other day. In fact I'd just finished work, when as you say, I was, "swanning around Victoria Street".'

'Oh, I didn't mean anything by that . . . ' Gabriella looked penitent and Viv laughed. 'It's okay. I'm not a skiver. I do other things besides cutting hair.'

Gabriella was over-compensating, and too eagerly said, 'Okay we'll get to that. But what made you become a hairdresser in the first place?'

'It's a long story.'

Gabriella nodded, encouraging Viv to continue. Viv sighed. 'Okay. I hated school and always wanted to be a hairdresser. Not any old hairdresser but one who would cut like Sassoon. No shampoo and sets for me. So I got a job in a good salon, did my apprenticeship and worked for a few years with them. But I'd always been a reader and one day I decided that cutting hair wasn't quite enough, so I went back to school, got some Highers, then went to uni. All the while I had to cut hair to finance the studies.' Viv hesitated but Gabriella nodded for her to go on. 'Once I got into the rhythm of studying I loved it and I enjoyed hairdressing even more . . . It gives me a kind of right brain left brain balance. So I went from one degree to another to another. My intention was never to collect degrees, although being called Doctor certainly had its appeal. Beats spinster.' She sighed. 'So here I am, a hairdresser with more degrees than I know what to do with.'

'What a great story. You should write about it.'

'Too busy cutting hair, writing columns and poking my nose into other people's business.'

Gabriella raised her eyebrows. 'Such as?'

'Well I occasionally get asked to investigate things, and sometimes I don't get asked but investigate anyway.' She grinned.

'Curious.' Gabriella blew a strand of hair from her eyes and stared at Viv.

Viv, embarrassed, looked at her nails and, mortified at how grubby they were, quickly bunched up her fingers. 'I've covered a few newspaper articles, and at times I've snooped around for the police.'

Gabriella smiled, but her disbelief was apparent.

Viv pressed on. 'It's true. I also used to be a part-time academic.'

This certainly had Gabriella pointing her fork. 'Now are you sure about that?'

'Yes, entirely sure. Trust me, I'm a doctor.' She started to laugh. 'What is this?'

Gabriella looked straight at her. 'Well, what is it?'

Viv looked away and felt herself colouring – had she made a huge assumption? She stammered, 'Well I don't know. You tell me.'

Gabriella grinned. 'Could be a beginning.'

Neither of them ate very much but nor did they seem too keen to get back on the road. They ordered ice cream but didn't eat much of that either. Then they ordered coffees, which they drained. Relieved when Gabriella accepted her offer to drive Viv was grateful to have something else to focus on. She slipped into the driver's seat, wiped her palms on her thighs and started up. Relieved to gain some control, she rolled her shoulders, and gave Gabriella the lowdown on what it was like to juggle three careers. They avoided chat about current or previous relationships, frightened to puncture the atmosphere of the day. During quiet moments, which were few, Viv imagined how the day might end. She would help Gabriella into the shop with the bits of furniture from the boot, but then they'd have to say cheerio. What then? She blinked the decision away. No amount of talking herself into the sanity zone worked. She imagined ways of keeping this woman's attention. They surely couldn't end the day on 'cheerio'. Viv's internal dialogue flitted from waking up in the morning with Gabriella by her side, to a night of regret and apologies for Walter. She knew which she'd prefer.

Once the boot was unloaded, however, Gabriella rubbed Viv's sleeve and looked directly at her. 'Your place or mine?'

Viv, surprised, hesitated, but smiled back. 'Mine's closer.'

Monday morning felt exciting and sunny and she hadn't even opened the curtains. Viv jumped up, pulled on a dressing gown, and headed to the kitchen to make tea. The muscles in her face couldn't resist smiling. As she waited for the kettle to boil she ran through the things she'd like to do today. The first of which was groveling to Walter. Well, not quite the first. She set up a tray with two huge china cups and saucers next to a Keep Hot teapot with matching sugar and milk set. She laid the tray on the end of the bed and opened the curtains wide to a glorious morning. Gabriella stirred, squinted and Viv imagined anyone faced with such a smile first thing in the morning would easily be hooked.

'Tea in bed. How good is this?' Gabriella plumped up the pillows then pulled the duvet up to her chin. She patted the space next to her and Viv slid in. They drank in silence. Viv became reflective. Felt misgivings rising, even though they'd only talked and cuddled. A parental voice inside her head screamed, 'What the hell are you up to?'

Gabriella cut into Viv's thoughts. 'I'll have to get going.'

Viv, trying to look disappointed, let go of a slow breath when Gabriella jumped out of bed still wearing underwear and a t-shirt, grabbed her trousers and shirt and bolted through to the shower.

Viv rubbed her face with both hands and whispered her thought out loud. 'What the hell are you up to, Fraser? Haven't you had enough drama for one week?' A little later, Viv got round to ringing Walter.

He picked up immediately. 'Hi, Viv. Is there any chance we could catch up today?'

Viv thought, 'catch up'? Mary, his wife, must be within earshot. Interesting that he didn't want her to know. Why wouldn't he?

She replied. 'Yes, I could meet you this morning if you like. But it would have to be in Edinburgh.'

'That's fine. How about that café in the Grassmarket?' He spoke as if they hadn't had an arrangement yesterday.

'That's good. What time?'

'I could get to you within the hour?'

iv looked at the time on her laptop, ten to ten. 'Eleven o'clock suit?'

He responded in a voice that was very upbeat, for a man who only two days ago sounded desperate. 'Excellent, Viv, see you then!'

She spent the next half hour online looking for info about the Eastern Brethren. There wasn't a lot on the Aberdeenshire group, but tons of mentions of Pennsylvanian groups. From what Viv read they were a lot like Plymouth Brethren only stricter. Their women weren't allowed to go out of doors without a hat. She recalled the sisters Louise and Emma who always wore hats. Apparently, they kept nasty angels from impregnating them. Viv guessed that the Eastern Brethren used the same biblical text to justify their own dogma. She could see the work of St Paul behind this, and shook her head as she spoke to the screen. 'Who are these people who think that some guy almost two thousand years ago had the right answers? Didn't he know that angels were clever enough to circumnavigate a hat?' Another couple of emails arrived in her box: one from Paula offering to meet, the other a promotional one, which she deleted. Viv checked the time. She'd answer Paula later.

Chapter Ten

Viv stretched out her hand as she approached the table, genuinely pleased to see him. 'Walter! How are you?'

He didn't look great. Although he was wearing an immaculate collar and tie, his pale drawn face told its own story. Viv nodded to Bella, the proprietor, who waved but seemed to sense that this was a business meeting and didn't come over for her usual catch-up. Viv, entirely at home here, slipped her jacket round the back of the chair, but before she was even seated Walter launched. 'I'm worried Viv.'

Viv nodded. 'I can see that. But what's going on?'

He looked round about him and Viv almost laughed. The steamer on the coffee machine swooshed full pelt trying to keep pace with people queueing for take-away latte and cappuccino. Walter practically had to bawl to be heard. They were the only two sitting in.

He leaned over the table. 'You're never going to believe this.'

Viv cocked her head. Then as he continued the swooshing stopped and Walter was bellowing into the now quiet room.

Embarrassed, Walter adjusted his volume. 'I've been having difficulty with an ex client . . .' He checked over his shoulder. 'She's stalking me and no matter how often I confront her about it she says it's simply coincidence. Coincidence that she's looking in an empty shop window outside my practice three or four hours a day. Coincidence that when I had, oh you'll love this, my haircut, she was in the salon at the same time. Guess what her presenting issue was?' He didn't wait for her to reply. 'Being obsessed by "powerful" men, but Viv I'm not a powerful man. You know that.' He was on auto-rant and completely unaware of it.

Viv nodded in acknowledgement, 'Yes, but I know what I know, and as you were always keen to tell me, I don't know what I don't know. And let's face it I don't know you beyond therapy. You could be an axe murderer.'

His face registered shock, and he shook his head running a hand over his grey stubble. Viv had never seen him in this state. Walter was so dedicated to neatness and routine that she fancied he must factor in a specific time for spontaneity. Life for Walter always appeared to flow seamlessly from one fifty-minute hour to the next. Viv, slightly alarmed by his obvious distress, remembered his infinite patience when she was in a similar state and decided she wanted to help.

She smiled at him as he rearranged the salt and pepper pots, an obsession familiar to Viv. 'You'll be relieved to know that I don't think you capable of criminal behaviour, but you get my meaning.'

He nodded. 'Of course. Of course.'

'What have you done to discourage this behaviour?'

Suddenly his fingernails fascinated him. 'The thing is . . . I have had coffee with her once or twice.'

Viv was dumbstruck. This was a complete no-no. To fraternise with patients outside of therapy was reason enough for him to be struck off. What had possessed him? 'Walter, is it my imagination or have you become a little lax in the ethics department. Not to mention arithmetic. Was it once or twice?'

'Okay, twice, but . . . '

She interrupted him by putting her hands up. 'Don't say it. Don't tell me there was nothing in it, because you and I know that . . . in fact, wasn't it you who taught me that the brain is a jail made out of bullshit?' Viv sighed and rubbed her hands over her face and into her hair. 'Okay, Walter. From the beginning. How did she come to you etc, etc?'

'Oh God.' He stared at her as the pause extended.

Viv's patience was beginning to be tested.

Before he blurted out, 'She said that you recommended me.'

Viv sat back in amazement and looked up at the cornice, racking her brain for anyone she knew that she'd have been comfortable sharing her therapist with. She couldn't think of a single person . . . 'Not Sal Chapman?'

He shook his head. 'No. Never heard of her.'

'Phew.'

He remained silent, staring at her over the top of his coffee.

'Well? Do I get to know or are we guessing?' He hesitated and she continued. 'And it's a bit late to play the ethics card.'

'Her name is Nancy. Nancy McVee. She said she used to work with you. She started to train as a hairdresser but couldn't hack it so took a job as a receptionist.'

Viv had no memory of anyone she had ever worked with called Nancy and shook her head. 'Don't know that name.' It was tricky though, because the hairdressing industry was notorious for people reinventing themselves, and if Nancy had a nickname her real name would have faded into obscurity.

'No matter, Viv, I hoped that if you knew her you could have a word with her and it wouldn't need to go any further.'

'But what do you mean? How much further does it need to go? You've already broken the patient–practitioner code by seeing her outside official sessions. And by the way, how does she know what your movements are?'

'That's one of the things I'm most worried about. She must be accessing my computer calendar. Okay I have my haircut on the first Tuesday of the month, so that's easy, but my dental appointments only happen once a year.'

'Lucky boy. Good teeth?'

He nodded. 'Yeah, at least I've got that in my favour.'

'So we could have an ex-client who is a hacker? She couldn't have access to a diary? I remember Mary keeping a house diary so that you both knew where you were.'

'God, Viv, that would be even scarier. It would mean that she had been in the house without our knowing.'

Viv visualised Walter's hallway. His notice board with hooks all along the bottom where all the keys hang, each key labelled for its own door. Anyone could take a key and have it copied.

'How old is she?' Viv had a vision of a young athletic female, stealthily creeping around Walter's house while he was seeing patients, and shuddered. She hated the idea that someone could have overheard her sessions. That was the point of going all the way to Fife to see him. She told herself to stay calm, that she had consulted Walter way before Nancy . . . but still. Walter stared into his cappuccino as if it was a crystal ball. 'She's twenty-five, twenty-sixish. Very beautiful. Photographed by Lichfield.'

Something about this tweaked a memory. 'She's not the woman who had the horrendous car crash and burnt her face? It was all over the papers.'

He nodded and took a huge breath. Viv waited what seemed like an age, before he released it and said, 'She's still beautiful. The skin graft was miraculous, and it was only at the edge of one side of her face.'

'But, Walter, her internal damage.' She tapped her temple. 'In here she'll never heal. And as you say she was stunning enough to be photographed by one of the most famous photographers in the world. How much d'you think she had invested in her face? Plenty. That's how much.' Viv sighed. 'When did you last see her?'

'Thursday. Mary and I were at a private view here in Edinburgh and she was there.'

'But it's not beyond the bounds of possibility that she had an invitation.'

'No. No, she didn't. I saw her arrive and watched her charm the man on the door. She said she'd left her invitation at home and he let her in.'

'Why wouldn't he? They want to sell pictures, and the more bums on seats, the better I suppose.' Viv took out her note pad. 'Okay, let me have her details and I'll see if I can find out what's going on. She hasn't threatened you with anything?'

Again he looked at his nails. This pissed Viv off. 'Your nails won't have any answers, Walter. Look, if you want my help you'll have to come clean. I can't be arsed with half-baked confessions.'

'She hasn't threatened me but she said I can't control her movements and if she wants to she can . . .'

'What? She can what?'

'She can make my personal life a misery. And I tell you, she's already doing that. She didn't want to end therapy, but I thought she was ready and explained that sometime she'd have to get on with day-to-day life without a therapist. She was having none of it. Had hysterics, so I gave in and said she could continue for three more sessions where we'd work on her endings. That was my first mistake. She agreed to the extra sessions but wasn't really doing the work. That's the thing about therapy, people think it's the therapist who has all the power but they don't.'

'What does your supervisor say about it?'

'She doesn't know about the stalking. But was adamant about me ending with her. Oh God, what a mess.'

'It sounds to me as if you need help. But not from me.'

'I have supervision monthly.'

'Yeah, sure you do, but you need to see a therapist, and your supervisor should have picked up on this.'

He looked out of the window then back at Viv. 'You're right. But who would I see? I'm not supposed to see anyone I know, and that's almost impossible. I know most psychotherapists on the Scottish register . . . I don't suppose you would consider it, Viv?'

Viv had practised as a volunteer therapist for two years, and decided she couldn't hack it. One client in particular, who had been recommended to have therapy by her solicitor 'as a way of reducing her sentence' had put Viv off. All that client had had to do was come and sit with Viv for an hour a week for ten weeks then their solicitor could tick a box marked, 'has been for counselling'. It was a total waste of Viv's time. The hour should have been given to someone more deserving, someone who really did want to do the work. With all this running through her mind she shook her head. 'No, Walter. I do want to help but I can't do that. Just give me the woman's details and I'll see what I can do. You'll have to find someone else to hear your story.'

He handed over a piece of paper with a mobile number on it. 'That's the best way to contact her.'

'Don't you have an email address for her?'

Reluctantly he took the paper back and wrote it down. His attitude wasn't what Viv would have expected, and she wondered what else was going on for him.

'How is Mary?'

A shadow crossed his already shadowy face. 'She's as she always is. A complete rock.'

'Have you told her about Nancy?'

He looked at her as if she was mad. 'Absolutely not. I still have to respect client confidentiality.'

Viv didn't believe him but nodded her head as if she did. 'Sure. Well look, I'll be in touch as soon as I make contact with her.' She stood to go but he didn't move, just stared out of the window, distraught.

When Viv passed Gabriella's shop on the way to her flat it struck her that their indiscretion could become a hassle. Gabriella had a customer with her but waved enthusiastically as Viv sauntered up the other side of the street. Her insides flipped, but not in a good way, as she took the stairs two at a time.

Chapter Eleven

Once inside, she checked her answering machine. A message from Mac. 'Viv! Where the hell are you?' Next, another message from Sal, which twanged her heartstrings, but she still wouldn't ring her. Instead she dialled Mac's number. 'Hey, Mac. I've been busy on a job. What can I do for you?'

'You can . . . No, first let me say thanks. That colleague's computer did show discrepancies. We're trying to marry those with the shifts of others.' It sounded as if he was with someone.

'I'm glad to be of service. But that's not why you left the message, is it?'

'No. I thought I'd take a look at that young missing person, the one in the photograph you gave Sandra. I came up with an odd religious group. They sound whacky, even by Aberdeenshire standards. Ruled by a control freak called Pastor Rawlins, an American, who appears to have bolted with the church's funds. The father of your young girl may have been involved.'

None of this was news to Viv but she said, 'Well done, Mac! You've obviously had a busy weekend!'

Her irony wasn't wasted. 'Well not as busy as yours *obviously*! By the way I think I saw that editor of yours going into the gym.'

'No way! Jules? Not a chance. She'd sooner have an amputation.'

He sighed. And she imagined him rubbing his hands over his face. 'She must have a double then.'

Viv snorted. 'Or she's lost her marbles.'

They laughed. Jules was the most unlikely candidate for a gym membership that either of them knew. Fags, booze, long hours – yes – but fitness never. Unless there was a new man on the scene. Even then Viv couldn't imagine it, as she continued, 'I must give her a ring. If there's been a story out there about a sect in Aberdeenshire she'll have had it covered.'

Mac was hesitant. 'How about lunch or . . . '

Feeling awkward she interrupted him. 'Sadly not. Absolutely up to my eyes . . .'

He replied. 'Okay. We'll speak.'

'Absolutely.' Had she heard disappointment in his voice?

No sooner had she laid the phone in its cradle than it rang again. It was Jules. Viv assumed this must be ESP. Jules and the gym – things must be bad.

Jules wasn't a woman known for social grace and she immediately set off. 'Hi, Viv. Need you to give me a thousand words on that young bird in the canal.'

Viv shook her head incredulously. 'That would be the young woman who is lying on a slab in the mortuary without any family or friends to mourn her.'

'Yeah. Yeah. What d'you have for breakfast that's made you into a puppy lover? They think they might have an ID. A student from Aberdeen.'

This confused Viv. 'But when was this girl found? Are we talking about the same girl here?'

'Pulled out of the Union on Saturday night. I just heard that she could be a student from Aberdeen.' Jules coughed and kept coughing.

Eventually it ended and Viv was able to say, 'Ah, so not necessarily from Aberdeen . . . only could be.'

'Viv, you all right? Not exactly hearing your cylinders firing.'

Viv imagined Jules perched on the window ledge inside her office, either hanging outside with a fag or just ducking in to light another. 'I heard you. It's just . . . '

Jules was on her. 'It's just what, Doc? Don't you go holding back on me now.'

Viv paused again. 'It's nothing. But if it becomes something I'll let you know.'

'You'd better or else.'

Viv smiled at Jules'audacity but was so used to it she just echoed Jules. 'Yeah. Yeah . . . Course. But listen, while you're on I need some info on a religious group in Aberdeen. Eastern Brethren. You heard of them?'

'Nope, but I'll take a look and get back to you.'

For all Jules's craziness when she said she'd do something, she usually followed through. 'Thanks. Speak . . . '

Her bad manners also never failed, and Viv was left listening to the dial tone. Viv shook her head distractedly, clicked on her inbox and read an email from Beccs with a telephone number and a message asking Viv to ring her.

Beccs immediately picked up. 'Hi. They've got my email address and my mobile number. She must have given it to them.'

Viv tried to slow her down. 'Hold your horses. Who's got your email and mobile number? And who is she? Are we talking Tess?'

'They're threatening to tell my dad about Tess and me. If they find out I'm interfering they'll definitely do it . . . Why now?' Could this be the result of her trip?

'Look, Rebecca, forward the email to me and I'll take a look at the source.'

The distress in the young girl's voice was evident as she shot back. 'No. I'm not doing that. They'll know that I'm . . . '

'You're what, Rebecca? They obviously already know something. If they're holding Tess we could get to her through that email. Come on, send it.'

Viv heard a stifled sob and said, 'Rebecca, your dad probably already knows. He's not stupid. I'm guessing he just doesn't think it's appropriate to mention it.'

Through her tears Rebecca managed to shout, 'You don't know him. It would really matter to him if this came out.'

'Well, as someone who works with the press, I know that a story like that would last five minutes tops, before it would be wrapping chips.'

She heard Beccs sniff. 'You're not allowed to wrap chips in newspaper any more.'

'I know. I know. But you get my meaning. It would be an overnight sensation if it was anything at all. It would rely on there being no other news and how likely is that?'

'You don't know what he's like. He's a perfectionist. We're meant to be a model family.'

'And so you are. The sooner he learns that perfection is a myth the better for him and his poor constituents. Go on, Rebecca, click send.' She heard tapping.

Within seconds the email was in Viv's inbox. Whoever sent this knew the hide–and–seek tricks of cyberspace. But as Viv was aware, everything could be traced if you looked in the right places, and thanks to an old university friend, Viv knew where those places were. Unorthodox skills in the computer department were part of Viv's toolkit. This said, it took her longer than she'd hoped but eventually she traced it through a data farm, then to an off-shore site. How convenient for them to be in the North Sea. But Viv reprimanded herself, remembering how easy it was to set up an account and access it from anywhere. Which meant the email may have been sent from the other side of the world. Going through an off-shore site made it look as if that was the source. She also understood that the account the email was sent from didn't necessarily give up the sender, but first things first.

Viv went into her own computer history and retrieved the articles she'd read about Tess's dad. When she found the name of the company that he worked for she hacked into his email account. This was also trickier than she'd hoped. But again with a bit of patience, which she was usually pretty short on, she managed to view his account activity. Only there hadn't been any activity for over two weeks.

She whispered. 'Curious! Or coincidence?' With her head down she felt herself being drawn into his correspondence, but decided she'd better scan for anything that didn't look work-related. 'Excellent!' she exclaimed, finding a feed on the account that filtered particular words. This proved useful, as did another account that she'd imagined might exist: one for receiving exclusively church correspondence. She was about to start reading when the door buzzer sounded. Not expecting company, she ignored it. It was probably the postman, then it occurred to her that it could be Gabriella, and she jumped up too quickly, and slightly giddy ran up the hall to answer it. 'Hello!' her voice nervous at the thought it could be Gabriella. But it wasn't.

'Hi, Viv, it's Mac, I'm sorry to bug you like this but . . .'

She was surprised – they'd only just spoken on the phone. 'Mac. Come up.'

Viv opened the door and leaned over the bannister, impressed at the ease with which he ran up the eighty-six stairs to her landing. 'Welcome. This is an unexpected pleasure.'

With his hands on his knees, and catching his breath, he looked at her quizzically. She could see that he was trying to work out if she was being facetious. But she wasn't. She was genuinely pleased to see him and shot him a convincing broad smile.

He stood, rolled his shoulders, relaxed and stepped forward as if he was going to kiss her, but he rubbed her upper arm instead and said, 'Thanks.'

She pointed down the hallway to the sitting room. 'Go through. I'll put some coffee on.'

As she filled the kettle she remembered what was on her screen and nipped through to make sure he couldn't see it. It was too late. He was already over by the window with his hands in his pockets, his huge bulk casting a shadow over her laptop. In two seconds the running water that was her screen saver poured over the illicit email.

Relieved, she grinned and asked, 'Milk?'

He nodded, and she returned to the kitchen. She already knew what he took in his coffee. She continued getting the cups and saucers out feeling slightly stupid. If anyone knew the tricks people play when they have something to hide, it was Mac. He shouted through, 'Everything all right with you?'

'Great!'

With the tray in her hands she pushed the sitting room door shut with her foot and laid everything on the Ottoman before turning to him with his coffee.

'Now what brings you to this neck of the woods?' She almost added 'you handsome bugger' but held her tongue.

He stood staring out of the window then looked into his coffee as if it was a crystal ball. But all he said was, 'I'm on my way to the Pleasance.'

She nodded, watched and waited, giving him the chance to elaborate. He was clearly struggling with something. In psychotherapy, silences are the breeding ground for the cure, and she knew to let him have the space to tell her whatever he needed to.

Sure enough Mac cleared his throat. 'You know that case we were speaking about earlier. The female who has been suspended?'

Viv nodded. 'Yeah, I remember.'

'Well . . . ' In a familiar gesture he rubbed the stubble on his chin. 'The evidence so far leads to another female PC in the same office. Only this female's uncle is the head of CID and we have to tread carefully, have all our facts absolutely water tight, before we move on her. You can imagine if we got that wrong . . . Well, life would be difficult for me especially, since I have to work with him every day.'

Mac was head of a team called the National Task Force, NTF, which focused on terrorist investigations. Of course, terrorism had changed its colours and was no longer just about suicide bombers, but a host of crimes, cyber sabotage being the biggest headache, so the NTF remit had widened. Mac's position was equal to the head of CID, so Viv couldn't figure out why he was involved in an internal case at all.

'Mac. Why are you involved in this case? Those guys in the department for internal complaints usually do the ugly work.' 'You're right. But St Leonard's asked for someone clean to take a look first. They didn't really expect that it would go as far as this. They already had another bloke in the frame and thought he might just need a bit of a fright and he'd back off. But it hasn't turned out to be that simple. The thing is, this female, whether we get her on this or not, has got to go. She's nothing but trouble. Sinister. Yeah, there's something sinister about her.'

'How the hell is it that her character is only being exposed now? Didn't she have to go through the usual hoops to get in?'

He looked sheepish and shook his head. 'Well, that's just it, it looks as if there were . . . doors opened for her.'

'The back scratching school of merit still alive and kicking then?' She nodded then gestured to the couch where he took a seat and perched his coffee on one knee. She admired his long fingers as they clasped the cup: feminine hands for such a blokeish bloke. Viv liked Mac, and could easily have been tempted beyond friendship with him. Seeing him taking up space in her sitting room had a strange effect on her. She guessed that what made him so attractive was that although he was big, he wasn't the slightest bit predatory. Viv had at times wondered how he had ended up in the same brutish profession that her dad had chosen, but working alongside him had shown her exactly how. His communication skills were amazing – definitely worth having him around in a crisis. Nor was it lost on her how like her dad he was physically.

'I'm not sure why you're telling me this, Mac. I mean, it has to go through the proper channels or you'll be for the high jump . . . if the press get hold of it.'

With the mention of press he sat forward. 'You wouldn't . . .'

She barked back at him. 'No, of course I wouldn't. But there are many others who will. I don't need to leak anything; the force is well capable of doing that for itself.'

They stared at each other until he said, 'I know. But it's just . . . '

'Just what, Mac?'

He put his cup on the floor at his feet and rubbed both hands over his face, 'Well, she's not only uploaded pictures of adults – there are children as well. She's taken them from sources that were already confiscated material, so she's breached security as well as setting up a colleague, and there's more.'

Viv steadied her breathing as she waited.

'She's actually in some of the photographs.'

'You mean . . . ' She turned to the window. 'Actually don't tell me.' His distress was obvious and she said, 'But, Mac, this is really crap for you and you need to get those complaints guys involved . . . You've no choice.'

'Always got choices, Viv. Always. This is about damage limitation. For her to breach security she'd have to have used encrypted discs . . . Oh.' He let go of a groan. 'Don't even know why I came. I shouldn't be telling anyone this stuff, let alone you.'

Viv knew exactly why he had come. People choose the person that they know they'll get the answer they're looking for from. 'Well, I'm flattered that you trust me.' She said with more than a hint of sarcasm.

'Okay, okay. Sorry. I do know why. You're easy to talk to.'

Viv laughed. 'Think of me as your priest. It will go no further than these walls. Want a top-up?'

He stretched out his arm and she took his cup and saucer. Their fingers brushed. She fumbled with the handle of the door. He jumped up to help.

'I'm fine. I'll manage.' This came out more defensively than she meant it to and Mac raised his hands in defeat, but followed her up the hallway and into the kitchen.

'Listen, Viv, forget the coffee. I'm already wired.' Then he brightened. 'Duty and honour call me to St Leonard's.' She smiled, and turned with arms folded, nodding towards the door.

'Bloody Wickham. I wish you luck.'

He nodded, and she sensed him digging deep for his parting smile.

She returned to her search through Andrew Grant's emails, and found a trail of deception from Pastor Rawlins. Although by the end of her reading Viv thought that the pastor had met his match. Their communication began as a discussion but ended in the strategic language used in military campaigns. Pastor Rawlins had found many ways to avoid telling Grant what had happened to this amount or that amount, and his exploitation of the Old Testament as illustration was admirable. Grant was politely persistent and Rawlins, clearly rattled, started to say that Grant had the devil in him.

Viv laughed and shook her head in disbelief. How come an intelligent man, as Grant must be to have the job that he did, put up with that kind of tosh? Grant continued to be polite and slightly deferential until the final two emails where he demanded to know where the money was and Pastor Rawlins retorted, 'God is taking care of it.' Grant tetchily asked for God's bank details. Viv laughed out loud.

Then the correspondence ceased. The dates on the emails were from two months ago and now the Grants had disappeared. Viv wondered if she could find the pastor and checked her diary for a time when she could return to Aberdeen. She found a church website which stated the times of the

Brethren's meetings. Sunday was not especially sacred, because they met every evening for 'prayer and praise'. It was a full- time occupation to be part of this group.

Viv recalled her own childhood worship with the Band of Hope. She'd loved it because all they did was sing happy songs, and give out prizes for good attendance. She'd won *The Mill on the Floss*, printed on really thin paper and in a tiny typeface. She mused that they'd inadvertently introduced her to feminism through the words of George Eliot. Humming a tune from an evangelical hymn, she pondered what to do next. There was so little on the Brethren's website she wondered at them having one at all. But they did have a contact email address, so she fired off a message asking if she could join one of their meetings.

She watched the gentle sway of the silver birch in Greyfriar's graveyard as the kettle heated up. Would she dare return to the hamlet where the Grants lived and ask the other people living there if they knew anything? The unfriendly man was definitely a disincentive, but she had overcome worse.

Before she did anything rash, she checked the email address that Walter had given her for Nancy, and tried to imagine what might be going on in her head. Walter could easily have given away something about his own life, something that he believed to be incidental, but that could have led Nancy to think they had a future beyond therapy. Viv's wording in this email was crucial. Honesty was a good policy, but was this the time for it? She decided it was and began, 'Walter Sessions has asked me to contact you . . . ' At least if he asked she could say she'd made a start.

Viv sipped her tea, and jotted down all that she had to do, but her thoughts were interrupted by the buzzer going again. 'Hi.'

'Hi. It's Gabriella. Just wondered if you fancy tea.'

Viv buzzed to let her in but Gabriella said, 'No, I meant in the shop. I've got the kettle on.'

'Um . . . Sure. I'll be right down.'

'If you're busy we can do it another . . .'

Viv interrupted. 'No no it's fine.'

'Excellent!'

Viv poured the remains of her existing cup down the sink and checked how she was looking in the bathroom mirror. Her teeth looked as good as ever but it didn't stop her from giving them a quick brush. Ruffling her hair and pinching her cheeks, she was out the door in a jiff. The Bow was as busy as always and she slid between two illegally parked cars to cross the road. Gabriella opened the door and kissed Viv smack on the lips. No ambiguity for her. She grinned and hugged Viv whose shock had only just begun to sink in. The shop was warmer today although the toxic smell still unequivocal.

'Sold that Radiogram already this morning.'

'Wow! That was quick. Did you have to demonstrate it?'

'I had it on when the guy came in. He couldn't believe his luck. Said he'd been looking for one forever. So that's the first month's rent covered.'

Since Viv had been left a legacy by Dawn, her previous partner, she hadn't had to think too much about money. She reflected briefly on her good fortune. Gabriella's eyes, wide-open and bright, lifted Viv's spirit and she grinned, feigning interest in the surface of the bookshelf they'd brought back from Aberdeen.

'I'm going back to Aberdeen tonight.'

Gabriella looked surprised, but not as surprised as Viv herself felt. She hadn't made the decision consciously. Where had that come from?

'Oh. Okay. I take it you've got unfinished business?'

'Yes. The stuff yesterday was more fruitful than I thought. I'll need to have another look and the sooner the better.'

Gabriella screwed up her eyes.

And Viv started to explain. 'I'll . . . '

Gabriella interrupted and put her hand up. 'No. No. Don't do that. If you've got work to do you've got work to do. I'll have to go home anyway and sort some things out.'

Viv stepped closer to Gabriella and gently put her hand up to her mouth but felt her tense.

'You don't have to do that either.'

Viv said gently, 'Give me all the numbers I'll ever need to contact you.'

At this Gabriella seemed to relax and she dropped her head onto Viv's shoulder.

'This is bad. I'm already in the shit.' Gabriella took out a little tartan-covered book and started giving Viv her numbers. 'I can never remember my mobile.'

Viv did the same. They chatted awkwardly until a client came in and Viv no longer had an excuse to stay. She rubbed Gabriella's back and said, 'I'll phone you later.' Then remembering how irritated she got when people were too general, she added, 'About ten o'clock if I've got a signal.' Gabriella's parting smile was enough to warm anyone's cockles.

Chapter Twelve

The journey to Aberdeen in the dark with a starry sky and a nip in the air was almost as beautiful as in daylight. It took her forty minutes to get out of Edinburgh and before she saw the Forth rail bridge and lights twinkling all along the Fife coast. She'd forgotten her iPod and had to settle for the *Bridge Over Troubled Water* CD. No hardship there. She pressed repeat and sang like no one was listening. 'Jubilation! She loves me again, I fall on the floor and I'm laughing . . . ' It would take a hard heart not to be lifted by that and Viv was already flying. By the time she reached the outskirts of Aberdeen she was hoarse.

The atmosphere felt entirely different as soon as she turned up the track towards the Grants's farmhouse. Almost blinded by a security light, she reversed out of its range before getting out of the car. The light stayed on for its thirty-second setting, and Viv, careful to avoid it, skirted along the edge of the hedge, then against the side of the house before she reached the walls of the barn. She asked herself what the hell she was doing – she should have gone straight to the other houses in the hamlet. There wasn't anyone here to answer her questions.

The door to the chicken shed was closed and had been secured with a padlock. Why? There was nothing in it apart from remnants of straw. Had she missed something? The barn beyond was open and a Zetor tractor was parked with its trailer sticking out into the yard. Viv stepped cautiously towards it, the condensation from her shallow breath leading the way. The engine was still warm and was making noises of contraction as it cooled.

Her eyes began to adjust to the darkness. In the far corner, sitting on top of wooden pallets, there were two huge unopened sacks containing fertiliser pellets. The concrete floor was marked by mud from tyre tracks left by other, smaller bits of machinery. She took out her torch and followed tracks near the right-hand wall. She spotted a straggle of straw sticking out of what turned out to be a hatch in the floor. There wasn't much evidence of straw anywhere in the barn, which struck her as odd. She crouched to take a closer look and a split second later she sensed a weightless step, then heard a light thud.

There was a bright light in the tiny space. It mightn't have been bright by anyone else's standards, but with a searing pain beneath her occipital bone, Viv's eyes were in no state to be tested. Bit by bit the room came into focus and she gradually and very gently moved her head to the right and left. She was alone, in the chicken shed, except for the forty-watt bulb dangling from the ceiling. She pushed herself up the wall of the wooden enclosure. Her gloved hands were covered in straw from the floor. She gripped the edge of a row of nesting boxes, just below her eye level, and levered herself onto her feet. Viv swayed, feeling nauseating pain in the back of her head. As she rubbed her hand across her neck she caught her glove on a spot of what must be dried blood. Her head started to spin and she sank to her knees, remaining on all fours for a few minutes and fighting the metallic taste in her mouth. Eventually, hand over hand she walked herself back up the wall until she was upright. She dropped her head onto her crossed arms, then tried to stretch. Viv patted her pockets: they'd been emptied. The light bulb dangling from the ceiling was a temporary fixture and she traced its make-shift wiring along hooks on the roof and down the wall towards the edge of the door. Why would they, whoever they were, bother to fix up a light when they clearly had no concerns about knocking her out? Did they plan to interrogate her? Viv wasn't good at feeling sick and again fought the burn rising up her throat. She took a few deep breaths and the cold sweat passed, but the pain in her head didn't ease. Leaning against the wall she thought about her assailant, the likely candidate being the bloke she had encountered here on her last visit. What was he so afraid of?

The silence beyond the hut was broken by the occasional hoot of an owl. She checked her watch but couldn't focus well enough to make out the time. She pushed the door, and was not surprised to find it well secured. She kicked it with the tip of her boot and extreme pain shot up through her foot. Her toes were frozen. She bent and laid her hands on her thighs, attempting to steady her breathing. The door had given slightly at the base, which was incentive enough to keep trying but using her heel instead. There wasn't enough space to take a proper swing at it but she kicked as high and as close as she could to the position where she imagined the lock to be. There was clearly a serious bolt. She swore and slumped, then recalled a movie where a man, trapped in a barn in mid-western America, had spent most of his energy kicking and punching the door to loosen its lock, when the hinges were its weakest point. She shook her head, which was a bad idea, and she had to rest for another minute before she started to kick at the hinges, mumbling her gratitude to Hollywood.

The bottom hinge was well on its way when she heard the approach of a diesel engine. It got closer and closer until its headlights showed beneath the hut door. She stopped, leant her backside on the ledge of the nesting boxes and waited. The engine kept running, but she heard a male voice cursing on the other side of the door. He unlocked the padlock and tried to slide the bolt from its mooring but it was trapped. Viv must have buckled it. He blasphemed again. She heard his footsteps recede and the sound of him rummaging about in what she imagined was a toolbox. Within seconds of his return he had wrenched the door off. His furious eyes, set in a face badly in need of a beard, settled on hers. Before he stepped forward, she raised her hand to shield her eyes from the car headlights, then dropped her head, feigning weakness. He raised the arm holding the metal bar, but as it began to descend, Viv kicked out and made serious contact with his groin. He crumpled, but caught her shoulder with the crowbar before he hit the ground. She squealed but kept moving, clambering over his bulk. He rolled on the ground winded, his face an unhealthy shade of ash.

Viv staggered towards his black Nissan pick-up, grabbed the key from the ignition, and stuck it in her pocket. She recognised her things lying on the passenger seat – mobile, keys, Swiss army knife: he was an amateur. She turned and watched him as he writhed on the ground. An expanse of flesh at the top of his waistband exposed a tattoo that read, 'Jesus Saves'.

Gripping her shoulder, she ran as well as she could towards the Rav. It purred into life and within seconds she'd reached the main road again. It wasn't until she was driving through the city centre that she realised she was holding her breath. The clock on the dashboard read two ten. A good reason for the roads to be empty. She'd been in that hut for three or more hours and her feet weren't the only things that were numb. She switched the heater up full blast and drove. Within fifteen minutes she'd reached the motorway south but a wave of nausea returned and, unable to breathe her way out of it, she pulled over at the next lay-by. As she stood leaning into the verge, bile rising and subsiding, she heard another engine approaching. As she straightened up a police car pulled in behind her. She groaned as two officers approached. The taller male asked, 'Everything all right here?'

She hadn't been sick but could still feel her gut threatening. She turned away from them, and bending over the ditch with hands on her thighs, heaved twice. She uncurled and tried to regain her full height but swayed and had to steady herself by holding the bonnet of the Rav. She pulled out a tissue from inside her sleeve, wiped her mouth and eyes before checking out the officers.

'A bit the worse for wear, madam?'

'Master of understatement, mate', is what she thought. She gave him a look. 'Quiet night officers?'

They weren't keen on this. Again the taller man spoke. 'We'd better have you inside the car, but first . . . ' He produced a breathalyser.

She shook her head in disbelief. 'Look I haven't had a drink . . . '

And was interrupted. 'Matter of routine, madam. Now if you'd blow into the . . . '

Irritated, she took hold of the device and blew into the mouthpiece. This was the quickest way to get moving again.

The breathalyser kit was put away. 'So what would cause a young woman from Edinburgh to be throwing up in one of our ditches at two in the morning?'

She was momentarily disconcerted, but remembered that their vehicle computer would show the registration and insurance details of any car before them. She was fully paid up so they had no reason to keep her. Involuntarily she reached up to rub her neck. This was, of course, spotted.

'Someone been giving you a bit of a knock then?' This from the sidekick.

He was a caricature, she thought. 'A bit, officer, but nothing I can't handle.'

His brow furrowed with concern. 'We'd take seriously even the smallest incidents of domestic . . . '

Viv held up her hand. 'It's all right. I'll be all right.' But as she said this, her colour drained and her legs wobbled. When she next opened her eyes she was travelling in the back of a car, with voices streaming through a radio. She closed her eyes and let go.

The smell of disinfectant inadequately masked the odours of bodily functions. The rattle of a trolley passing nearby had woken her. She was on a solid hospital bed surrounded by curtains. She fingered a waffle blanket. The sheets, white and crisp, were tucked in so tightly that she could have been in a straitjacket. She wouldn't be going anywhere in a hurry.

Dim lights were a sign that it wasn't daylight yet. She was no longer wearing her clothes. She tried to lift her head but it started spinning and thumping. Her head wasn't the only thing that was in pain. Her shoulder and arm were bound in a sling, the agony unbearable. She closed her eyes again and felt an involuntary tear roll down the side of her face into the creases on her neck. Eventually a nurse bustled through the curtain and gently said, 'Doctor Fraser. Can you hear me?'

Viv opened her eyes and replied softly, 'Perfectly.' The formulation of the word was difficult, and her desire to keep her eyes closed was overwhelming, but the nurse insisted on lifting her head to give her a sip of water.

'We'll need to keep you hydrated but you're not sorry enough for a saline drip.'

This twisted Aberdonian attitude, Viv thought, must date back to the Reformation. She definitely felt sorry enough for a drip. The nurse gently plumped up Viv's pillows, humming a familiar tune. Viv couldn't quite place it.

'Your visitors will be back in a jiff. They just went to make some calls.'

Viv was confused, then remembered the police officers. A movement near the bed forced her to open her eyes again. The curtain was drawn back and the taller officer stood like a tower, staring at her. What did he want now?

Gently he said, 'Doctor Fraser.' He drew closer, leant forward. 'Doctor Fraser.'

Viv felt tears running down her face and into those creases again. It was a disaster when someone was nice to her when she felt rough. Embarrassed, but with nowhere to hide, she lifted her free hand to shield her face and mumbled, 'I'm sorry.'

'That was quite a bump you took there. Good job you didn't try to drive on to Edinburgh.'

'I take it I passed out and you brought me here?'

'You sure did. You came round for a few minutes but were shaking so violently that we thought you were having a fit. Apparently it's not uncommon in cases of shock. Your adrenaline goes off the scale.'

'A bit like now then?'

The officer smiled. 'You'll be fine. But you're not going home today. Is there anyone you'd like me to contact?'

The first and only person she wanted was Mac. 'Could you ring a friend of mine in Edinburgh. He's one of you.'

The officer raised his eyebrows. 'Is he now? What's his name?'

'DI Marconi, he's at Fettes.'

He didn't register any recognition of the name. 'I'll get hold of him. But you rest. You don't happen to know what the weapon was, do you?'

Viv sobbed and he didn't push her for an answer.

When she next woke up Mac was by the bed. 'How . . .'

'Don't try and speak, Viv. Not yet. I'll get the nurse.'

He parted the curtains and gestured to the nurse. She didn't come at once but when she returned there was a doctor with her. He shone a light into Viv's eyes and took her pulse, nodding to the nurse as he waited. When he'd finished Viv tried to sit up, but pain ripped through her shoulder and she sank back. She tried again. This time Mac came to help but the nurse batted him out of the way and hooked her elbow beneath Viv's armpit, at the same time shoving a huge triangular pillow behind her. This position felt less vulnerable. It took a couple of minutes before she was able to focus properly but when she did she was alarmed by the look of distress on Mac's face. He took her hand, but she withdrew it. It only made her want to cry again.

'I had no idea . . . ' She covered her face with her free hand. 'Oh boy, does this hurt?'

'I bet. Do you know who did this?'

She nodded. 'I don't have his name but I'd know his face anywhere.'

The nurse returned with a tray carrying buttered toast and tea. Mac coaxed her to have a nibble, and once she'd had one it was an easy step to another. Reassured by his presence, little by little she told Mac the details of her search for Tess Grant, and her encounter with the crowbar enthusiast. She tried to describe the location but ran out of steam. Mac held up his iPhone and said he'd be right back. Within five minutes he returned and showed her an aerial photograph on Google Earth. She nodded, and again he headed back out between the curtains.

Viv drifted in and out of sleep for some time before a different nurse shook her and offered her more tea and toast. Viv accepted; if she refused food they'd keep her for longer. Sleep came again but this time with dreams of being trapped and hyperventilating in a tight space where she couldn't stretch out her arms.

Chapter Thirteen

The soft touch of Mac's hand woke her and this time she gripped it.

He whispered, 'I think they've got him.'

She looked bemused. 'How long have I been asleep?'

'Getting on for five hours, give or take the few minutes when you gave me the story. He got the shock of his life when Grampian's best turned up on his doorstep. Denied everything of course but they've already matched his tyre treads to the farm track. Apart from his four by four, the tractor and one or two other tracks, those are the only vehicles that have been up there recently. We'll have to eliminate the other sets.' He stared at her questioningly with eyes wide open.

'One could be a Volvo. I was driving a Volvo Sunday.' He didn't take his eyes off her, hoping for further clarification.

'It belongs to . . . a friend of mine.' She gently shook her head, regretful of having to mention Gabriella. Mac raised his eyebrows. 'Anyone I know?'

Viv gave another slight shake of her head. 'D'you think they'll let me out of here?'

'I doubt it. Another twenty-four hours of observation is what the nurse told me. But she was only guessing.'

'Can't you pull some strings? Say you'll take responsibility for me, or something. That's what they need. Someone to take the flak if I pop my clogs.' She tried to lever herself up, but grimaced with pain. 'I've no intention of doing that. But I can't stay here.' Mac reckoned her recalcitrance was a good thing, and probably the first sign of recovery. She watched as he screwed up his eyes weighing the pros and cons of taking her into his care.

Then he nodded. 'I'll see what I can do.' He ducked out of the ward and Viv made another attempt at sitting up. But putting any weight on her shoulder caused pain like nothing she'd ever felt before. She almost bit through her lip, but managed to take a huge breath before rolling onto her good shoulder instead. By the time Mac returned, an ashen-faced Viv was sitting with her legs dangling over the edge of the bed looking young and more vulnerable in her NHS gown than he'd seen her since the explosion at Morgan Clifford. She caught his look and tilted her head in a question.

'Oh nothing. It's just . . . never mind. I've signed a form. Which means I'm in the driving seat . . . both physically and metaphorically. Did you get that? I am in control – you do as I say, otherwise.' He ran his hand across his throat in a cutting motion and winked.

She didn't answer but he pressed. 'Do you hear me?' When she didn't answer again he parted the curtain to leave. 'Fine. Your call.'

She shouted as best she could to his retreating back. 'Okay, okay, you win.'

He turned, fingers splayed over his hips, an expanse of pale pink shirt strained over his abs, and nodded. 'That's more like it.' Then he added, 'I've never met anyone more obstreperous than you. And given the circs . . .'

She interrupted him. 'I said okay. I'll do as you ask . . . if you're polite. Now can I have my kit . . . please?'

While Mac went in search of her clothes Viv tried to put her feet on the ground. The shock of the cold floor was nothing compared to the room spinning. She gripped the bed, feeling that she might lose consciousness. Slowly she lifted her head and steadied herself, mindful that Janice Galloway was right, the trick was to keep breathing. Even with old yoga skills the task of calming the breath was hard work. But the more she breathed deeply the more the pain eased. Mac swung back the curtain and was shocked to see her standing by the bed. He tutted, but handed her a clear poly bag containing her clothes. Courteous to a fault, he turned his back, but eventually the noise of her struggling to dress made him laugh, and he turned round to give her a hand. She hid behind her jeans.

'I've got three sisters, Viv. If I see anything I haven't seen before I'll shoot.'

She was unconvinced, but her yelp as she attempted to pull on a sock made him sharp. 'For God's sake, Viv, let me do that.' To add insult to injury she blushed. 'Hurry up and stop making a meal of it. My feet don't hurt.'

He ignored her and smiled. 'Calm down. I don't see any fire.' He blew a few strands of dark hair from his eye, a familiar gesture, which had Viv welling up again. With as much clothing on as her bandage allowed, she accepted Mac's offer of his arm and they slowly meandered out toward the car park.

'How are we going to do this?'

'Trust me, Viv, I've got this covered. I came up here in a car with a colleague. She'll take the police vehicle back and I'll drive you. Okay?'

Viv nodded, exhausted with the effort of walking even that short distance. 'Okay.'

Chapter Fourteen

Viv dozed for most of the journey but instead of taking her to her own flat Mac took her to his. She'd never been before and was surprised when the car came to a halt in Learmonth, the posh end of Comely Bank.

'What?'

Mac put a finger up to his lips. 'No arguing. You said you'd do as I ask and for one night I think you need to be here. I have work to do on my desktop.' He could see she was about to argue and pre-empted her. 'This is not negotiable, Viv. My spare room is very cosy.'

That was all she needed to hear.

Even though she had to grip the handrail to struggle up his three front steps, she still managed to take in the detail of the flat. The hallway was cavernous, with a wide set of steps leading to a floor below. A large Persian rug overlaid a dark green carpet. She trailed her hand gently across what she thought was Chinese-red wallpaper, that turned out to be fabric. She traced its raised pattern beneath her fingers, the repeat was as big as she'd ever seen. A gilt mirror hung directly above a desk with a telephone, an answering machine and other, neatly laid out, office paraphernalia. If it hadn't been for these modern necessities she might have believed she'd landed in the nineteenth century. Such opulence was not at all what she'd visualised when he'd been on the other end of that phone. As if being recalled from a dream Viv shook her head at the sound of Mac's voice.

'In here.' He gently pushed a door and stood back to allow her to enter first. She loved his manners and wondered, not for the first time, where they came from. The room had a high ceiling with a central chandelier that would grace a ballroom. Three immense bowed windows, still with their original rippled glass, took up the whole of a curved end wall. Two sofas covered with brocade sat adjacent to a veined terracotta marble fireplace. Mac bent down and lit the gas flame fire, which immediately made the place seem warmer.

He shrugged out of his own jacket and laid it over the back of a sofa. 'Let's get your jacket off, then I'll get the kettle on.'

'Mac, you don't need to do this. I just needed a way out of hospital. Let's have a cup of tea and then you can take me home.'

He looked disappointed. 'Viv. I told them I'd take care of you, and I'd like to do that . . . I'm guessing it'll only be for one night anyway. Why don't you chill on the sofa and I'll be right back with the tea.'

Too fragile to argue she sat down tentatively. Everything about the place shouted 'money'. She couldn't imagine it had all been Mac's doing, and ungraciously thought he'd inherited someone else's taste. It was pretty fabulous. The same dark green carpet from the hallway continued into the room, but she couldn't see much of it with the selection of oriental rugs that covered it. She looked up at the ornate plasterwork on the ceiling, but regretted it when her head started to spin. She sat back and closed her eyes for a few minutes while her head settled. Mac returned carrying a tray adorned with a white linen cloth and a china tea set. She really had missed the measure of this man. She'd imagined a domestic life of minimalism, wall-to-wall white, with unlived in echoing rooms.

He poured. 'Viv, the guy in Aberdeen. They think his name is William Harvey. He denies any knowledge of Tessa Grant. No surprises there, but I think since he was willing to whack you the way he did, there's no telling what he's capable of. I'm pretty concerned to find Tess. The Grampian guys will have to question everyone down here who knows anything, which will include your mates Margo et al. I'll do what I can. I was at Tulliallan with a guy who's pretty senior up there.'

Viv sighed and rubbed her temple. 'I'll get onto Margo as soon as . . . '

'No. That's not what I was getting at. I was hoping you'd give me all those details and I'd be able to delegate them to . . . How about Sandra? Would it help if you worked with Sandra? You do realise this could have been, in fact may still be, a murder enquiry and . . . '

She had considered this when she was lying in hospital. 'I know. I was lucky he didn't kill me.' She lifted the thin porcelain cup and blew across the tea: an oddly reassuring ritual. She sat back, the sofa so wide that even her long legs draped over the edge without reaching the floor, and continued. 'I'll pass on Margo's email, and Rebecca Younger, Tess's girlfriend, will need to be handled with kid gloves.'

His brow wrinkled.

'Her father is Malcolm Younger.'

'Oh! I see.' He nodded knowingly. '*The* Malcolm Younger, campaigner against same sex marriage?'

'The very same. But get this, that means her mother is Dr Betty Bates.'

He looked confused. 'Who is she?'

'Psychiatrist. Campaigner for women's rights, also pro ECT. A bit of a crazy herself, if you ask me.'

He gave her a wry smile, 'Never a dull moment for you, is there, Viv?'

'I must say this . . . ' she pointed to her head, 'isn't at all what I signed up for. I thought I'd find Tessa's family and they'd have some ideas on where she might be. But if they've scampered, and crowbar William is now the keeper of the gate, there must be something to hide up there . . . I did find some details of the Grants' involvement in a church that has recently been having financial issues. As you found for yourself. Looks as if their pastor has bolted with the church funds, which, by the way, is not our issue.'

He nodded. 'How much are we talking about?'

'Two hundred and fifty.'

'That's peanuts. Why would . . . '

She interrupted him. 'Two hundred and fifty thousand is quite a lot in my book.'

He nodded again. 'And mine. How did you find out about this?'

'The net. No details.' He knew not to press her and shook his head. 'Could we use any of this?'

She knew what he meant and nodded. 'I think so. Tess's father was the treasurer or secretary or something, but when he started to question Pastor Rawlins on one or two unauthorised withdrawals, the pastor didn't like it. Now Mr Grant is nowhere to be found and his daughter has been taken in mysterious circumstances.'

'And you know all of this . . . illegally?'

'No, some of it comes from Tess's girlfriend, some from Tess's emails.'

He shook his head again then dropped it into his hands. 'Shit, Viv. You can't look at someone's emails and get away with it.'

She didn't say anything. He raised his head and looked at her, sighing before shaking his head again.

She stared at him over the top of her teacup. 'You'd better watch. If you keep shaking it like that it'll fall off.' She smiled. 'Come on, Mac, spare me the dramatics. Everyone is at it. You don't need to know or say how I got my information. I can say I've got sources. Which is true.'

'Okay. So you have your sources and I have a concern about the girl that was pulled out of the canal, Aberdeen student. And now, all of a sudden, having never been in Aberdeen since I was a lad, I find myself racing up the road to rescue you.'

'Sir Galahad. Thank you. But you don't . . .'

He cut in. 'No, Viv. I've got a sense that there could be a connection between the girl from the canal and this stuff that you're working on.'

'How do you figure that out?'

'Oh I haven't figured it out; it's just a possibility.'

Viv knew him well enough to understand that he was not likely to speculate without good reason. They had had many discussions about their resistance to New Agey stuff. Intuition must be followed by deduction. She wondered what was tickling at his brain for him to believe there was a connection. She looked round the room, now warmed by the fire, and guessed that the central heating had also kicked in.

'Is this your doing?' She gestured with her free hand.

He smirked. 'You think someone else must have done this, don't you? Well you'd be wrong. The carpets were here but everything else was designed, if I can say that, because it wasn't really a design, more happenstance. But, yes, all my own work. Even that muckle thing.' He pointed up to the chandelier.

She lay back, trying to find a position that wasn't so painful, to get a better view of his fantastic acquisition. She wondered how on earth it stayed attached. The weight of the glass could surely bring down the plaster ceiling.

'It is amazing. Amazing! How the hell . . . ?'

'Quite something to hoist it up there. Took us . . .'

She looked at him quizzically. 'I had a team of guys from Lyon and Turnbull help me get it in here.'

She shook her head in marvel. 'This is your very own place then?'

'Yep. Parking for guests can be a bit of a bummer, which reminds me, I'd better go and put a notice on your car before it gets a ticket.' He jumped up and from the top drawer of an oriental cabinet scooped out a laminated sheet of A5 and flashed it at her. 'This should do the trick.' And he was off. The warmth of the room was soporific. She struggled to lever her boots off but once they flopped to the floor she pulled her feet up, curled onto her good side and allowed her eyelids to drop. The next thing she felt was Mac gently covering her with a duvet then she heard him tiptoe out of the room.

Tuesday. She woke up in a bed, bigger than a single but not quite a double, wearing over-sized tartan pyjamas. She snuggled into their brushed cotton and caught the smell of lavender water from the pillowcase and white duvet cover. The small room was painted pale blue. A dragging technique had been used on the walls and continued onto the headboard: impressive. She dropped her legs over the bed and ran her feet over a thick silk rug in creams and greys. Motivated by a whiff of frying drifting up from below, she wandered into the hall and pushed a door to the left of Mac's desk. Relieved to find it was a bathroom, she struggled with the necessities, then headed down the wide staircase to where the smell of bacon began to canter round her system.

Mac didn't hear her approach and Viv leant on the doorjamb, taking in the view of Fettes College through the kitchen windows. The College, a magnificent Victorian building, with towers and turrets and an entrance that would put a palace to shame, is one of Edinburgh's architectural gems. To its right sat the ugly seventies monstrosity that was Mac's home turf, Edinburgh's police HQ. The radio was on and she watched as Mac, standing with his back to her, sizzled bacon in a pan. She coughed. 'Good morning.'

He turned and smiled, his wet hair plastered across his scalp. 'You look better. Feel better?'

'Yeah. Much.' She looked down at the pyjamas and asked a question with her hand.

'It took a bit of negotiating but, promise, I didn't compromise your modesty.'

She did feel much better and was so grateful for his help that she grinned and forgot to be alarmed at how easily and how often she'd been undressed in the past few days.

'I believed you when you said you'd shoot if you hadn't seen it before.'

He held up the pan. 'Bacon?'

She nodded eagerly and wandered round the kitchen as he elegantly flipped the bacon over and shoogled the pan.

'Work today. For both of us if you can take it, Viv.'

Not sure what he meant, she tilted her head. 'What do you mean?'

'I think we should head back up to Aberdeen. The sooner you identify your assailant the sooner we can press charges. He's bound to start talking when he knows we've had a positive ID.'

'Can't we do that from here?'

He paused. 'We could, but it would speed things up if we went.'

Viv ran through all the things that she should be doing. The first was to contact Gabriella who probably thought she'd done a runner. She hated the idea of having to explain what had happened and yet it wouldn't be possible to hide the bruising, which was already developing the most amazing deep purple hues.

She crossed the warm tiled floor, stepped into a small glass-roofed porch, leant on a chair, and looked back into the kitchen, comfortable with what she saw. Copper pots and pans hung above a solid wood workstation, their handles hooked onto a circular rack. The ceilings were lower down here, which made it cosier. Viv's client, Ailsa, lived at the other end of this street but her flat didn't have the views, or such stunning décor.

She swept her good hand round the room. 'Is this also your doing?'

He grinned. 'Most of it. I like to cook, to wind down somewhere completely different from the grey corridors of Fettes. But so do you. Sherlock Holmes would be at home in your place. And I'd like to think he wouldn't be out of sorts here either. We've got more in common than you think, Viv.'

This sent off an alarm bell inside her head. 'Those bacon butties ever going to be ready?'

He fiddled about with rashers of bacon, roasted tomatoes and garlic mayo on warmed ciabatta rolls with olives in them. She salivated, and with her good arm, pulled the chair out from the table. It was heavier than she'd imagined and the reason soon stirred. Two cats curled up on a green velvet cushion opened their eyes and peered at the strange apparition who was disturbing their peace. She took another chair and watched as one of the cats jumped onto the floor, stretched and sauntered towards a shaggy sheepskin rug. Adjacent to it sat a pagoda shaped box decorated with red and gold oriental motifs. Viv stared as the cat disappeared through a flap in one end. On reappearing it sat licking its back paw, in a posture that would take even the most committed Yogi a lifetime of practice.

Mac brought the plates over and they tucked in with only the odd 'Mmm' and 'Ahh' by way of appreciation. After a second cup of blow-your-head-off coffee Viv said, 'My God. Dee-bloody-licious. D'you always make this kind of effort?'

'Not all the time. It's nice to be nice. Food's about commensality, building allies.'

Surprised by this, she exclaimed, 'But I'm not your enemy, Mac!'

'No. But you still don't trust me. Do you?'

'What's . . . Nearly. I nearly trust you.' She grinned and nodded gently, aware of the pain that was lying in wait if she moved too vigorously. 'I must get going. If we're going back up today I've got people to see and things to do.'

He raised his eyebrows. 'You're still in my care, remember?'

She wiped her mouth and hands on a napkin then pushed her chair back and headed towards the stairs. She threw over her shoulder as she went, 'Yeah, my cordon bleu minder, not about to trade you in anytime soon.' She giggled on her way to the bedroom where she found her clothes in a neat pile on a chair opposite the bed. How had she missed them?

Once she'd dressed she made for the kitchen. 'I'll come back when I've got through the things on my list.'

'List, eh? Nice try, Viv. But you ain't going nowhere without me.'

'I don't need you to come with me. I'm going home to change and have a shower. I'm not about to exert myself in any way. I've a few emails to catch up on and someone to see. Then I'll be back.'

He looked at her, resigned, and heaved a huge sigh. 'Okay. How about we meet at Fettes.' He checked the clock on the kitchen wall. 'Midday?'

Viv looked at the clock as well. 'Should be able to do that. If I'm running late I'll ring you.'

'Fine.'

Viv walked towards the stairs again, but turned. 'Thanks, Mac. I'm really grateful that you came to fetch me.'

'I'd rather you were glad.'

She thought about this a moment then slowly nodded. 'I am . . . Thanks again.'

Chapter Fifteen

The West Bow had been closed off for filming, and an outside broadcast lorry was taking up six parking spaces, forcing Viv to circle even more than usual. She cursed and eventually had to leave the car on King's Stables Road and walk slowly back through the Grassmarket.

When she reached the Bow a man in a day-glo vest with a walkie-talkie stopped her. 'No access this morning. You'll have to . . . '

Viv squeezed with some effort between him and the metal fence. 'I live here.'

He started to splutter but she ignored him. She wanted to see Gabriella. The door to the shop was locked so Viv tapped on the glass door in the hope that Gabriella was down in the basement. She looked around. There was no sign of the Volvo but it was no wonder. The street was empty of cars and there was a layer of muck over the street covering any evidence of the twenty-first century. A carriage with a man in a top hat stood outside what used to be a church, now converted into a variety of eateries. Viv knocked on the glass again, convinced she could hear music coming from inside. No luck.

As Viv put her key into the lock of her outside door something made her glance round. Gabriella stood staring at her from inside the shop. Viv removed the key and started back towards the shop but Gabriella turned and disappeared down into the basement. Viv banged on the door, to no avail. 'Shit.' She took out her phone, scrolled for Gabriella's number and waited. She heard it ring on the other side of the door; Gabriella's bag must have been beneath the counter, but wasn't visible. It rang and rang but Gabriella ignored it. Viv checked her own messages and counted twenty-seven missed calls from Gabriella's number. Disconsolate, she returned to the flat. She'd find another way to explain. The mailbox in the passage was full of correspondence, which she loaded into the sling on her arm as she climbed the stairs. There wasn't anything beyond junk and she'd bin the lot. When she reached the top landing Ronnie, her next door neighbour, was at her door wearing an apron and rubber gloves. 'What . . .?'

'Oh hello Viv.' He continued wiping down her door. 'I came out and interrupted someone. They'd smeared marmalade all over your lovely brasses.'

Viv couldn't think straight. Who would do such a senseless thing?

Ronnie said, 'I'm almost finished.'

Viv realised that Ronnie wasn't stammering. Then he turned and looking straight at her opened his mouth but couldn't get his sentence started. 'Thanks Ronnie. I owe you.'

He smiled, picked up his bucket of soapy water and retreated inside his own flat. Viv put her Yale key into the lock and made a note to self to buy Ronnie a bottle of wine. Who would do such a thing? Surely not Gabriella.

Her in-box had a number of messages requiring attention, not least a pleading request from Margo on behalf of Rebecca, who had changed her tune about her father getting to know about her sexuality.

'Too late was the loud reply,' Viv muttered to herself. 'Too late.'

She didn't have an email address for Gabriella but found a website for the shop which she could use. Unsure where to begin she wrote and deleted, wrote and deleted three or four attempts, no easy task with one arm out of commission, then sighed, staring at the screen. She leaned back and said out loud, 'Okay, Gabriella, what do you need to believe in order to behave like this?' A number of scenarios ran through Viv's mind, but the one that made the most sense was that Gabriella believed that Viv had lied and had been with someone else. Which was actually true, but not in the way that it might look to a potential new playmate. In her NLP days Viv remembered doing an exercise with a woman who didn't trust her husband. Whatever he did, the wife made up her own fantasy about what he was up to, and never gave him credit for doing what he actually was doing, which was usually work. What fantasy was Gabriella entertaining at the moment, in order to demonise Viv? She decided to tell Gabriella every detail of her story and if Gabriella couldn't hack it perhaps she was not for Viv anyway. In fact, as she typed, doubts began to settle in, and she guessed it was already too late. Once the email was winging its way Viv sat on the couch and looked round her little flat. She could see what Mac meant, that they had a lot in common. His flat was on a much grander scale but they definitely had a similar theme going. Deep coloured walls and lots of old velvet made for a spooky Victorian stage set. If it wasn't for the hundreds of modern books on her shelves, she could certainly convince herself that Mrs Hudson might come through the door any minute. Her own Persian rug was shabbily frayed at the edges but was all the more welcoming for that. She stroked the dark red velvet curtain that she used as a throw for the chesterfield, gaining a strange comfort from the way the colour changed as light caught the weft.

She put a hand up to her neck and gently pressed the bruise. 'Ouch!' How lucky she had been that the crowbar didn't hit the top of her head. She'd have been a goner. If he had wanted her dead, he could have killed her while she was unconscious. And why had he left that light bulb on? He mustn't have had a plan otherwise her keys wouldn't have been left exposed in his truck. What exactly was he hiding? Was it Tess or the others or both or something else entirely? The phone ringing startled her. 'Hello.' Silence. 'Hello. Gabriella is that you?'

'No, lady, it is not Gabriella. I'm someone you haven't met and wouldn't want to . . .'

There was a scuffle in the background and the line went dead. She dialled one four seven one and a voice said. 'The caller withheld their number.' The caller's strong American accent definitely didn't belong to anyone she knew. Pastor Rawlins was the only American that she had been interested in recently. 'Crikey! Another threat.' When her mobile rang her belly clenched. She checked caller ID and found it was Mac. Relieved, she held the phone to her ear. 'Hi, Mac.'

'What's going on?' As if he'd already picked up her anxiety.

'Just had a call. American voice. A caricature of threatening . . . '

'You do one four seven one?'

'Yeah. Number withheld.'

'You really up for another journey, Viv?'

She sighed and shook her head. 'Not really, but as you say the sooner I ID him the sooner he'll be out of our hair. And maybe he'll talk . . . Can you ask the Grampian guys to find out if my attacker knows anything about Pastor Rawlins? He's the chap who ran off with the church funds.'

'You get here asap . . . you sure you're all right?'

The idea of driving had no appeal to her. 'Actually, Mac, if there's any chance that you could pick me up I'd really appreciate that. I'm knackered and I'm parked a million miles away.'

He knew she'd never accept a lift, let alone ask for one unless she was desperate. 'Give me half an hour or so.'

'Okay. And Mac, I'll wait for you at the war memorial. There's filming in Victoria Street and parking's bedlam.'

'Sure. Half an hour.'

After a hot shower Viv plastered her shoulder in arnica gel, dressed losing the bandages, then headed out the door. She passed her new neighbour, a Spanish post grad, who had taken the flat below her. She had only met him a couple of times, the last when he invited her in for coffee but produced endless plates of food that he'd been sent from his home, an organic pig farm in Salamanca. They exchanged pleasantries and she nodded a vague answer to his request that they get together again.

The film crew were still at work with their cameras set up on Victoria Terrace. She glanced across to Gabriella's and saw her speaking to a customer, but her back was to the street so she didn't see Viv. There were a few men sitting with cans of beer on the steps of the war memorial, so Viv hovered outside the joke shop window until she spotted Mac's Audi turning in. As she opened the car door she looked back and saw Gabriella at her shop doorway still with the customer. Their eyes met but Gabriella quickly looked away.

The leather strap of Viv's rucksack got caught in Mac's car door and she blasphemed trying to untangle it from the recliner switch. 'Shit! Shit! Shit!'

Mac smiled. 'Everything all right there?'

'Don't even . . . '

She didn't finish, remembering this was not Mac's problem. 'Sorry.' She took a deep breath and leaned back into the headrest. 'Give me a minute and I'll be fine.'

Mac performed a nifty U-turn and they were on their way.

Mac laughed. 'I heard from Aberdeen just now. Get this. Your attacker says that he was trying to free you from the shed when you kicked him in the groin.'

With a fair bit of effort she turned in her seat and looked at him in disbelief. 'What a nerve . . . '

'Your word against his.'

'Yeah, sure, Mac. I whacked myself on the back of the head then locked myself in a shed and, unprovoked, booted some guy, who was trying to save me, in the balls. And I don't think.'

Mac smiled. 'Did you hear what I said? Your word against his.'

She shook her head. 'I don't fucking believe this. How can the Aberdeen guys . . . '

He interrupted her before her rant took off. 'They're not stupid, Viv. They'll be doing everything to gather evidence. When he knocked you out you must have fallen and he must have lifted you. There will be fibres if not DNA. But it will take time, and he is saying that you walloped him. I'm just trying to prepare you for what's about to happen. Stay calm.'

There was nothing worse than someone telling you to stay calm. 'Well, indebted I'm sure,' she growled under her breath.

'Oi! Don't shoot the messenger.' He shook his head. 'Now let's you and I go over the whole story again. Starting with your night out to the Dragon with Margo et al.'

'Oh God. Do we have to?'

He thrummed his fingers on the steering wheel. 'I think it would help if I have as much information as you do. I don't need to remind you that you got me involved in this. So everything, come on, spill.'

Viv went through the process of explaining how she had been asked by

Margo to find Tess Grant. Firstly, her meeting with Rebecca, going through Tess's room and the emails between Tess and the person she referred to as 'Si'.

'The guy that's banged up in Aberdeen, saying I beat him up, must be involved in the church. When I first mentioned going to speak to other members of the congregation about Tess's dad, he got really tetchy. I wonder if there actually is a building where they worship, or if they meet in each others houses.'

Mac gave her a searching look. 'You mean no building with an altar or a font?'

'Church didn't originally mean bricks and mortar. It applied to the followers. They can worship anywhere, indoors or out, altar or not. We could be talking about someone's back room, even a chicken shed.' He raised his eyebrows and she continued. 'Andrew Grant, Tess's dad, works for an oil company, so I'm sure we'll be able to trace him through their offices in Aberdeen. If we get hold of him we'll be well on our way to finding Tess. I have a funny feeling she'll be with the family. Wherever they are now.'

He pondered what she'd said. 'It'll be interesting to see what we can pump from William Harvey.' He nodded. 'Why do so many religious groups attract crazy folk?'

Viv stared out as they swept past green fields, her view occasionally interrupted by an efficient single stroke of a windscreen wiper clearing light drizzle.

She answered. 'The Eastern Brethren is a pretty popular sect in the USA, but who knows what could have become of them in Aberdeenshire. The committee that chose Pastor Rawlins obviously weren't too hot on judging good character. By the way, the guy that bashed me has a tattoo with 'Jesus Saves' on his butt.'

Mac didn't answer but shook his head. As they turned off the motorway towards Dundee Mac pressed a button on the radio. 'I'd be surprised if the local radio haven't got hold of this yet.'

Viv hadn't given this a thought, but of course they were bound to pick it up. She could even have made the local newspapers. They listened to traffic news before a young woman gave the headlines. Sure enough they ran a story where a man had been taken into custody after 'allegedly' attacking a woman on a farm.

Viv sighed. 'Thank goodness it happened in Aberdeen and not Glasgow. Imagine . . . actually I guess nothing short of a stabbing would make them turn out at the Glasgow courts, and even then I'd have to be dead.' They laughed knowingly. Scotland was one country, but many lands.

Chapter Sixteen

When they arrived at Grampian police HQ there wasn't a soul in sight. Mac opened Viv's door and helped her from the car. She hissed, 'I'm not an invalid,' then yelped as she caught her shoulder on the edge of the door. Mac looked away and whistled, but turned back with a grin on his face. She, with eyes bulging, pointed a finger at him, daring him to utter a word.

Once inside she was reassured that Mac immediately switched into autopilot and the whole form filling process, second nature to him, was over before she knew it. One of the officers who had taken her to hospital appeared, his tanned face incongruous in this grey walled corridor with grubby linoleum and industrial strip lighting.

'Due for a refit any time soon?' offered Mac.

The officer raised his eyebrows. 'I don't think décor is high on anyone's priority list . . . ' He opened a door and stepped aside to let them through. Mac said, 'What's the story?'

The officer filled Mac in as he led the way. 'He swears that he was trying to help Doctor Fraser here to get out of the chicken shed, when she went for him.'

Viv drew in a huge breath and shook her head in disgust.

Mac put up his hand. 'You don't have to say anything yet, Viv; relax. This is going to be fine.' He turned back to the officer. 'What did forensics find?'

The officer looked from Mac to Viv and back again. Mac nodded his permission.

'They've not had much luck . . . '

Viv interrupted him. 'All they have to do is take a sample from the inside of my jacket pocket, and a sample from his passenger seat and they'll find all manner of matches. Mainly biscuit crumbs, but fibres and tissue paper fragments probably with my DNA on them. He emptied my pockets when he knocked me out the first time. When . . . ' choosing her words carefully, 'I got free I retrieved them from the front passenger seat of his Nissan truck.'

Mac nodded again to the officer, who then gestured to Viv to remove her jacket. He handed her an evidence bag which she dropped the jacket into. He left with the jacket in the bag, while they waited in tense silence for him to return.

'Tea anyone?' A cheerful female PC stuck her head round the door.

Mac responded. 'I'll have a cup.'

'Milk and two?'

He nodded and smiled at the PC.

Viv looked at Mac. 'You don't usually take sugar.'

'No, but it could be grisly and sugar will get it over.'

'Crikey, Mac, does nothing change outside the capital? Female still on crap tea duty.' She blew out her disdain.

'Every unit is different, Viv. Inverness is totally switched on. They've even got a female DCI.'

'Yeah, they might have but the fact that you say "even" means it's still nowhere near standard procedure. Neanderthal policing or what?'

'You'd better save your breath for your broth until these guys get you out of what could become a fiasco if we're not careful.'

As if her message had got round, a male PC knocked and entered with their tea and a plate of chocolate digestives. Mac threw a 'watch it' look at Viv that made her grin.

'Digestives. Mmm, my favourite.'

Mac threw her another look. The tea wasn't bad.

The officer returned and, speaking more to Mac than Viv, said, 'This guy has more names than Di Caprio. He told us he was William Harvey but his wallet and glove compartment turned up a selection of cards with different names on all of them.'

This made Viv sit forward in her seat. 'Any chance that we could see what those other names are?'

The officer turned to Mac, who nodded. 'Don't see why not.'

The officer poked his head out of the door and spoke to someone in the corridor. Then returned. 'So what's going on, Doctor Fraser, that you're in Aberdeenshire on investigative work that we don't know about? It's manners to let the local police know when you're nosing about in something illegal.'

Viv screwed up her face. 'Wait a minute. I haven't done anything illegal. I was only looking into a matter for a friend who is worried about someone.'

'It's all a bit of a coincidence that we've been trying to get a handle on a group,' he continued, his tone sarcastic. 'You might have heard of them: the Eastern Brethren. Their pastor has gone missing with a large sum of money.'

Mac interrupted. 'Two hundred and fifty thousand.'

The officer looked surprised. 'How did you know that?'

'Viv, I mean Doctor Fraser has been looking for a young girl, unofficially reported missing, and among the girl's emails and correspondence she discovered the troubles at the church.'

Viv's mouth twitched at this suitably vague summary. The officer wasn't daft and shook his head in disbelief.

'The more information we all have,' his emphasis on all, 'the better, wouldn't you say? Now I'm guessing that's why you were at the farm. I'd like to hear the whole story. So from the top, Doctor Fraser, and don't be shy.'

Viv told him about her first visit on Sunday at noon and how even then the guy, whatever his name turned out to be, was on edge. Keen to warn her off. Then on Monday when she returned she'd been taking a peek in the barn when someone crept up behind her and whacked her on the back of the head. When she woke up she was in the chicken shed. As she recalled this she still couldn't imagine what his motivation was. Unless he believed it was some way of torturing her. The actual escape sounded completely unreal when she described him blinding her with the headlights of his truck and her instinctive reaction when he began to bring the crowbar down towards her head.

'The rest you know.'

'Wait a minute. Was he really aiming at your head?'

Viv sighed. 'Of course he was. And I wasn't about to die in a chicken shed in . . . '

Mac sensed where she was going with this and kicked her beneath the table to prevent her from offending her best hope.

'Yes. Go on.'

'I'm not ready to meet my Maker and you'd have done the same as me if faced with a crowbar-wielding nutcase.'

'I've no doubt you're right. But how am I to prove that he wasn't acting in self-defence?'

'Does he have character references or something? He threatened me on Sunday and then walloped me twice on Monday. There'll be enough DNA around him. He must have carried me into the chicken shed. His tee-shirt, jacket, jeans, car seat: somewhere out there is proof in the form of my hair or fibres from my jacket, scarf.' She rolled her free hand. 'Remember he took everything out of my pockets and left them on the front seat of his truck. It's not frickin' rocket science.'

Mac gently kicked her again.

The officer stood with his head cocked and eyebrows raised. Then quietly in his soft Aberdeen accent, 'It's all right, Doctor Fraser. We get the same resources as your chum here does down in Fettes.'

Mac butted in. 'She just meant . . . '

'I know what she meant. We've already got forensics onto stuff from the truck. Rome wasn't built in a day. His story is that he was trying to help . . . '

Viv lost it. 'His story is a pack of lies. D'you think I whacked myself on the back of the fucking head?'

Mortified, she felt her eyes filling and put her hand over her face.

'As it happens we don't think that you whacked yourself over the head, nor do we think you fell and bumped it. But, as you probably know, what we think and what we can prove are two different things. Now what else have you got that will help me build a convincing story to keep him for another day. Everything mind.' The warning in his voice was obvious.

Viv went through the whole thing again, right down to the details about emails and the letters redirected to Tess from her home.

This time the officer nodded. 'Right, that's better. We can get a look at his computer. See what's going on there. You weren't planning on going south again?'

Viv turned to Mac, who asked, 'How long do you think you'll need her here?'

'There's not much more apart from the ID that she's got to be here for. But I'd want to know she wasn't planning to leave the country.'

Mac smiled. 'I'll vouch for her.' He sensed Viv's eyes boring a hole in the side of his head. Viv sat, incredulous that they'd just spoken about her as if she wasn't there.

'Right, Doctor Fraser, if you follow me we'll let you have a look at him.'

She was led into a room with a window through which she could see into another room. Her attacker was brought in and Viv gasped. It was definitely him.

'Could you ask him to turn round and lift up his tee-shirt? He has a tattoo just above his butt that says "Jesus Saves".'

After a few minutes an officer entered the custody room, and indicated for him to lift his shirt. Her attacker stared at the mirror defiantly. Then he grinned and suddenly lunged towards it, flicking his studded tongue at her. She leapt back, knocking over a chair. The officer in the other room grabbed his arm. Viv quickly recovered herself but felt unsettled knowing that he knew she was there even though he couldn't see her. Her knowledge of the tattoo convinced the officer that he was her attacker and he led Viv back to where Mac was waiting. Her ashen face was a sign that she'd had enough.

'Let's get out of here.' Mac took her arm and they headed out to the car. 'Everything's going to be fine, Viv. They just can't show you any preferential treatment.'

She pulled her arm away. 'I wasn't expecting preferential treatment. I only need them to use their brain cells.'

'Yes, and you were not very tactful about that, were you? If someone spoke to you the way you spoke to that detective you'd have gone off your rocker. I know you're feeling vulnerable . . .'

'Do I fuck!'

He opened the car door and blew his cheeks out. 'I rest my case. Get in.' He held the door as she edged into the seat.

The journey home was bound to be a long one. She sat staring into the space beyond the window with silent tears rolling down her face. The weight on her chest felt physical, solid, as if she could lift it off in one piece, only she couldn't. She knew enough about her own psychology to understand that her reaction was disproportionate to the event. Was this about Dawn's loss again?

When they reached the Forth Road Bridge she turned and looked at Mac. His profile was calm and reassuring and she heaved a huge sigh. He stretched across and rubbed her hand briefly. There were very few men that she could tolerate the way she did Mac, and she suspected this sentiment worked in reverse. He took her straight to her own flat, and if she was honest this left her feeling a grain of disappointment.

'Thanks, Mac.' Genuine words.

He nodded and bit the inside of his cheek. 'Take it easy, Viv. And don't go anywhere that will get me into trouble.'

She remembered that the officer in Aberdeen was only happy to let her come home because of Mac's position.

'I'll be here.'

He waited in the car until she was inside the building.

A hot shower and bed were all she aspired to.

Chapter Seventeen

Wednesday Viv spent recovering in bed ignoring every form of communication until teatime, when she mustered the courage to punch Sal's number into her phone. Relief flooded through her when a recording of Sal's voice said, 'Please leave a message.' As she did so, Viv recognised her own familiar pattern of resistance for what it was. Fear. Fear that rose in equal measure with the quickening of her heart at the thought of Sal's beautiful face, her razor sharp intellect, and her emotional wisdom. The knowledge that she was someone that Viv could spend a long time with was much more scary to her than any Aberdeen heavy with a tattoo. Somewhere in Viv's soul she knew she needed Sal, and there was no stronger reason to resist her.

Wallowing in bed had given her ample time to reflect on her behaviour over the last few days. First, her indiscretion with Almond Eyes. She shook her head in despair. What the hell had that been about? Then Gabriella. Who was probably a nice enough woman . . . very generous, Viv. But God, what was Gabriella next to Sal? What was she thinking? A night with the telly was the only way out of her head.

By Thursday, a hair day, she still struggled to stretch, barely able to raise her arms to wash her own hair. She flicked through her diary checking the kinds of haircuts that she might have to tackle. She decided that she was being pathetic. Most were more than doable. Only one client with long layering, who even on a good day had Viv feeling as if she'd had an hour of body-pump. She rang and left a message asking to postpone the appointment. With that done she went into the hall cupboard and raked around for a large canvas bag with wheels on it; a discarded Christmas gift from her mother that had been gathering dust for a couple of years. To get to it she had to shift all manner of things, including a box of old photographs. She made the mistake of glancing at the top of the bundle. Before she knew what she was doing she was on the hall floor going through them one by one. They spanned her adult life. Viv sat with her back to the wall and let her tears flow, until the telephone rang. Wiping her face with the back of her hand, she took a huge breath before lifting the receiver. 'Hi. Viv here.'

At first she imagined it was a repeat of yesterday's threat but then Gabriella's defensive voice broke the silence. 'It's Gabriella. I got your email . . . We need to talk.'

This had Viv on the starting blocks, ready to run in the opposite direction. 'We need to talk' was the kind of non-negotiable statement that Viv had shrunk from all her life.

'Gabriella. I've got to work today . . . ' Viv heard the dead tone and sighed, thankful not to have to explain any more and resigned to Gabriella's reaction. Dawn had had many faults and couldn't be trusted, but strangely enough she had trusted Viv, and that had mattered more. Returning to the photographs lying on the floor, she gathered them back into the box. She spotted the bag beneath the hose of an old vacuum and eased it out. Her mother had said it would come in handy one day. Viv smiled at the recollection of her own response and how, more often than she liked, her mother turned out to be right.

Before she left for work Viv checked her emails. There was a short, badly written response from Walter's alleged stalker, arguing that Walter was the one with the issue. That he was always turning up at things, and in places where he knew that she would be; including the hair salon. This should be easy to check. Viv sent Walter an email asking where he had his hair cut. Then she tucked her rucksack into the bag and shrugged as best she could into a jacket. After locking up she headed towards her car.

Viv's first client was in Cluny, an area of Edinburgh regarded as the superior fringe of the muesli belt. With its large houses within walking distance of good comprehensives, the area had a real mix of ageing hippies and lefty conservative corporates. Viv counted four different school uniforms on her way.

Ricola Wedgewood, with her distant connection to Josiah and therefore a tenuous link to Darwin, was a tiny, shy, intellectual woman whose husband, a company director whose name she hadn't taken, worked abroad. She spent too much time with the NCT group and people at the school gate, who wanted to discuss nothing more than breast-feeding and anything else to do with their children. Consequently when Viv arrived there was often some more testing question hovering on Ricola's lips. The door was ajar and Viv pushed it open and shouted, 'Hi Ricky! It's me, Viv!'

Somewhere above another door opened and Ricola rushed down the stairs with a towel on her head. 'Have you heard of this new digital programme that can make an exact replica of your bones?'

Viv smiled at Ricola's back as they strolled through her hallway to the kitchen. 'I have, as a matter of fact, but only because I saw a piece on the news about it. Surely if your bone is defective you don't want an exact replica. You want something new that works better than the old one.'

Ricky furrowed her brow. 'You've got a point there. I hadn't thought of that.'

They laughed as Viv began to set up. 'What's the plan today?'

Viv knew that whatever the 'plan' it made no odds. Ricky never had her hands at peace. Once Viv had counted Ricky ruffling her hair twenty-two times, which was quite something given that for most of the forty-five minute slot Viv had been cutting and blow-drying her hair. As Viv laid out her gardener's sheet, Ricky took bread out of the oven and laid it on a cooling tray.

Viv nodded towards the loaf. 'It'd be safer to put that somewhere else. I'd hate to get hair on it. Besides the smell would be a delicious form of torture.'

Ricky smiled and removed the bread to the utility room. As Viv waited, she glanced at a tabloid lying open on the kitchen table, unusual for Ricky. The page three headline read, 'False alarm at Country House Ball'. Viv only got the chance to start the first paragraph before Ricky returned. 'Have you read this?'

She pointed to the article and Ricky stood on tip-toe to look over Viv's shoulder. 'Oh yes. It's about a famous diamond going missing then turning up in the family vault.'

Viv was intrigued but had work to do. She would wait to get the lowdown online later.

Ricky, however, had other ideas. 'I've met them, you know. Bryce is on the board at Gordonstoun; the Newhall boys were there. Amazing what you learn at governor's dinners. That story is a follow-up.' She pointed to the paper. 'The other day the headline was "Jewel Theft!".' She laughed and ran her hand through the air describing an imaginary headline. '"Cat burglar comes to Scotland. Has Monaco run out of jewels"?'

Viv smiled and dug into her kit for her scissors. It was unlike Ricky to get drawn into local news. Her usual idea of a chat would shame the academics that Viv used to work with.

Before Viv started cutting, Ricky said, 'If the phone rings you'll have to excuse me for a minute. I'm waiting for a call from my GP.'

'No problem. So are we having a change today or sticking with your safe bet?'

Ricky sat straight as a rod, as Viv had taught her, with her feet firmly planted shoulder-width apart. A squint body meant squint hair. 'Not sure I'm strong enough for a change. Let's just keep it as it is for now.'

Viv continued to cut into Ricky's short choppy layers. The phone didn't ring until Viv had almost finished the blow-dry and Ricky leaped up to the handset and took it into the hall. Viv was party to all sorts of personal stuff, often stuff that she didn't see needed to be a secret, but she had long since understood that the stories she encountered were not hers to tell. When Ricky returned she was grinning from ear to ear. 'Good news. Tests are all clear.'

Viv smiled. 'Great.' No notion of what had been tested but delighted that whatever it was Ricky was relieved.

Ricky let go of a huge breath. 'You can do what you like with my hair now.' Unable to resist, she ruffled it then sat, her body language completely transformed. 'Where were we?'

'You were saying that you weren't strong enough for a change but it's too late now. I'm almost through.' Viv stepped round in front of Ricky and pulled at tendrils reaching for her cheekbones. 'Yes. That looks really good. Not many women can get away with this elfin look, but you can. Eat your heart out Twiggy.'

Ricky snorted. 'I wish. The eyes are beginning to sag. Not much I can do about that though. I'm definitely not up for surgery. Although Bryce did suggest it.'

Viv was horrified. 'You don't need surgery! I'd kill for peepers like yours.'

'You're a sweetie for saying that. But you know what Bryce is like. Never satisfied.'

Bryce wasn't the only husband who was a full-time critic. He wasn't exactly George Clooney himself, but it didn't stop him. God help their children.

Viv was keen to get more information about the false alarm at Newhall but had another client to see before she could go home. She arrived slightly early and sat in the car outside the house, only a short distance away from Ricola's, and checked her phone. There was a message from Walter. She rang him back. 'Hi, Walter. How's it going?' She was aware that this kind of social fluff was an irritation to him but, hey, tough.

'I was just wondering how you were getting on with . . . ' He must have put his hand over the speaker because all she could hear was his muffled voice speaking to someone else.

'If you're busy I'll ring you back.'

'No. No. It's fine. I've had an email from you know who. Explaining a few things, things which make sense in the context of . . . '

Viv interrupted, sensing that he was backing off. 'I have also had an email from her.'

'Ah! So what story has she spun you?'

'Whether it was a story spun or not, Walter, are you sure you would like me to carry on my search? It didn't sound like the kind of thing that I'd be able to help with.' She cleared her throat. 'After all you're the one with the legendary people skills.' When in doubt she appealed to the ego.

He gave the slightest chuckle. 'Perhaps the stress of work made me exaggerate. I appreciate your trouble, Viv, but I think I'll be able to handle it after all.'

Viv shook her head. 'I didn't go to any trouble. I only sent her one email.'

'I'll square up with you if tell me what your fees are.'

'Let's call it a favour for old times' sake, Walter. And if I were you I'd still find someone to speak to. Your supervision clearly isn't cutting the mustard. Everybody needs someone to talk to . . . even you.' She knew she'd lost him at 'if I were you' but it was worth a try.

Viv got slightly nervous in the company of her next client, especially if there was no one else around. She'd spotted his huge frame towering over a small female in the crowd at the book launch the other night but she didn't think he saw her. He was on sabbatical, which meant working from home. Viv usually did his hair at his office, a safe place with secretaries knocking and entering at any moment, in the New Royal Infirmary. On one foolish occasion he made an inappropriate suggestion, allegedly in a joke, which Viv batted straight into orbit, giving him a look that had made him wither. Ralph Mullan was at the top of his game, a neurosurgeon whose attention to detail had always been admired. He was not shy and wore his intellect heavily on the sleeves of his Savile Row linen suits, some of them now a fraction too tight. With too many conferences his belly had begun to droop over a belt that was bound to have cost more than Viv's whole outfit. His hair, a mane of shiny dark locks, was his crowning glory. He believed he could trace this to his Spanish ancestry when sailors from the Armada swam ashore off the Ardnamurchan peninsula on the west coast. Viv rang the bell and Ralph answered, specs on his forehead. He looked surprised to see her.

'Oh, Viv. Is it that time already?' He stood aside and beckoned her in. 'Can you just give me a minute? I must save what I was doing.'

'Go ahead. I'll set up in the kitchen.' The kitchen was shambolic. Dishes piled up by the sink, unread newspapers on the table, among them the Red Top that Viv wrote an occasional anonymous column for. Lucy, Ralph's wife, must be away. She was also a doctor but had decided to go part-time until the children were a bit older. Viv sensed that the children had been something of a shock to Ralph whose Porche 911 didn't have space for a conventional baby seat.

'I'll go and get this mop washed. I'll only take a minute.' He gestured to a high- backed chair at the table. 'Grab a seat,' he said, as he took off towards the stairs.

At the other end of the table lay a copy of the book from the launch, sitting next to his laptop, which sprang into life when Viv accidentally nudged it as she reached for the book. She was tempted to look but only glanced at a screen full of graphs before lifting the book and leafing through it as she leaned against wall beside the double patio doors.

When Ralph returned he was dripping all over the floor. No idea that he should have given his hair a good rub with a towel before traipsing back through the house.

'I don't know how I could have forgotten. It's desperate. In fact I wish I'd had it cut last week. I was at a white tie do at the weekend and it looked a bit theatrical.'

Viv's ears pricked up and she laid the book back on the table. There are very few such events in Edinburgh and it was too much to think that there'd be more than one in a weekend. Without thinking she said, 'Oh, that must have been Thurza's,' then immediately wished she hadn't. She fiddled around getting her kit ready.

He shot her a quizzical look. 'The Countess of Newhall.' He doesn't pronounce the h. 'You know her then?'

Viv looked at him with knitted brows.

'Of course you do. Silly me. There are very few whose locks don't come under your tutelage.'

'Did you have a nice time?'

He shrugged. 'As fundraisers go it wasn't at all bad. Why were you not there?'

Viv laughed. 'Not enough dosh. Did you have to take a table?'

'No. I was invited by some other rich sod who had been talked into it. You'll have heard about the diamond.'

Viv nodded, trying not to look interested.

'What a crazy bitch she is.'

Viv was even more intrigued, but wrapped a gown round his shoulders and combed his wet hair back from his face. 'You looking for a change or six weeks' worth?'

He laughed. 'That's what I love about you, Viv. No messing about. Straight to the point. Six weeks' worth, please.'

Viv set to work, and he, not beyond being impressed by aristocracy, carried on his story about the ball.

'Apparently at some point during dinner, a woman sitting at Thurza's table took a close look at the diamond and commented that the thread that had been used to secure it was different from the thread used for all the other jewels on the dress. Thurza said that it wasn't surprising given that the diamond was a newer addition. But the woman insisted that the diamond had been sewn on with cotton thread, which was completely wrong for the silk fabric. Thurza tried to argue that it was fine, but by this time Toddy, her dullard of a husband, had overheard some of their conversation and was intrigued. The upshot of all of this was that Thurza had removed the real diamond and put it in the family vault for safe keeping, then replaced it with a piece of cut glass. Said she was worried that someone would steal the dress. I'm amazed you haven't heard the details if you're her hairdresser.'

'I saw her on the morning of the event. It sounds like a sensible move to me.'

'Ah, but Toddy thinks she was squirrelling.'

Viv shook her head. 'Thurza doesn't need to squirrel.'

'Well apparently . . . '

Viv clasped her hands over her ears. 'I don't want to hear it. Don't tell me any more. If Thurza tells me then fine, but I'm not interested to hear goss.'

He laughed again. 'We're lucky to have you. You could dish the dirt on all of us anytime you fancied.'

'Yeah. And how long would my business last if I did? How's Lucy?'

'Oh she's fine. Down south seeing her aged parents and leaving me to my own inadequate devices.' He gestured round the kitchen. 'I need looking after, Viv.'

'My heart bleeds. Where's the au pair?'

'She's around but her remit was only to care for the children and I'm not included.'

This really did make Viv laugh. 'It's a tough life. You living on calorie-counted dinners?'

He looked hurt and patted his belly. 'Suppose I could do with it. Luce left me food in the freezer.'

'God, Ralph! What are you like? Did you not have a mother who cooked?'

He raised his eyebrows. 'No. My mother was a nippy Glaswegian politician who didn't have time to cook for us. She was too busy looking out for everyone else's kids.'

Viv had forgotten about his early family life. 'Never mind the sob story. You're a grown-up now and it's about time you started caring about that waistline.' She grinned. 'Otherwise you'll have to give up on the Boss belt.'

He patted his belly again, a gesture which had obviously become a source of comfort. Viv, concerned, shook her head. 'It's nothing to be proud of, you know. And as a proper doctor I'd have thought you'd be on the case.'

'Cobbler's bairn. That's me.' They both laughed.

'Spare me.'

Viv lifted Ralph's hair, thinking how many men would be envious of his mane. 'So what's the project that's keeping you at home?'

'An offer for another job, actually. It's not common knowledge, but I've been headhunted for a post in Sydney, and even though I'm not sure I'd want it, I've got to consider their not insignificant terms. Lucy wasn't keen but now that she's seen the amount of money they're offering, and the state of the art unit that I'd be running, she's coming round. How d'you fancy coming to Sydney to cut my hair?'

He laughed, but Viv knew just how concerned he would be if he had to find someone else. Before Viv he'd had so many bad haircuts, always too short, always making his head look like a pea on a mountain. He was a big bloke and Viv was the first to give him permission to have longer hair, proportionate to the rest of him. It seemed as if every one else had judged what he, a surgeon, should look like. For Viv 'should' was shit, and was usually the loud voice of an over-bearing super-ego. It would be a great loss for Edinburgh if he went. He was one of the best neurosurgeons of his generation, but more than that, his ebullient personality had been an asset to the fundraisers. She blasted his hair dry using her fingers instead of a brush and once it was done she tucked her dryer into her kit bag. He stood and headed into the hall to check in the mirror.

'Great, Viv. As ever. What would I do without you?'

'Oh, you'd find someone. You just have to be more assertive.'

It was ironic that a man with so much power was terrified of anyone wielding a pair of scissors. She had seen a photograph of him with one of the disastrous cuts, and could see why he'd never want that to happen again.

'Communication. You must be excellent at communicating with your patients otherwise you wouldn't be so popular. So you'll just have to imagine you are talking to a patient.'

'Whoah! I haven't accepted yet. It's still in the very early stages. And it really isn't common knowledge.'

'Your secret is safe with me. It'd be a pity for Edinburgh if you were tempted away.'

'I like the way you generalise. Edinburgh would miss me, but you wouldn't.'

They had never discussed his veering off track. Viv had made herself so clear at the time that it had never been brought up again. Viv busied herself disposing of the hair and emptying the water spray. Ralph sat on an old church pew that had found a new life at his kitchen table and took out his Filofax. Security was another appointment with Viv in the diary.

Chapter Eighteen

Back in her car Viv checked her mobile and picked up an odd message from Lynn asking her to ring as soon as possible.

While Viv waited to be connected, she ran through the possible reasons for the call, first of which was what she had done with Lynn's hair. 'Hi, Lynn, it's Viv. What's up?'

'Oh, Viv. I'm sorry to bother you. You know I wouldn't have called if I didn't really think it was necessary. Have you seen the papers? The article on Thurza?'

'Well, I did see something about the stone going missing but then it wasn't missing at all. What's wrong?'

'The night of the party, when all hell was let loose about that bloody stone, Thurza pointed the finger at my Martin. He didn't know anything about it but that didn't stop the police from giving him a going over.'

'What do you mean "a going over"? Was he hurt?'

'He says no but he's in such a rage about it. She humiliated him in front of hundreds of guests, and he was only there to do her a favour, helping with the cars.'

'Hold on. Are you saying that Thurza said it was Martin who stole the stone when it was actually her?'

'Yes. The bitch. After all we've done for her . . . and to save her neck.'

'I'm not sure what you mean by that but . . . what made you ring me? What can I do?'

'Well Thurza has to apologise to Martin. He's totally humiliated but his mates . . . '

'Go on . . . his mates?'

'Well, his mates are threatening revenge. They're saying that because she's a toff she thinks she can get away with anything. If Thurza would apologise . . . '

'Have you spoken to her about this?'

'Sure I have. But she said she didn't mean anything by it and that he shouldn't be so touchy. You can imagine how that went down. Martin is a nice boy but he's embarrassed and angry. She's known him since he was a baby. How could she do that?' Lynn's voice cracked, and Viv said hastily, 'Lynn. I'm still not sure what I can do.'

'Speak to her, Viv. Try to make her see that there's an easy solution to this. Martin isn't threatening her but his mates are and I'm not responsible for them. One or two of them are really . . . bored and looking for excitement. They could do something daft, crazy even . . . and I'm not sure what I'll do myself.'

Viv heard a different tone in those last words. 'Don't do anything stupid, Lynn, she's not worth it.'

'You can say that again.'

Viv sighed. 'Okay. I'll give her a call.'

'No, don't do that. Could you drop in? Convince her that . . . oh God knows. She's so stubborn. And I can see her getting all high and mighty, but something has to come from her and soon.'

'I'll think about it and ring you back.'

Viv could see Lynn's point. To head this off at the pass was definitely the sensible thing to do but she sensed there was more to Lynn's anger than Martin's humiliation. Martin was a nice boy and she could imagine how he must have felt being accused of theft in front of Scotland's great and good. What could have possessed Thurza to do such a thing? Maybe what Viv had to do was speak to Martin's chums. She started the engine, and with a bit of effort managed a u-turn and headed towards the Forth Bridges.

Thurza wasn't a bad woman. At times misguided, but this episode seemed out of character. Before she reached Newhall she pulled into a lay-by and took out her phone. With her finger hovering over Thurza's number, Viv glanced up and spotted Thurza's four by four racing in her direction. There was no doubting that she was over the speed limit. The crazed look on Thurza's face as she passed, bawling into her mobile phone, made Viv alarmed.

But before Viv had the chance to give chase she heard the screech of rubber on tarmac. In her rearview mirror Viv saw the Range Rover shudder into silence in the middle of the road, about a hundred yards from where Viv was parked. Thurza made no attempt to get out or start up again. Viv's belly contracted at the thought of what might be under the wheels but she jumped out of the Rav and jogged towards the enormous four by four. Thurza was slumped over the wheel. Viv opened the door and Thurza struck out with her elbow, narrowly missing Viv's face.

'It's okay, Thurza, it's Viv.'

The tracks of mascara on Thurza's swollen and bloody cheeks shocked Viv into action. She rubbed Thurza's arm, gently coaxing her out of the car. 'Come on, let's get you home.' Like a rag doll Thurza flopped out of the driver's seat and Viv led her round to the passenger door. Once Viv had her clipped in she took a look beneath the wheels and at the pavement on either side of the narrow road but saw nothing untoward. She jumped in, turned the Range Rover around, and headed back to Newhall. Thurza sobbed into her hands without uttering a word. There was a back entrance through the old stable block, which was now used to house garden machinery, and was a no go area for the public, so Viv parked in the courtyard and checked for stray visitors before leading Thurza upstairs to the kitchen. Thurza heaved a sigh and dropped into a chair at the table while Viv automatically put the kettle on the stove. After a few minutes Thurza's sobs subsided and Viv said, 'Who did it?'

Silence.

'Come on. You didn't do that to your own face, so who did?'

Silence.

Thurza took out a huge pink spotted handkerchief and tentatively dabbed at her face before lifting her head to look at Viv. 'How come you were in Queensferry?'

'On a job.' Which was kind of true.

As if she was beginning to wake up Thurza shook her head.

'God! I'm losing it. I've done the most awful thing.' As if the whole world didn't know about it, Thurza continued. 'The night of the ball I did the most ridiculous thing.'

Viv remained quietly at the stove filling a teapot, allowing the story space to emerge.

'The thing is I had no reason to do it. I had no reason to take the stone off the dress and put it in the safe. There were guards. It was perfectly secure where it was. But I got it into my head that someone would steal it and I decided I'd double cross them . . . it didn't work out like that but in the process of trying I've let myself down badly.' She covered her face with her hands and drew in a huge breath. Then turning to look at Viv, she continued. 'I tore a strip off Martin. Lovely, shy, insecure Martin who will never look me in the eye again. All in an attempt to save my own skin.' She started sobbing again and Viv brought two mugs of tea to the table.

'The way I see it . . .' Viv paused until she was sure she had Thurza's attention, 'it wouldn't take much on your part to mend your relationship with Martin. But he's not responsible for doing that to your face . . . Was there anyone specific that you thought might harm the dress?'

Thurza ignored Viv's questions and looked directly at her. 'And how might I do that? I've known Martin since he was born. He's always been a lovely sensitive kid. Oh God, why him? What was I thinking? Lynn will never forgive me either.'

Viv, resigned that she might never get any answers, said, 'If you apologise, sincerely apologise, then it would surely be up to them. The ball would be in their court . . . Perhaps offering him some work would help. It would be a sign that you do actually trust him.'

'Toddy is going mad . . . It's not the first time I've made things difficult with . . . '

Viv nodded. She was aware of Toddy's temper but needed to hear that this was actually him. But Thurza wasn't ready to tell.

'With Martin and Lynn?'

'No, not them, but with . . . oh, never mind. But you're right. I do have to apologise. I'm sure Lynn won't answer her door if she knows it's me but I'll give it another go.' She stood and looked at her reflection in the microwave door.

'Holy shit. Do I look awful or what?' Hints of mid-atlantic surfaced through years of clipped vowels and consonants, proof if ever it was needed that you can take the woman out of the USA but you can't take the USA out of the woman. Viv's recollection of the last time that Thurza was in Toddy's bad books made her blood boil. Then a snippet of conversation with Isla, one of Thurza's daily helpers, came back to Viv. Something to do with a gamekeeper, but it was before her or Viv's time. Viv took a deep breath. 'Look, Thurza, is there anything you'd like me to do?'

Thurza caught Viv's enquiring look, but glanced away. 'Sorry. I didn't mean . . . '

Viv persisted. 'I'm not worried about what you meant. I just think that you don't need to put up with this kind of thing.' She pointed at the swollen cut cheek. 'Lynn and Martin are the least of your worries . . . Look, I shouldn't even be here.' Viv shook her head and let go of a deep breath, poured the remains of her tea down the sink and walked toward the kitchen door. She stopped with her hand poised on the knob. 'I'm guessing that there's something else going on, T, that you're not talking about.'

'You won't tell anyone . . . ?'

'You shouldn't need to ask me that. '

Thurza stared at Viv, her eyes screwed up as if she was making a decision, but the moment passed and Viv opened the door.

'Good luck.'

Viv sauntered back through the gloomy maze of tack rooms until she reached the back lobby, where she bumped into Toddy. The surprise on his face was obvious. 'Oh . . . Viv. I didn't know that you were coming today.'

'I wasn't.' She looked him straight in the eye. He held her stare. He was wearing bright orange padded chainsaw trousers and heavy metal toe capped boots.

'Chain needs sharpened.' He held up a chain and stepped to the side to let Viv pass.

Viv looked beyond him and he turned to see what she was looking at. There was nothing to see apart from tools but Viv was weighing up what she might do or say that wouldn't make Thurza's life more difficult. She decided that silence was the best option for the moment, and edged past him to the outside door.

With smoke belching out of every orifice she jogged over the courtyard and round to the front of the house. She ran alongside the eighteenth-century haha onto a belt of smooth far-reaching tarmacadam. The immaculate lawns, known as the Deer Park, stretched for half a mile on either side until she reached the gates where she turned and looked back at the house, swallowing again the secrets it concealed.

The distance between the gates and house was impressive. In the early days Viv had made a deal with Thurza so that she could park at the front door. The paying public parked half a mile away in a shaded, muddy area, and Viv wasn't up for that trek once a month, laden with her hairdressing kit.

Within minutes Viv reached the Rav and drove home, seething over all the reasons that women gave for staying with violent partners. She'd done it herself but that was no justification for her silence.

Chapter Nineteen

Back in Victoria Street, she was still unable to get the image of Thurza's bloody face out of her head. Should she butt out and let them work it out for themselves? She'd never been a successful by-stander, and domestic violence relied on people being willing to do nothing. She'd ignored Gabriella's shop until her key was poised to open the stair door. She glanced across Victoria Street and wondered, not for the first time, if Gabriella, controller of terms of endearment, had also been crazy enough to pull-off the marmalade trick.

Viv bumped her shoulder against the edge of the bathroom door and blasphemed. She pulled off her jacket and checked in the mirror to see how her own bruises were healing. The dark purple was fading and spreading out into an ochre yellow sunset. Pretty impressive. She stretched her arm above her head, pushing the pain barrier until tears stung her eyes. She reckoned in a couple of days she'd be ready for a swim.

She opened her emails, relieved to read them on a bigger screen than her iphone. She ignored one from Walter, but was irritated to see another from the guy with the almond eyes. The content was embarrassing – trying for non-committal but with a covert invitation to meet again. Viv, still alarmed at how quickly he'd found her personal details, deleted it as if by keeping it he might materialise. No sooner had she deleted the message than she hovered the cursor over the trash half-thinking of retrieving it, but was distracted by a message arriving from Mac.

There was something about Mac that she yearned for, and it wasn't simply access to police data. The message said that Grampian police had started a search of the farm property. She grabbed her mobile and punched in Mac's rapid dial number. He answered on the second ring.

'Hi, Viv. I've just sent you an email.'

'Yeah, that's why I'm ringing. Any more news?'

'Well, they've found a cellar, actually more of a cupboard under the stairs kind of thing, with evidence of habitation: empty bottles of Iron Bru, a wrapper that had the remains of pies in it. Very little chance of finding the person alive who has eaten that lot.' Viv visualised him sitting at his desk in Fettes pushing a fountain pen round with his elegant fingers.

'Does it look like the home of one person or more?'

'They didn't say but it sounds to me as if it was just one. There are a couple of bales of straw that someone had been lying on.'

There was a pause as they each considered the implications of this. Was the someone alive or had that someone been dead?

Viv broke the silence. 'Don't suppose there's anything either of us can do? I guess Grampian will want to keep the reins.'

'It's their patch. There's no reason for them to let us get involved.'

'Even if one of their possible victims lives on your patch?' She emphasised the last words.

'Look, Viv, they're on our side, and as competent as any other force. Let's just wait and see what they turn up.' Then, 'Wait . . . They've sent me another email . . . '

Viv chewed the edge of her lip. It wasn't inevitable that they'd find Tess's body but it was her biggest fear.

'Clothing. A jacket and a cap . . . in the cab of a tractor.'

'They could belong to the farmer.'

'Apparently too small, and the cap has Edinburgh University embroidered on it . . . Listen, I'll have to go, but I'll keep you posted. And remember, Viv, while there isn't a body there's still hope.'

'Okay. Speak later then.'

Her imagination already in overdrive, she visualised the barn and recalled the smell of the chicken shed. She paced round her sitting room like a distressed elephant but then recalled the cap and jacket left in such an obvious place with no attempt to hide them. On autopilot she sought out the kettle, which gave her a chance to structure her thoughts. In her mind she walked over the floor of the barn and remembered the area that had been disturbed, but had there been a trap door? Perhaps the tractor was parked over the top of it. Too bad her search had been hampered by the small matter of being knocked out. It briefly crossed her mind to return to the farm, but the idea of a rollicking from Mac made her think again. She wasn't gifted with patience and would have to dig deep to wait until Mac got back to her with the next report from Aberdeen.

The many 'what ifs' of Tess's disappearance crept through her mind. Viv's sitting room, too furnished to make pacing satisfactory, allowed her only to tread from door to window with the odd pause at her computer to check her inbox. Eventually she sat tapping her pen against the notepad on the desk and scrolled back through the emails she'd received from Rebecca, hoping she might see something that she hadn't before. This process was interrupted by the sound of her mobile ringing. It was Margo. 'Hi, Margo. How are things?'

'I'd ask you the same question but I probably have more than you do at the moment. Beccs just rang to say that she received a letter this morning. She's hysterical. It's apparently so horrible that she can hardly stand to handle it. It's from Tess or someone claiming to be Tess.'

'How does she know it's not from Tess?'

'Well, she can't be sure, but she claims that Tess would never say the kind of things that are in it . . . '

Viv sighed impatiently into the silence. 'And you're going to tell me what those things are sometime soon? And was there a post mark?'

'I'm just getting to it. It's all religious stuff as if she's found God . . . or has had a lobotomy, and I sure know which I'd put money on. She can't make out the post mark.'

'I need to see it. Could you scan both, the envelope and the letter, and email it to me?'

'Yes, if I can get it from Beccs. She's so distraught she might have destroyed it . . .'

'For God's sake! Make sure she doesn't do that. She can't be that stupid. It's the only evidence we've got.'

'Calm down, Viv. I've already told her all of that but it sounded as if there was some threatening stuff in it. You know the kind of crap . . . that Tess was possessed otherwise she'd never have let Beccs near her and that it was Beccs who forced Tess.'

'It doesn't say anything about outing her though?'

'No. Not that I'm aware of. She just read bits of it out and as I said she's hysterical. Look, Viv, I'll ring you back once I've got the letter. The sooner I get my hands on it the less chance there is of Beccs putting a match to it.'

'That would be such a big mistake. If someone is holding Tess, and they've written this letter, our having it will be the best chance of finding her. By the way handle it with gloves or tweezers. Ring me as soon as you've got it.'

'I'm not daft, Viv. I'll get it.'

Viv stared at the phone and wondered about letting Mac know there had been a development. Instead she threw on her jacket, grabbed her rucksack, and headed out.

Fifteen minutes later Viv sat drumming her fingers on the steering wheel as she waited for a man wearing a flat cap to vacate a parking space in a resident's bay in Broughton Place. On the first ring of Rebecca's buzzer there was no answer. Viv stepped back onto the pavement and looked up at the building. The voiles on the window of Rebecca's flat were trembling. She rang again and Beccs's shaky voice said, 'Come up.' As Viv reached the landing she heard furniture being scraped over a wooden floor. After the sound of keys unlocking two double locks and a mortice, Beccs's ashen face appeared round the door. Viv smiled and squeezed through the gap. 'I see you're expecting trouble.'

Rebecca didn't smile. 'I'm not taking any chances. In fact I think I'll go home to my mum's.'

Viv followed the girl to the kitchen where Rebecca clicked the kettle on. Then hearing the element crackle, she took it to the sink and filled it. 'Tea?'

'Sure. Peppermint if you have it.'

Beccs looked at her with a slight smile. 'It's almost the only thing that I can guarantee.' She nodded at an envelope at the end of the kitchen table. 'That's what you've probably come to see.'

Viv raked around in her rucksack for a pair of latex gloves. She held them up. 'Just in case,' then inspected both paper and envelope. The envelope could have come from any stationer from Wick to Wiltshire but the sheet of paper inside was thick and heavily embossed. Viv recognised it from letters Tess had received from her parents, and gently ran her fingers over the raised symbol to double check. She held it up to the light but that didn't improve it. It could be a crest.

She settled her concentration on the content of the letter and concluded that the grammar was too poor to have been written by a university student. Then she remembered some of her own students wrote like this. Even students aiming for articulacy said 'like' at the end of every sentence, although they tended not to write it. This writer had, only once but still it was a sign . . . of what, though? Rebecca dotted around the kitchen like a pied wagtail until eventually Viv said, 'Why don't you take a few deep breaths, and a seat? You're making me nervous.'

'*You're* nervous? How the hell do you think I feel? Have you read what it says? It's a pack of lies. Tess would never say things like that . . . unless someone was forcing her.' She shook her head. 'Shit. If they made her write it there's at least a chance she's still alive.' Her eyes darted round the kitchen. What was she expecting?

Viv couldn't concentrate. 'Whoa! Relax. We can't say when it was written. The postmark is the day before yesterday, but that only tells us when it was posted. It may have been in their care for longer. But okay, it is possible that they forced her to write it and sent it straightaway.' Viv suddenly dropped the paper onto the table and headed for Tess's bedroom. Beccs followed her. 'What are you doing?'

'I'd like to find her brother's number. It's got to be in here somewhere.'

'I don't think it will be. She'll have had it on her mobile. Why would she need to write it down?'

This made sense but Viv still wanted to take a look at Tess's family's correspondence. Beccs huffed and puffed in the background until Viv threw her a scathing look. 'Do you mind?'

The girl skulked off to the kitchen leaving Viv searching. Without finding anything, other than a few spare sheets of the embossed paper, she returned to the kitchen where she startled Beccs, who was tucking a slip of paper into her trouser pocket.

'What's that you've got there?'

There was no denying that she'd put something in her pocket so she said, 'Oh it's just a bank receipt.'

'Well in that case you won't mind letting me take a look at it.'

Rebecca hesitated then pulled out the paper and quick as a flash ripped it to shreds, staring defiantly at Viv as the pieces fell onto the table.

Viv ran her hands through her hair then dropped them onto her hips. 'What the fuck's going on, Rebecca?'

The girl stood her ground. 'No one gets to see my bank details.'

Viv agreed with this in principle but the point was that Beccs had something to hide, and whatever it was it wasn't to do with her overdraft.

'You want to fill me in on what's really going on here?'

'Not really.' Her voice was suddenly strong and defensive. Viv watched as Beccs braced herself. 'I'd like you to leave now.'

Viv's confusion must have been evident.

Rebecca grinned and pointed two fingers like a gun. 'Gotcha! Now move along, I've got things to do and people to see.'

This change was remarkable. Viv shook her head. 'I don't get it. You'll have to fill me in . . . I really just don't get it. Did you write that letter?'

Beccs's body swelled up before Viv's eyes. 'Did I fuck!' So with added sarcasm Viv said, 'Then who the fuck did?'

Beccs's face crumpled as if she might cry and she took a step towards Viv, who managed not to flinch, but whispered, 'Where is she, Rebecca? Where . . . is . . . Tess?' Nothing.

Viv tried again. 'Where is she?' As Viv looked at Beccs's thin but muscular form, it crossed her mind that it could easily have been her who whacked Viv in the barn. Viv adjusted her own posture. Feet shoulder width apart she shook her hands out at her sides, then rolled her shoulders and cracked her neck. A little bit of theatre goes a long way, and as Viv intended Beccs stepped back.

A deodorised sweaty mix filled the space between them but still Beccs refused to answer. Viv made a quick move towards a kitchen chair and Beccs leaped back and crashed against the sink. Viv grabbed the chair from under the table and sat astride. She gestured to the chair on the opposite side of the table and looked at her nails while Beccs decided what her next move would be.

Slowly, staring at Viv, she pulled the chair out and crossed her arms on the unwelcoming surface.

Viv, smiling. 'Nervous? . . . There's a lot you need to tell me.' Viv continued to stare. 'There is a way of making this easier, Rebecca.'

Rebecca looked at her fingernails but quickly curled the fingers into a fist. Viv noticed the chipped aubergine varnish and wondered at the many contradictions of this young woman.

Viv tried again. 'If you know where she is we can go there right now.'

Rebecca looked up. 'You've no idea what it's like.'

Confused, Viv said, 'No. But you could tell me. Look. The sooner we find Tess the better things will be for you.'

This was a leap, but proved worth taking because Rebecca jumped to her feet. 'Okay, let's go.'

Viv hadn't expected action quite so quickly but recovered her composure and headed for the front door behind Beccs who grabbed an oversized leather biker's jacket on the way out.

Once they were settled in the car, Viv said, 'If you're thinking about taking me on a wild goose chase, I wouldn't.'

Rebecca responded by asking, 'How long will it take to get to Aberdeen?'

'Three hours if the going is good.'

Chapter Twenty

Viv pulled out from the kerb and drove north towards the Ferry Road, the easiest way to get to the Forth Road Bridge without getting snarled up in the west end. She was tempted to put the radio on but decided that silence was more likely to encourage Beccs to speak, and sure enough by the time they had woven their way through Davidson's Mains and Cramond, Rebecca had thawed and begun her story.

'I went to visit Tess's family at the Christmas break. Just as a "friend" but her brother seemed to know that we were more than that. He started to make jokey asides to me and Tess went ballistic, which of course just confirmed his suspicions and gave him more reason for blackmail. You've got to understand, the whole family are religious freaks, even Tess was getting drawn back in over Christmas. Simon's a good looking . . . ' She looked into the darkness of the fields on the left. 'He's a really handsome bloke. It all started as a bit of a tease and a laugh but as I said, Tess began to freak out. She hates him with a passion and when I didn't show signs of hating him as well she went off in a strop accusing me of disloyalty and everything.'

Viv turned to look at her. 'And were you?'

'Was I what?' This angry retort caused Viv to curse to herself silently. She said, 'Sorry I didn't mean . . . '

Still scowling, Beccs continued. 'We were only mucking about but Tess couldn't handle it and asked me to leave. Simon didn't want me to leave. He was having more fun than he'd had in ages. He'd been expelled from uni.

Well, not a proper university, one of those agricultural colleges. He'd got into bother for not turning up at practicals and eventually they sent him home. Their dad got him a job on the farm, shovelling shit. I'm talking literally. Anyway that doesn't matter.' She waved her hand dismissively.

Viv guessed it might very well matter, but didn't risk another interjection. She checked the fuel gauge and decided they'd make it to Perth before she had to top up.

Rebecca stared out of the window and gave a moan. 'What a mess.'

This was good. When someone owned their psychological turmoil, there was a strong chance of recovery.

Beccs continued. 'It was just meant to be a laugh. But I suppose it got out of hand. Si started taking me seriously. Talking about us being together. I felt sick at the thought of it in the end. But I'd played him like a fiddle . . . He won't have hurt her?' She glanced at Viv for reassurance but none came.

Viv pulled down her collar and exposed the healing bruise. 'I suppose he didn't mean to hurt me either. That's the good version. You should have seen it when it was newly done.'

With her mouth gaping Beccs shook her head. 'Oh God. Did he do that? Surely he won't hurt his own sister?'

Viv considered. The connection must be the church. Or was Harvey the same person as Si? She replied. 'Depends how mad he is with her, or with you. He might use you as an excuse to get at her . . . You didn't notice if he had any tattoos?'

Beccs shook her head then turned her gaze to the outside world.

They pulled in at the first petrol station on the Dundee road after Perth. On her way back to the car Viv pressed the fast dial number for Mac on her mobile but got his machine and didn't leave a message. Back on the road she pointed to a sign. 'Right, we're almost at Rait. Should take another hour and a half, two hours max.' She tossed a packet of Minstrels at Beccs. 'Here, these should keep you going.' As soon as Rebecca started chomping Viv regretted giving her sweets that made so much noise. When she chewed, the jewellery on her face moved about with consummate ease. Her eyebrows, her lips, her nose, and her ears were all home to some sort of stud or ring. Viv understood why such a lovely looking girl might wish to destroy what nature had given her, but how could she be intimate with anyone given such defences? When Viv refused the offer of a sweet Rebecca shrugged and resumed eating.

By the time they were on the outskirts of Aberdeen, Viv's brain had shifted into overdrive. 'I'll head straight to the farm and we'll see what's happening there. That's if there aren't cops all over the place.' She sensed Rebecca nodding but there was no comment.

Before they reached the turn-off to the farm, Viv pulled onto the verge and took a pair of binoculars from the glove compartment. She pressed a button and Rebecca's window slid down, allowing a blast of cold fresh air into the Rav. The trees on either side of the farm track cast long shadows, but Viv spotted tail-lights sticking out from the barn and decided it was unwise to simply swing into the yard.

'Okay, Rebecca, are we a team or not?'

The young girl's eyebrows furrowed. 'What d'you mean?'

'I mean are you going to melt at the sight of Simon and leave me in the shit? Or worse. If you leave me in the shit you'll be abandoning Tess.' The next few seconds were silent. The fact that Beccs had to think about it had Viv worried, but she waited. When the answer came she was unconvinced.

Rebecca stared across at the farm complex and then turned to Viv. 'Is there a plan? Or are we winging it?'

Viv, defensive, said, 'No we are not winging it. You take a walk up the drive and if Simon appears make like you are desperate to see him. Remember you've travelled all this way because you wanted to see him and you're worried about the police. With any luck he'll be a long way away.' As she spoke she spotted the tail-lights reversing out of the courtyard. It was too late for her to move so she stuck the reading lamp on and said to Beccs, 'Heads together. We're map reading.' Beccs did as she was asked and put her head down together with Viv's until the car drove by. Viv checked over her shoulder and managed to get the registration number. She pulled out her pad, jotted it down and returned the pad to her inside pocket. If she hadn't been there 'illegally', she'd have asked Mac to run it through the system, but she was and he'd have a fit. It would have to wait.

Once the car was well on its way Rebecca opened the door and jumped out. 'We are winging it, aren't we?'.

The question didn't require an answer but Viv nodded. 'Yup, we sure are. We'll be fine so long as we know which side we're on.' She didn't take her eyes of Rebecca until she nodded. 'Good. I'll not be far away. By the time you're up the track I'll be on my way across that field.' Viv pointed to the field beyond the drive. Rebecca hesitated and Viv said, 'You okay? We can go up there together if you'd rather.'

Rebecca looked toward the farm and then back at Viv. 'Okay. How about we both skirt the field and snoop around the other side?' Viv's suggestion changed Rebecca's manner and she nodded enthusiastically and jumped back into the Rav. Viv pulled out and they drove about half a mile before reaching a place to park off the road. In the cold air their breaths could have given them away but Viv nipped round to the boot and grabbed a scarf and a large handkerchief. She held them up. 'Which would you prefer?' Rebecca looked confused. 'We'll be safer if we tie them round our mouths.'

Rebecca released a nervous giggle, took hold of the handkerchief and tied it round her mouth like an outlaw. Viv did the same, then patted her pockets, making sure she had everything she needed before locking then unlocking the Rav. If they had to make a quick escape it wouldn't do if the car was locked.

Together they walked through the dark in the direction of the farm. The field was rough going with pits from cattle hooves now beginning to freeze, but cowpats looked recent and hazardous. Viv scanned the perimeter just in case she had missed a sleeping bull but there was nothing to see. The light in the farmhouse was still on but it could easily have been left on by a negligent police officer. The noises of the countryside going to bed or waking for a night's work broke into the quiet. Cars were infrequent but there was a rookery nearby and hundreds of birds took off from the branches of a huge sycamore tree. The racket of this covered any noise that Viv and Rebecca could have made.

Half way across the field Rebecca slowed her pace. 'There is somewhere else.'

Viv stopped and tried to keep her voice steady. 'What? Am I getting this right? It's taken you until now to mention that you know of somewhere else that Tess could be? Or do you mean is?' She tightened her lips to prevent her anger from spilling over. Rebecca kicked at a lump of earth, her silence an eloquent sign.

Viv stepped closer to her and quietly asked, 'Has he threatened you? I mean beyond telling your family that you're gay.'

Beccs swung round and through gritted teeth spat, 'I'm not!' Then more gently, 'I just fell in love with Tess.'

Even without light, when Beccs rubbed her face with the back of her hand, it was obvious that she was wiping away tears. This was all Viv needed, a blubbing adolescent on a stake-out. She took the girl by the arm and led her back to the car.

Once inside she quizzed her. 'Okay, from the beginning. There's no point in us risking trouble with Grampian cops or your friend Simon unless we really need to.'

When Rebecca got herself together she blew into the tissue Viv offered her and began, 'Simon has a weird friendship with their pastor. So Tess could be in the hall.'

Viv interrupted. 'What hall and where is it?' She started the engine. 'Do you know how to get there from here?'

'I could try. I only know because we all went in Tess's dad's car to church and the hall is at the back. I think we carry on along this road and at some point turn left toward,' she pointed, 'that hill.'

Viv drove slowly, hoping that Rebecca would continue to tell her story, but she started sobbing again. Viv's mum's voice echoed in her head, 'Let her have her greet.' A nugget of wisdom finding its way up through her mother's verbal garbage.

After about a mile there was a turning on the left and Viv gestured at it, but Rebecca shook her head. Same for the next turning, but at the third Beccs lifted her head and nodded. They wound their way up a steep single-track road until it flattened out. Viv couldn't see anything on the horizon except a single cottage off to the right. It was properly dark and Viv was sure that the road was traversing a bog. Tough-looking reeds encroached onto the passing places and there wasn't anywhere that they could turn if they needed to. Viv said, 'Are you sure about this?'

Beccs scrabbled about in the pocket of her trousers and pulled out another handkerchief that looked well past its sell-by date. 'Yes. I'm almost sure this is it. We came in the daylight but I remember that steep brae and this moor. Just keep going.'

Viv thought she'd caught something odd in Rebecca's tone but put it down to nerves. The occasional light on the horizon meant that there was some life out there. When they ran out of tarmac, Viv thanked God for the Rav's high-performance tyres. The track became rutted, the potholes filled with granite chips. Beccs picked at her nails while scanning the horizon. After a few minutes she put up her hand. 'Wait. That could be it. '

Across the moor a shadowed outline of a large building came into view. Viv glanced at Beccs. 'You sure?'

Beccs retorted. 'No, I'm not fucking sure. Have you got a better suggestion?'

Viv sighed and slowed the car. 'Calm down. I'm only asking.'

The buildings were in complete darkness. Viv pulled into the next passing place and switched off the engine. 'Doesn't look as if there's much action going on.' She leant over the steering wheel and tried to work out if there was somewhere to turn if she took the car any further. She decided that it wasn't worth it. She jumped out and indicated to Beccs to do the same. 'Come on. Let's take a look.'

Viv patted down her pockets, checking again for the usual tools: torch, picks, army knife. When she was satisfied that all were present, she stopped herself pressing the fob to lock the Rav and set off ahead of her companion. The track they'd just driven was rough but the one to the church hall was much worse. She was tempted to lead them over the field but her torch beam caught the reeds of a small pond and she edged back onto the track. Better safe than stuck in a peat bog. Rebecca lagged behind, but when Viv turned to reassure her Rebecca didn't look much like she needed it.

Viv stopped. 'What's going on, Rebecca?'

Rebecca also stopped. 'Nothing. Nothing's going on.' Her tone was all wrong.

'No?' Viv put her hands on her hips. 'Okay. I guess you're taking the piss. But I'm the one with the car keys so you're not going anywhere soon without me.'

Beccs shrugged. 'I've walked further than this loads of times.'

Whatever she was up to it would seem that Tess was not at the top of her agenda. But who was? Was it Simon? Viv continued walking towards the church and threw over her shoulder, 'You could live to regret this. If Tess doesn't survive this game of yours, you, at the very least, will be an accessory to murder.' She didn't turn to see what affect this had, but continued towards the front door of the church. She hoped that using the word murder would give Beccs a wake up call.

Viv's torch flashed over the concrete slab steps leading up to the door and she scratched her head. With this movement she threw light up into a tiny bell tower, causing the flapping of wings to break the dense silence. Her worst nightmare, or one of them, was having a bat caught in her hair and she quickly put her arm over the top of her head until the flapping stopped.

Patches of grey harling that remained on the walls were stained with rust from old iron downpipes. It was such an ugly grey box that Viv couldn't imagine anyone being spiritually inspired here. She turned the handle and was surprised when the door shifted and scraped along the floor until there was enough space for her to squeeze inside. She ran her fingers along the wall for a light switch but didn't find one.

Her torch-beam didn't reveal much in the cavernous space. No pews, only stacks of chairs lined up against the walls. Her footfall echoed on the wooden floor as she made her way to another door at the back. A musty smell laced with disinfectant reminded her of primary school. A vision of Ronnie Robinson's vomit on the gym floor covered by sawdust ran through her mind. No indication that Rebecca was trailing her.

There wasn't even a pulpit, only a low platform where, Viv guessed, the pastor gave his sermons. Viv hated buildings where the windows denied you a view of the world beyond. It made her think of a Victorian schoolroom where anything outside was regarded as a distraction rather than an inspiration.

She flicked the torch round the room again and began to retrace her steps.

Then she spotted the remains of 'Vestry' written in barely visible gold paint on the inner door. Someone had had a good go at removing it. Viv tried the door, but although it sounded as if the lock was moving there was something jamming it. She pushed with her shoulder and it moved a couple of millimetres. There was no way she was going to move this by herself and little chance that Beccs would lend a hand so she headed back to the front door.

Beccs was leaning against the wall playing with her mobile.

'Don't suppose you'd give me a hand moving the door in there?' She thumbed toward the inside of the church. Beccs didn't even look up.

'Rebecca! Did you hear me?'

She looked indignant but still didn't speak. Viv took in a huge breath then let it go slowly. Instead of giving Beccs the good shake she'd like to Viv made her way round to the back trying to visualise the position of the jammed door. The windows were too high up to allow a view of the inside.

At a guess, the main building was nineteen thirties, and the hall a seventies addition. But there was an even newer annexe, a glass box which connected the hall to the church. When Viv ran her torch round the glass corridor, it appeared to double as a Sunday School room. Low plastic tables and chairs with drawing materials were arranged along one side. A door at one end led into the church through the defunct vestry; a second, at the opposite end, opened into the new hall, another ugly grey box, this time with a flat roof.

Viv edged round the perimeter on a pebbled pathway in search of another entrance. She found the fire exit, which had no external lock to pick. To the right of the door there stood an industrial sized bin. She checked inside but it contained only a couple of supermarket bags, used teabags and the wrappers from two large packets of digestives. Not a sign of anyone battening down for the duration. Viv retraced her steps to the front of the church. Beccs was stamping her feet and rubbing her hands against her upper arms.

The sound of a vehicle approaching made them both turn towards the noise. Whatever it was the engine struggled with the brae but then, grateful for the reprieve of flatter land, it purred back to normal. One dim headlamp wove its way across the winding road on the moor, passing the turn-off to the church and continuing on its way.

Viv glanced at Beccs, who was pretending not to have noticed either the car or Viv's return. Viv snorted and took off at a jog towards the Rav. As she switched the engine on she looked back and watched the silhouette of Rebecca on her mobile. Pissed off, she reversed the Rav onto the rough track and drove back the way she had come. If Beccs was used to walking further then she'd have no difficulty in doing it again.

Chapter Twenty-One

'Mac!' Viv shouted into her mobile.

Nothing.

'Mac!'

Again, nothing.

Then a female voice that Viv didn't recognise, said, 'Hello? Hello?'

'Who am I speaking to? I'm looking for DI Marconi.'

'I'm his PA. He's in a meeting, but left his phone in his jacket. D'you want me to get him for you?'

'PA? I didn't know . . . I need to speak to him. It's urgent. Tell him it's Viv and it's to do with Tessa.'

The woman said, 'I'll take the phone with me.'

Viv heard footsteps clicking along a corridor and felt a pang of jealousy. Then she heard a tap on a door. Viv visualised where she could be in Fettes.

'I'm looking for DI Marconi.'

A cacophony of voices indicated that they too would like to know where he was.

The woman spoke into the phone again. 'Hello. You probably heard that. I don't know where he's gone. Shall I try his special line?'

Viv, ignorant of this line, raised her eyebrows. 'If you would.'

'You want to hold or will I get him to ring you back?'

Viv chewed the edge of her lip and replied, 'I'll hold on.' As soon as she heard Mac's voice she shouted, 'Thank God! Where have you been?'

'Where the hell are you, Viv? I've been trying to phone you and it's been engaged for about two hours.'

'I'm in Aberdeen.'

'What . . . '

She interrupted him. 'Before you start bawling at me just listen. Rebecca said she'd help so we got into the car and drove. We've ended up at the church that Tess's family use. There's nothing doing here and I think that Rebecca's just been taking the piss. She took me to the house first but there were cars that I thought must be Grampian police but couldn't be sure. Anyway she suggested we go take a look at the church. Which was a spoof. I'm guessing she's in cahoots with Tess's brother and he has Tess somewhere on or near the farm.'

Mac interrupted. 'The Aberdeen guys have searched the farm and there's nothing there. You need to back off. I'll phone them and tell them what you've told me. Is Rebecca with you now?'

'Not a chance. She was completely pissing me off so I left her at the church. It's a bit of a walk but nothing she can't handle.'

'But Viv, if he does have Tess, or has had her, and he knows that Rebecca is about, what's to stop him getting to her too? She's just a pawn. Surely you can see that. If this is about what I think it is, he'll no more want Rebecca than his sister. He wants rid of both of them. Christ, Viv, get back out there and pick her up.'

Viv didn't need a second telling. She sped back to where she had left the girl and caught Beccs in her headlights walking along the track. When she reached her she wound down the window and said, 'Want a lift?'

Rebecca shook her head.

'Look. Just get in. I'll drop you wherever you like.' She brought the Rav to a halt, and Beccs sulkily got in. 'Dump me back down on the main road.'

That would never happen. But Viv nodded and they drove in silence for the few minutes it took to reach the main road before Rebecca said, 'This'll do.'

Viv slowed the car but didn't pull over. 'Look, Rebecca, whatever he's told you he won't stop at harming his sister. If that's what's happened?' This was a question but Beccs didn't pick it up. Viv continued. 'You're an intelligent woman. If Simon was upset with Tess and willing to do this to me, someone who was only having a look around . . .' She pulled down her collar again. Rebecca didn't flinch this time.

Viv continued. 'What has he told you? If he's told you he wants you, you mustn't believe him. He's not a good guy. If he was a good person he wouldn't be all wound up about you and Tess being more than friends.' This struck the wrong note.

'So what if we were more than friends? It was only once.'

Viv remembered the cosy set-up at the flat. 'It's nothing to be ashamed of.'

At this Rebecca swung round in her seat and Viv braced herself. The girl shouted, 'How dare you tell me what is and isn't shameful. I'm going to have an easy life not a life that's complicated by filth.' She spat out this last word and Viv couldn't let that go. 'Filth? How can you say that? Two people loving each other isn't filth. I thought you were doing psychology. You must know that there are nutcases out there who will use any argument to back up their prejudices . . . ' She shook her head and stopped abruptly.

Rebecca's eyebrows knitted, and she pushed up her sleeve to rub her arm. Viv glimpsed scars on her shiny white wrist. Suddenly the depth of the girl's self-hatred was staring her in the face and Viv reminded herself to go gently. 'Okay. Say he does want you. It would still be better if you were together without anyone being hurt in the process.'

Rebecca didn't answer. Viv went on. 'I take it he's been in touch?' Still no answer. Then Rebecca's phone vibrated. She checked the caller's number and hesitated. Viv watched as her finger hovered over the answer button. Seconds passed before she put her phone back into her pocket.

As they approached the turn-off to Tess's family home Viv noticed a downstairs light going out. She braked and pulled into the side. Beccs made to open the door but something prevented her from leaping out. She leaned forward and pinned her eyes on a movement outside the farmhouse. 'It's him.'

'Are you sure?'

'Of course I'm sure. It's definitely Simon.'

Viv couldn't get her head round this. There was a police presence there less than an hour ago, and now he was brazenly wandering around the house. He had to be mad. Within a minute or so the sound of an engine starting broke the tension inside the car. A rasping noise, like a serious motorbike, filled the air, but when headlights appeared between the house and the barn they belonged to a quad-bike. Whether the driver was Simon or not he was making his way towards the steep hill at the back of the farm.

Viv pulled out from the verge and turned up the drive to the house. She'd expected to see some evidence of police activity but there was nothing, but why would there be? There was no body – yet. The only crime that had been committed so far was someone bashing her on the head, and the culprit was in custody. Or was he? Mac would surely have said if they'd let him go? Viv cut the engine and they both jumped out and stood listening to the quad's engine fading into the distance. Viv guessed that if the rider needed a quad-bike to get to where he was going there probably wasn't a smooth way out. No hurry to follow him.

Viv stepped through the garden gate onto the gravel, passing a curtain-less bay window before she reached the front door. When she pushed the door, it gave. She stretched in to the right for the light switch but didn't enter. Just inside the door a few lumps of mud still holding the shape of a thick tread lay in perfect formation. Someone had left a trail that lead off to the right into what appeared to be a kitchen. Viv slipped out her phone, crouched down and took a photograph before lifting a cake of mud and waving it under her nose. It was peaty mud. Rebecca, a few steps behind her, screwed up her own nose and said, 'What the hell are you doing with that?'

Viv ignored her, took out a tiny poly bag from her inside pocket, and tipped the crumbling mud into it. Nothing ventured and all that. 'Well, Rebecca. Are we going up the hill or what?' 'I don't see why we need to do that.'

'Not keen to see Simon after all?' Viv fastened her jacket, closed the house door then retraced her steps to the car. She turned and stared at Rebecca, whose hands were deep in her jacket pockets and her mouth covered by her scarf.

'Your call . . . You know, I can't make you out. Even if things were not working with you and Tess, there's no need to become a criminal over some bloke who's clearly unhinged, and if I'm right, not really interested in you or anyone but himself.'

Rebecca didn't reply but turned away and walked down the track towards the main road.

Chapter Twenty-Two

Viv jumped into the Rav and followed the track behind the farm round the contour of the hill. It was bumpier than it looked from below and she slowed to second gear. With her headlights off it was a serious challenge for her night vision but her eyes gradually began to adjust to the dark and she sat back trying to imagine what could be up ahead. She reset the mileage so that she could keep track of how far she'd gone and sat forward, peering vainly into the distance. The clouds began breaking up, and a sliver of a new moon made an appearance – not enough to create decent light. Viv put the window down and drew in the smell of the moist earth. The front wheels hit a pothole and the Rav shuddered to regain stability.

This had probably been a drovers' road at one time. An offshoot of it appeared to continue up over the top, possibly reaching one thousand feet, following the line of a crumbling stone parish boundary. If she hadn't been anticipating trouble this would be a lovely place to spend time, night or day. The still night air must surely have amplified the thrum of her engine, but there was not a blind thing she could do about that.

The sound of the quad-bike had gone. Almost a mile beyond the farm the din as she rolled across a cattle-grid shook her to the core. It was the best early warning signal a man could have. The road continued to undulate, at one point flattening out into a strath with a fast-running burn splashing on her left. Up ahead she caught a reflection of light onto a large body of water.

There was no passing place so she did a two-hundred-point turn, with her heart in her mouth as she skimmed the ditch. She managed to switch the engine off with the wheels facing down in the direction of the farm. She'd have to cover the rest of the way on foot. It was further than it looked and after ten minutes of striding out she had to loosen her scarf and undo her top button. The light was coming from a cottage nestled at the end of the reservoir. It could have been the scene on a chocolate box with its windows lit up and a thin line of smoke rising from a single chimney.

Viv scanned the landscape, figuring out which way to reach the cottage. The land rose behind it and she decided she would approach from this angle. In order to get there she had a huge detour round the edge of the water. With any luck they wouldn't have heard the car, but if they had they'd be on alert. Viv couldn't imagine any vehicle using this track unless it was for Hydro-board business.

A noise to her right startled her and she watched the back end of a red deer take off up the hill. Her heart took a minute or two to stop thumping. Then the image of men in tweeds, driven in four by fours, stalking in all weathers, entered her head. This vision went some way to calming her anxiety. If there was stalking up here there should be the odd rough path in the heather. Although she knew it was not a great idea to go off the track, she decided it would be worth the detour. So, following the hind, she scrambled over a ditch and up onto a steep bank grabbing at handfuls of heather until, heaving herself up, she regained her footing.

The sky had completely cleared which meant she didn't need to use her torch. As she got closer she caught a whiff of some kind of pine burning, a familiar country smell. She clambered quickly up a steep bank which continued to run in a ridge immediately behind the little house, slowing down as she reached a position where she could see into the cottage through a side window.

The scene before her looked like a rural idyll. A slim, youthful man was stacking wood at the side of an open fire that was already roaring. No sign of anyone else. Simon, if indeed it was him, moved out of sight and Viv's heart leapt. She hit the deck when the back door opened and he stepped out and began to refill his basket with logs. If he had heard her engine he was showing no concern about it.

Viv's heart stopped skipping and she held her breath, nervous that if she exhaled the sight of her warm breath could give her away. Eventually, satisfied with his load, the man returned inside. Viv exhaled into her scarf but remained lying on the ground and watched as he came back into view by the fire. Then to her astonishment a woman entered the frame and laid her hand tenderly across his back and rubbed it as again he organised the logs in neat rows. This vision came completely out of left field. Surely this couldn't be Tess? A metallic taste rose into her mouth but she didn't take her eyes off the scene.

Eventually with logs stacked Simon stood and stretched. The woman embraced him then slowly pulled his shirt-tail out from inside his jeans. She ran her hands up his back in a way that wasn't remotely sisterly. Viv shook her head with eyes widening, decidedly uneasy with what was unfolding. What happened next tipped the scene from ambiguity to certainty. Tess knelt before him, slowly undid his zip, and darted her tongue into his flies. Viv rolled onto her back in disbelief. Regaining composure, she rolled onto her knees, and with eyes on stalks, stared as Tess eagerly nuzzled into his crotch, licking him like an ice-cream cone on a hot summer's day.

'Oh my God!' Viv whispered. And as if they'd heard her he pulled away. But he didn't move toward the door as Viv expected, he began to undress the girl. They were obviously familiar with each other, and once she was naked he gently laid her down onto a rug in front of the fire. Viv felt a stirring in her own loins and looked away, then back.

'Shit!' If she was seeing what she believed she was, there was nothing she could do. Tess was alive and having an affair with her brother. Illegal it might be, but it wasn't part of Viv's remit. She was only involved because Margo thought Tess could be in trouble. And whilst this constituted trouble it was not the kind she'd be expected to deal with.

Viv sat on the ground and watched as the two young people traced the other's pleasure. Neither was in any hurry or forcing the other to do anything. In fact there was considerable relish as far as Viv could see. How weird to be a voyeur.

Eventually she became aware of how cold she was, and decided to retrace her steps. She'd seen enough to convince her Tess was definitely not being held against her will.

Back in the car Viv rubbed her hands together and blew on them, coaxing some life back into her circulation. She released the hand brake and let the car glide down a few hundred feet before the steering lock prevented her from continuing on course, and she'd no choice but to switch the engine on. Her mind flipped over all the explanations and possible outcomes and acknowledged to herself that incest had never been in the running. Poor Rebecca.

As Viv approached the farm she mulled over whether this information had to be shared with Rebecca or if there was a way of softening the blow. She also asked herself again if there could be another explanation but didn't reach any plausible conclusion. Beccs's reaction to her own sexuality was extreme enough and Viv guessed incest might be a challenge too far.

As she passed the farm she wondered again where the mother and father could be. This whole drama had been a wild goose chase. But what about the guy who had whacked her, how was he involved?

She slowed and stopped on the track. The battery on her mobile was low but she hoped she still had enough power to speak to Mac. She pressed his number and to her relief he answered immediately.

'Hi, Mac . . . ' The headlights of a car approaching up the track almost blinded her and she said, 'Oops! I think the cavalry have just arrived. I'll ring you back.'

Mac shouted, 'No. Tell me what's happening.'

'Incest. That's what.'

Silence. As this sank in she waited. 'Okay, Mac. Once I've spoken to your guys here I'll ring you back.'

Obviously distracted, he managed a barely perceptible, 'Okay.'

When Viv stepped out of the car the officer shook his head and tightened his lips. He stretched his ample body to its full size and hooked his thumbs into his belt loops.

'And you are here because?'

Viv enjoyed his accent but sighed. 'Well. I thought I'd take a look around.

There might have been something I missed the first time . . . like a trapdoor or something.' She looked at him directly. He returned her gaze then nodded, as if to encourage her to continue. 'I didn't expect to find a love nest.'

He looked confused.

Viv gestured with her head to the hill. 'Up at the head of the reservoir, the cottage.'

'Carry on. The Hydro-board cottage.'

'Yes. I found who I was looking for in there.'

'We've got the couple in there as . . . ' He took out a notepad from his breast pocket and flipped through it. 'A Mr and Mrs Symmington.'

Viv sniggered.

'Something funny, Dr Fraser?'

Viv turned away. 'Look I'm still only guessing but the bloke I just saw up there could be Simon Grant and if I'm right his wife isn't a wife at all but his sister Tessa Grant.' She pointed to the farmhouse. This was, or perhaps still is, their family home. No sign of their parents though.'

'Mr Grant has been transferred. This is a company house.'

'What? Nothing to do with the farm then?'

'No. The farm is leased to the bloke who . . . ' he hesitated, 'you had your little run in with.'

Viv didn't like the sound of this. 'You mean the man who, unprovoked, attacked me and locked me up?'

'Your word against his, I'm afraid. We've released him.'

Viv felt the colour rise up her neck and knew she should get back in her car. But knowing and doing were two different things. Trying to keep a lid on it, she said, 'So. He could be right here in this very place.'

'I expect he'll be tucked up in his cottage over there.'

He pointed to the little group of houses beyond the field on her left.

Viv bit into her cheek and stepped back toward the Rav. But she wasn't getting off that lightly, and he thumbed to the police car.

'You might want to take her back with you before I charge her with something.'

Viv craned her head and, shielding her eyes against the headlights, saw Rebecca in the back of his vehicle. He sauntered over to the back door and opened it.

'Okay, young lady. Here's your lift.'

Viv snorted in disbelief. 'You.' She walked away pointing her finger at him. 'Were clearly asleep through political correctness classes or haven't those reached Aberdeenshire yet?'

He shrugged bemused.

Rebecca edged out of the police car, ducked under his arm and ran to the passenger side of Viv's car. Once she was inside Viv backed up and mounted the verge, squeezing the Rav through the tight space between the police car and the fence. She watched the officer in her rear view mirror, who stood staring at their rear lights until they turned onto the main road.

They didn't speak until they reached the motorway south, when Rebecca twisted round to Viv. 'I'm sorry.'

'Sorry for what?'

'Sorry for not warning you, for not . . . being able to believe it . . . '

'Did you hear?'

'Yes. But I'd already suspected. I just couldn't . . . ' She swallowed. 'Disgusting. It's so disgusting.'

Viv recalled the fireside scene. To anyone who didn't know they were related, what they were doing couldn't have been described as disgusting.

Rebecca continued. 'Tess was so weird about him. Said she hated him.'

'Could've been a lover's tiff.'

Rebecca shuddered. 'Don't. I can't stand to think of them . . . he must've just been using me to get to her – to make her jealous or something. He's . . . so manipulative. Tess is trapped or he's trapped.'

'It didn't look that way to me.'

Rebecca swung round again in her seat. 'What? What did you see?'

'Enough.'

They were silent for the next few miles then Viv said, 'What will you do about the flat?'

The girl replied immediately. 'Leave . . . My God, who'd want to stay there?'

Viv was unconvinced.

Rebecca managed to nod off for the last bit of the journey, giving Viv time to think. The local boys back in Aberdeen would have to make a choice about whether they followed up Viv's allegation, or, she supposed, they'd more than likely just drop it.

Her belly rumbled and the idea of a fish supper occurred. She checked the clock, one fifty in the morning. No chance of anything being open at this time. The road after the Forth Bridge was glistening. Her headlights bounced over enormous puddles that hadn't yet drained away. Viv glanced across at Rebecca, whose hand was squashing her face as she leant her head against the window. The piercings looked distorted and even more ugly. As if she had felt Viv's eyes on her Beccs stirred and rubbed her hands over her face.

Viv flinched. 'God sake! I don't know how you can do that to yourself.'

'What?'

Viv pointed. 'Those studs and rings. It must be sore when you do that.'

Rebecca shook her head. 'I don't feel anything.'

Viv wondered if numb was Beccs's general state. Those scars were testimony to serious inner turbulence whatever she said out loud.

It took another twenty minutes from Cramond Brig to Broughton Place, where Viv double parked and Beccs jumped out. Viv opened the window but Beccs just waved and fumbled in her jacket for her door key.

As luck would have it there was a tight parking space opposite the bottom of Viv's stair. She eased the Rav in, only slightly nudging a Silver Merc. She climbed up to her flat as if her legs were filled with lead. Once inside she flopped onto the couch, pulled a woollen throw over her shoulders, and fell into a deep sleep.

Chapter Twenty-Three

Viv woke the next morning with a crick in her neck, and decided there was nothing else for it but a swim. Within fifteen minutes she was pushing through the turnstile at Warrender Baths, prepared to challenge her own record. She didn't break her record, but felt a whole lot better after twenty lengths and a long hot shower. As she meandered back across the Meadows she recalled the couple the previous night, and how weird it had been to watch. She examined the light cloudy sky and thought of the day ahead. As she trudged upstairs she almost bumped into Ronnie, her almost silent and all but invisible next-door neighbour. 'Oh, hi Ronnie. How you doing?' She hadn't seen or heard him since the Marmalade incident but noticed his normally pasty complexion was even paler than usual.

' . . . F-fine . . . Just . . . P-posting . . .' He held up an envelope.

She smiled and carried on upstairs. 'See you. Take care.'

Ronnie made an indecipherable attempt at an answer.

The light was flashing on Viv's answering machine and she pressed the button to listen to her messages.

Margo's voice echoed into the room. 'Viv, could you ring me asap? I think there's a problem at Broughton Place.'

A breathless Margo, clearly on the hoof, answered Viv's call.

'Hi. I passed Broughton Place about ten minutes ago and there was an ambulance outside the girls' tenement. Could be nothing. Could be someone else. But you and I are not ones for coincidences, are we?'

'No. No, we're not. I dropped Rebecca off at about two this morning.'

'What the hell were you doing with her at that time?'

'We decided to take a drive up to Aberdeen and discovered . . . Well, it'd take a while for me to explain, but let's say our little friend Bambi was pretty disillusioned. An ambulance is a sign that it's too late for us to do anything but should mean, if it is Beccs, that she's now in good hands.' Viv paused. 'How about lunch?'

'No can do, I'm in meetings all day. Could do an early supper though? Lind's gone south to a Thomas Lawrence exhibition. I'm dining on my tod.'

'Okay, I'll try and get a table at Kushi's for half six.'

'Sure. Speak later.'

Viv spent the next couple of hours faffing about, putting a washing on, tidying anything that sat still, and answering emails, but put off responding to the guy with the almond eyes, who had sent another request for them to meet for coffee.

An email from Mac said, 'Heard from Grampian. You must have remained calm and charming from what they report! Let's meet and go over the whole case.'

Viv shouted at the computer monitor. 'It wasn't a case.' The phone ringing interrupted her. Slightly embarrassed for shouting at a machine, she answered prepared to be calm and collected.

'Viv, it's me.'

Viv didn't recognise the voice at first.

'It's Gabriella.'

There had been so much going on that Viv had all but forgotten about their recent night. The feeling that she swallowed had nothing to do with ardour and as if Gabriella sensed this she said sheepishly, 'I thought we might clear the air.'

Viv looked at the handset. 'What? You think that wasn't my plan when I was ringing your phone off its hook? I think the air at my end is as clear as I need it to be

. . . '

Silence.

Then Viv spoke less aggressively. 'I'll be polite when we meet if that's what's worrying you. I'm not the explosive type. Look, let's just call it quits. Okay?'

A very small voice from the other end said, 'Okay.' And the receiver was replaced.

Viv did the same and blew out a stream of hot air. 'Well handled, Viv. Well handled. The woman wants to apologise and you shoot her down. Nice work.'

Before she spiralled into self-flagellation she reminded herself that tiredness with pain made her a tiny bit pissed off. The last few days had been mad. 'Jeez,' she said through gritted teeth. Grabbing her mobile she pressed Rebecca's number. It rang and rang before going to answering machine. Viv left a message. 'Just wondered how you're doing. Give me a call when you're up and about.'

She flicked the TV onto the news channel. Nothing much of interest. Back to the laptop. She navigated her way round BBC Scotland news and eventually found an update on the girl in the canal. Her dental records had shown that she wasn't from Aberdeen at all, and had had all her treatment here in Edinburgh. They still weren't releasing a name.

Viv checked the time, and reluctantly headed for the car. A visit to her mum could be done in an hour, maybe less, depending on the mood she was in when Viv appeared. The sheltered housing complex at Haymarket boasted two parking spots, one for the ambulance, the other for a visitor. Viv parked in the space reserved for ambulances. Her mum was surprised to hear Viv's voice and pressed the buzzer for her to enter. So far so good. Viv took the stairs to the first floor two at a time, and found her mum waiting at the door.

'Hi, hen. What a nice surprise. I wasn't expecting to see you. Amanda phoned, she's on her way.'

'Great to see you, Mum. You're looking well.'

Her mum hated to hear those words. The competition to be the most ill was fierce in places like this, and Viv's mum had forgotten what a good thing it was to be in good health.

'I'm no all I look. I've had the doctor in . . . '

The buzzer shrieked and Viv stood aside to let her mum out from her tiny kitchenette. She already had a tray with two cups and saucers, and a plate of biscuits, laid out. Viv watched and smiled as her agile old mother repeated her passage through to the front door. Ten steps in total and not even remotely unstable on her pins. To move in here was the worst thing her mum could ever have done. It was a ghetto of ailments for those embracing the sunset of life, with no youth to aspire to, no kids to admire growing up, and only the endless comparison of aches, pains and pills. Viv heard Amanda arrive breathlessly and kissing their mum. Still undoing her scarf she came wafting her expensive scent and glossy, dark haired, willowy figure into the tiny sitting room, to find Viv.

Amanda's face fell, and through clenched teeth asked, 'What brings you here?'

'Hi, Amanda. I'm fine thanks – how are you?'

Amanda threw Viv a death stare.

And their mum said, 'Right. I'll get the kettle on.'

'Not for me, Mum, I've got a meeting.' Viv checked her watch. This wasn't designed to get Amanda's hackles up, but true to form the look on Amanda's face indicated she was about to launch. Viv was beyond smoothing the path for her. There was a time, before her sister's 'corporate' marriage, when they had found some level ground. Mand, whose course in Legal Administration hadn't been going well, had asked Viv to help her with assignments, which Viv did. So when Mand decided to opt out and go travelling the world with a man who should have advertised for an automated device for lifting his socks, Viv was less than sympathetic. Since her global jaunt Manda had filled her time wearing Escada, having facials and manicures, doing his laundry, and picking fights with Viv at every opportunity. Guilt was a strange animal.

For Viv, Mand's turning up was a good thing, because now she wouldn't feel bad about leaving her mum on her own. 'Look, Mum, since you're looking so well you don't need me to hang around. I'll come back during the week.' This ambiguous time frame was one that she usually used. Her mum, who clearly hadn't heard everything that Viv said, called from the kitchenette,

'Amanda, give me a hand and lift this tray.'

Mand, ever dutiful, shot Viv another death stare and obeyed the summons. When she returned, Viv had her hand on the handle of the sitting room door.

'Right, that's me off then, Mum.'

'I've made tea.'

'No thanks. I'm fine, Mum. Got to get back to work.'

Mand didn't look up and commenced pouring tea. Viv stepped over to her mum and rubbed her on the shoulders. 'See you later then.'

'Aye. But how much?' Her mum shook her head.

Viv stepped out. But before she reached the top of the stairs Amanda came after her. 'Mum probably won't remember to tell you but incase you're interested . . .' she looked away. 'I'm pregnant.'

Viv, utterly gobsmacked, said, 'Wow, that's fantastic.' But seeing the look on Mand's face she said, 'isn't it? I thought . . .'

Mand's eyes filled and Viv stepped towards her but she shrank back. 'I just thought you should know.' Then she turned and walked back into their mum's flat.

Mand's news was incomprehensible. Viv couldn't imagine Douglas as a father, as for their white wall-to-wall carpets and leather Corbusier furniture that would have to go. It must have been a mistake otherwise Mand would be delighted. The idea of a baby in the family certainly gave Viv reason to smile but was Mand okay? Was the baby okay? 'Shit!'

As she approached her car, thoughts of Manda having a baby were sidelined by the fact that the over-zealous warden from her mum's building had been out policing, and had slapped a white sticker telling her she'd parked irresponsibly, on the driver's side of the windscreen. Viv scrabbled about in her glove compartment for an ice scraper. It took a good dose of screenwash and ten minutes' elbow grease to get it off. Viv cursed under her breath. 'That woman hasn't got enough to do.'

Chapter Twenty-Four

Distracted by both the baby and sticker business, Viv took a left instead of a right at the traffic lights at Haymarket, and since she'd made the mistake she made a snap decision to head to Fettes and find Mac. The sooner he was satisfied with her story the sooner she could move on. Another keen parking attendant at Fettes stopped to look at her as she crawled round looking for a space. Eventually she squeezed the Rav into a tight space knowing she'd need to exit through the passenger door. She watched in her rear view mirror as the attendant hovered at the back of her car. Viv clambered out and all but swaggered over to him. 'I'm seeing Marconi. DI Marconi.'

'I ken who Marconi is. But he's not in the building. His car's no' here.'

'It doesn't follow that because his car isn't here he isn't in.' She walked towards the steps and turned. 'I'll be back with a permit.'

This was a shot in the dark but she struck lucky, because Marconi was in. Viv skipped back out to leave the permit inside her windscreen. By the time she returned to reception Marconi was waiting. He was cleanly shaven with a telltale nick on his cheek. 'I didn't expect to see you here, Viv.'

'I was just passing and thought it would be better if I gave you the lowdown face to face. But if you're busy I could come back?'

'No. No. You're all right. Come through.' He gestured to a door on the right of reception and they entered the corridor that Red had taken her through a couple of days ago: different room this time. He held the door open and when Viv entered she understood why Mac was so compliant. A man she'd met before stood and stretched out his hand. Viv returned his healthy shake, then shot Mac a 'what the hell?' look before turning back to the man in tweed.

It would have been easy to assume from the man's ruddy complexion that he was an alcoholic, but this simply demonstrated his Celtic warrior genes.

Viv eyeballed him and with her sweetest smile said, 'Nice to see you again . . . I've forgotten your name.'

The ruddy man smiled at this. There had never been a formal introduction at their previous meetings. He knew Viv's name but she only knew him as the man in tweed.

Viv tried again. 'This is a coincidence. Mr . . . ?'

At this he responded, 'Isn't it? A very happy coincidence for me.'

This had Viv on alert. 'Oh no. Not another proposal?'

'I hear you're still in the journalism game.'

She'd forgotten about his accent and how easily the Invernesian lilt in his voice could lull her into a false sense of security. She reminded herself that that was his job. Whatever he said always had a dual purpose. He might look like Santa, but Santa he was not.

'Yes, I'm still at that "game", as you call it.'

'I'll come straight to the point, Viv. We need your help. '

She interrupted him. 'And who exactly might "we" be? You see that's what I've never been clear about. And as you know I'm a woman who likes clarity.'

'We've noticed that, but you're also a woman who likes a challenge and we could help you with this – call it mutuality.'

He pointed to a seat on the opposite side of a large table, but she waited until he sat down before pulling out a chair. She sighed and shot Mac a dagger, which he ignored.

Ruddy clasped his hands together on top of the light wood table, and said, 'We've been keeping an eye on you.'

At this she swiveled and fired another dagger at Mac. Who didn't bite, just continued twiddling the pen in his hand and looking straight ahead as if she wasn't anticipating a response.

Ruddy continued. 'You wouldn't expect it to be otherwise, so no need to feign surprise. Now, what would we need to do to get you on board?'

Viv smiled. 'If this is to do with one of my clients, you already know my answer.'

He took in a deep breath. 'I understand.'

When he didn't elaborate, Viv continued. 'I thought we'd been through this? I've got a moral obligation to my clients. I'm not willing to breach that at . . . any price.' Her slight hesitation let her down.

'Are you sure it's at any price?'

Viv mulled this over. 'You know that I don't have anyone that I'm particularly close to.' Then she hesitated. 'Apart from my mum and my . . . sister.' She might not be Mand's best friend but she was still family and now there was a baby on the way. Ruddy's expression didn't change. 'There's a very small thing that,' he paused, 'I think you might help us with if you . . . '

Viv put her hand up. 'Don't!'

He continued. 'He's got to be stopped and you could be crucial.'

'I can't stand this cryptic stuff. Who's "he" and what's he done that you think would make me change my mind about my contract with my clients?' Viv really didn't want to go to the place that she imagined he was about to ask her to.

'One of your clients is endangering the lives of children and he's just about to be transferred abroad to stop the stink. But his intentions won't change just because he's in Aus . . . '

Viv's eyes widened. She knew that they wouldn't name him if they weren't sure. They could only mean Ralph. She recalled his vast intimidating bulk looming over that tiny woman at the book launch. Also, her last visit, his wet hair dripping all over the floor while he chatted about nothing in particular.

'Are you sure? I know he's a letch but what exactly has he done or is he doing?'

'You know he has a child with a rare genetic disorder?'

'No, I didn't know that.' She couldn't believe that over the years neither Ralph nor Lucy had mentioned a disabled child.

'Well for the last decade he's been experimenting.'

'How many?'

A confused look crossed Ruddy's face. 'Do you mean how many has he killed or how many has he experimented on?'

Viv shuddered. 'What exactly would you need me to do?'

Ruddy glanced at Mac and almost smiled. 'His "research" isn't on any computer that we've accessed in the hospital so he must have one at home which he uses specifically for this. Are you with us?'

Viv looked at Mac. 'Looks like it.'

Ruddy pushed back his chair, came round the desk and perched on its edge. 'Excellent. He's away at the moment at a conference so we'd like you to go in and have a look around.'

Viv raised her eyebrows. 'There is the small matter of a wife called Lucy who isn't going with him.'

She remembered the laptop lying at the end of Ralph's kitchen table. How close she had been to taking a peek but, unusually for her, discretion had kicked in. She knew it'd be easy to get back in. 'I'll say I've mislaid my scissors.'

Ruddy was about to object when Viv continued, 'They're not just any old scissors. They cost me nearly four hundred quid and have my signature on them.'

He raised his ample eyebrows at this, but nodded. 'Okay, that'll get you in.'

'Lucy will let me wander and poke about. Presumably she doesn't know?'

'No, she doesn't, but he'll have made it clear to her that whatever he's been working on is precious and not to be disturbed . . . We trust you to find a way to copy his files.'

Viv stood, walked to the window and crossed her arms and stared down into the car park. 'What are the chances of his computer, whether laptop or not, being accessible to me? He's not stupid. He'll have the stuff on a USB and taken it with him.'

'Marcus here said that you have creative skills in the technology department, one of the Digirati I believe.'

Viv shot Mac a look that said, how could you? She did not respond to Ruddy's comment, but said, 'Here was I thinking I'd just update Mac on a missing person that's turned out to be a false alarm.'

Mac smiled. 'Speaking of which, Sandra said that your MisPer had a tattoo.'

'Yes, still does, I imagine.'

'Well, ours doesn't, it washed off. Must have been henna or a transfer.'

'How's that going?' Viv caught Ruddy looking at his watch and said, 'I guess you've got bigger fish to fry, but Mac and I could do with a catch-up.' Ruddy stretched out his hand again and she took it and said, 'God, I hope this is worth it.'

'Trust me, it is.'

Once he had closed the door behind him Viv put her hands up in a question to Mac.

'I didn't know he was coming here today and for that matter I didn't know that you were either, Viv.'

'Great! Two birds and all that. What exactly am I getting into, Mac? Is there more to this than he's said?'

His hesitation told her all she needed to know.

'Okay. There's not much more to tell you about Aberdeen. Incest. Says it all. But how about this? The sod that bashed my head? He's out and about and they said it was his word against mine.'

Mac rubbed his hands over his face and through his hair, a gesture that she was now familiar with. 'And it is, Viv. What else can I do? I think they'll, as a courtesy, let me know about Tessa Grant but they haven't yet.'

She shook her head. No point in fighting a battle that she couldn't win. 'Right. I'll make contact with Dr Mrs Mullan then.'

'No, wait. I have a mobile phone and some tools to give you. He's clever.'

Viv wasn't sure who he meant at first. 'Mullan, you mean?'

'Yes. It goes without saying that . . . ' He was about to name the man in tweed but smiled. 'Nearly, Viv. Nearly. Not knowing is for your own good. Follow me.'

'This is all a wee bit Alistair MacLean for me.' She skipped to keep up with him as he strode down the corridor to the front desk, then across the foyer to another corridor. Mac punched in a code on a panel by the door. Restricted access, then. No carpets, another sign that the 'public' were not invited here. At the far end of the corridor they descended a set of steps into a secure underground area with passageways branching out in all directions. Mac turned. 'Impressive, isn't it?'

Viv continued to trot to keep up with his long stride and nodded. 'Sure is.' Then more to herself she whispered, 'My dad never brought me down here.' Mac was too far ahead to catch it. They arrived at a metal door – to its right, a receiver with another key-pad. Mac picked up the handset and spoke into it. Viv thought he'd said "Gold Finger" and sniggered but was impressed when the door slid back and they entered a buzzing techie area. She'd never have imagined this hive of activity in a million years, but now that she was there she understood that it should be like this. Intelligence had to be collected and stored somewhere.

Her belly rumbled and Mac turned. 'Hungry? I can have something sent down from the canteen.'

'No, thanks. I'll get something when I get home.'

There was nothing at home, but she'd had Fettes food before and it had little to recommend it. Besides she was intent on taking in what was going on around her. She didn't need food distractions.

But after a few minutes of passing monitors the idea of a decent lunch at Bella's seeded itself, and her tetchiness began to take root.

'Will this take much longer?'

'No. Here.' They'd reached a huge double door, which Mac opened by keying in a number. He stretched up to a high shelf and retrieved a black pack, like a slim toilet bag. 'Everything you need is in there.' He pointed at the bag. 'If not ring me on number one on this phone.' He handed her a mobile.

'What. It's pre-programmed?'

'Yep. Goes straight to my . . .'

She smiled and interrupted. 'To your "other line"'. You two have thought of everything. You must have known I wouldn't take much persuasion.'

'We had a sense that he wasn't your favourite man anyway.'

'How the hell did you know that?'

'Don't ask.'

'How long have I been under surveillance?'

He shrugged. 'If I knew I wouldn't tell you. But I'm guessing probably since you took the MI5 test at uni.'

She heaved a huge sigh. 'For fuck sake!' One of the techies looked up from his keyboard and smiled, but with a glance from Mac he immediately returned his attention to his screen. 'I didn't follow it up.'

'No, you didn't, but guess what? They followed you up. Look at it this way, Viv. You were obviously slightly interested and you've obviously not done anything that they're worried about, otherwise they wouldn't have kept you in their sights.'

She was incredulous and whispered, 'But who the frickers are "they"?'

'You'll work it out. That's why they want you.'

Viv grasped the bag to her chest and turned to leave. 'Right, get me out of this place.'

Before they reached the stairs, Mac said, 'Viv, you do realise that you can't actually be a journo any more?'

'He didn't say that. What better cover could I have?'

Mac didn't answer until they were in reception. 'You're possibly right. But be prepared to disappoint Jules.'

Viv raised her eyebrow, then winked. 'I haven't so far.'

Mac laughed. 'You are the limit. You know what I mean. Writing for her will be . . .'

'What, Mac? What will it be? Don't make a mountain . . .' She rolled her hand to finish her sentence.

Mac rested his hands on his hips. 'Look. I've put my head on the block for you.'

'Well, you shouldn't have. I can make my own future. You obviously need someone with access, but it needn't be me. There's bound to be . . .'

'Okay. Okay. You are in exactly the position that we need.'

Viv bowed her head knowingly. 'So give me a break. Ease off with the pressure.'

Rain had started lashing against the main glass doors. 'Where the hell did that come from?' Mac, who hadn't noticed the weather, looked confused, until she pointed outside. They stood for a minute watching people racing to and from their cars.

'Mac, trust me, I'm a doctor.'

At least this raised another smile and he nodded. 'Sure. Keep me in the loop.'

'There is no loop . . . not yet anyway. But if I've something to report and you're the man to hear it, you'll be the first to know.'

She ducked out into the rain and bolted for the Rav, taking time to have a look at her mobile before starting up and heading south to the Grassmarket.

Chapter Twenty-Five

Not a single free parking space was to be had after her third round so she dumped the car on a yellow line where she could keep an eye on it from Bella's. The heart-warming smell of fresh coffee lifted her mood as soon as she opened the door.

'Hey, Doc. You just go ahead and grab your usual seat.'

Viv's 'usual' seat gave her a terrific view of the east and west entrances into what had once been a medieval market place. She grabbed a paper off the seat and threw it onto the table in front of her. A familiar view of the Forth Bridges stared back at her. It was Lynn's view. The ESPC was the freebie from the Edinburgh Solicitors Property Centre and as she read through the article on 'Edinburgh's Best Views' she was horrified to realise that Lynn's flat was on the market. Confused, she checked the address. It was definitely Lynn's. What could possibly have happened that she would put her home up for sale? She slipped out her phone and tried Lynn's number but it rang out. No answering machine. That was odd.

'Coffee or food?' Bella smiled and passed Viv a menu. 'Specials are on the board. There's probably only one portion of the venison casserole left. It's rich.'

'Sounds great. What veg have you got with it?'

Bella snorted. 'You havin' a laugh?'

'Sorry Bella, I'm not with it. Been circling on empty for the last fifteen minutes. Blood sugar's hitting rock bottom.'

Bella offered the same veg everyday because no one would let her change it.

Before Viv had her jacket off, Bella had brought an espresso and a jug of water and placed them on the old scarred wooden table in front of Viv.

'Been busy?'

'Not too bad. The venison shifted at the first sitting. Snow off a dyke.'

Viv smiled at Bella's Scots-Italian accent, which made the phrase sound exotic. The casserole arrived piping hot with a bowl of veg and homemade ciabatta. Viv blew over her first forkful but still burnt her tongue and squealed. Bella shouted from the back of the counter, 'Go easy, Doc. Don't go spoiling those taste buds, I've got a lemon drizzle with Madagascan vanilla custard.'

This was just the kind of comfort food that Viv was in the mood for, and she salivated at the thought of it, never mind dinner out later on. Half way through her main course Bella joined her.

'So how are you? I've seen you dotting about the market . . . not that there's anything new about that.'

Viv nodded and between mouthfuls said, 'Been busy. Here and there.'

Bella didn't pursue her question. 'Seen the new Deco shop across the road from you?'

Viv kept eating, swiping at the gravy on her plate with a chunk of bread. Then without lifting her eyes, 'Yes. She's got some nice stuff.'

'Pricey?'

'Nah. Fair I'd say. I bought a plate on the first day she was open and she gave me discount without me having to ask.'

'Great. I hate that asking thing. Don't get me wrong. I'd do it but I hate having to.'

Viv decided that Bella's question was innocent and raised her eyes to look at her. Bella was tall and slim with a sallow complexion, a woman who would never know how beautiful she was, which made her even more desirable.

'You want some of that drizzle cake?'

'Sure. I've left a drizzle-sized gap just ready for filling.'

Bella stretched and threw her dishtowel over her shoulder. 'I'll be right back.'

Viv, already feeling more human, caught sight of a warden and leapt out of her seat. Fumbling in her pocket for her keys she ran out towards the car, shouting as she pressed the remote, 'Be right back, Bella! Blue Meanie alert!'

She jumped into the car just in time and again drove round the block in search of a space. She found one at the bottom of the Bow and jogged back to Bella's where an unexpected figure had taken a seat at her table.

'Well, this is a coincidence,' said Viv, with no small measure of irony.

With equal irony the guy with the almond eyes responded. 'And your email isn't working?' Viv was caught off guard. She'd forgotten about his RP.

'You from these parts? . . . Because you don't sound as if you are.'

'Wellington. That's what you're really asking, isn't it? What school did you go to? The least creative question in Scotland.'

Viv grinned. There was a school, well more of a Borstal, outside Edinburgh, with the same name, but locals called it 'The Welly', a whole different set of entry requirements.

He stared up at her questioningly until Viv took her seat and Bella brought out her pudding. His eyes almost popped out. There was nothing modest about the portion that Viv was about to attack.

'Wow. Are you hungry or what?'

Viv didn't look up. 'Feeding two.'

The guy's back straightened and his face dropped. 'Oh my God!' Then he spotted the smirk on Viv's face, and accepted the spoon that was being offered across the table. Viv withdrew her hand as their fingers met and her internal voice screamed out a warning. For a few minutes they were silent with only the odd nod of acknowledgement at the delicious cake. Eventually Viv sat back and wiped her mouth with her napkin. 'So . . . how long have you been stalking me?'

He was about to protest but Viv put up her hand. 'Don't. You're not telling me this is coincidence. So what is it you want from me?'

'I thought we'd had a good time and so I don't understand why you haven't responded to my emails.'

Looking at the vision across the table Viv wasn't sure either. Apart from the small detail of his being a student in a department where Viv had been a guest lecturer, Viv couldn't think of a real reason. 'Okay. Would you like coffee?'

He grinned and nodded. 'Black please.'

Viv caught Bella's eye and ordered. 'Two black coffees please . . . I'm worried about the fact that you are a student . . . '

This time he interrupted. 'Actually. Technically we're colleagues. I have a teaching fellowship so if you're worried about ethics?'

He left his question hanging as Bella approached with their coffee.

Viv reflected on the last few days and let out a sigh. The idea of a further complication wasn't in her game plan, but equally she liked what she saw.

'Look, I'm sorry that I didn't email you back. I've been busy. I'm not looking to have a serious relationship . . . ' Viv stopped when she realised he was shaking his head.

'God. Who asked for a relationship? I was hoping we could talk about Freud. The other night we got carried away with those cocktails but my partner wouldn't take kindly to . . . '

Viv flushed, mortified. 'Oh. Okay. Freud it is. What is it that you'd like to discuss?' Her phone rang, interrupting him with his mouth open, poised to speak.

Viv nodded and put her forefinger up, 'Sorry, I have to take this.' She scraped back her chair and headed for the door. It was Mac. 'Viv, you won't know, but the Grampian guys have pulled your girl in.'

'You mean Tess?'

'Yep, the very one. They've also got her boyfriend brother. You know I'm not big on making judgements about what folk do in their spare time, but I can't get my head round this one.'

Viv didn't know whether he was judgemental or not. In fact in the time that she'd known him he'd never once asked her about her sexuality. Occasionally a look passed over his face that conveyed his curiosity, but no question ever materialised and she liked it that way. Viv recalled what she'd witnessed in Aberdeenshire, two young people demonstrating love for each other. The crazy bit was their gene pool. They must be as freaked out about what was going on between them as anyone else. If what Beccs said was true, then Tess had been resisting him. But not any more.

Viv remembered that she was holding the phone. 'Sorry, Mac. It's just that what I saw looked so normal . . . until I remembered what their relationship is. Just two people . . . '

'Yeah, Viv, but brother and sister? Even you've got to find that weird.'

'What do you mean EVEN me?' Her hackles rose when he didn't answer. 'What is it with you guys? You've got to learn that you can't keep lumping everyone who isn't doing what you do into the same pot. For you guys there's no line between . . . '

'Don't even go there, Viv. What you're about to say is not true of me, or anyone on my team, so back off with the accusations. And by the way you just did the very thing that you were accusing me of . . . lumping us all together . . . "you guys". Like there's only one cop mould.'

'But . . . '

He interrupted her again. 'Don't, Viv. All I'm saying is it's weird and I don't know anyone who would think otherwise . . . including you.'

She calmed and said, 'That's better. I do think it's weird.'

'Look, if you'd give me a chance to finish. Simon is saying, with no small amount of smugness, that they've done nothing wrong. In fact he says that when he was a child he found papers that stated that Tess was adopted.'

Viv said, 'Ah!'

But Mac continued. 'The Gramps are checking that out as we speak. Tess, of course, had no idea. Been under the impression that what they've been up to, until now, was the most disgusting, but irresistible, thing in the world, she "couldn't resist him" . . . Oh, and by the way, they reported that she's covered in scars.'

An image of Rebecca's scars flashed into her head.

Mac continued. 'He, Simon, I might add, did nothing to enlighten her. Thought it was a laugh to keep her thinking that they were real blood relations. Little bast . . . Viv?'

'Yeah. I'm still here. It's disbelief. He's such a nasty piece of work and yet if what he says is true the "Gramps" as you call them, won't have anything on him.'

'No they won't . . . Incidentally, they're only keeping me posted as a matter of courtesy, and I thought since you have an obligation to Ms MacDonald . . . '

'Yep. Okay, okay. I'm really grateful. I'm seeing her tonight.'

He made a comment that she didn't catch and decided to let it go. Glancing back into Bella's window she watched as the guy with the almond eyes played with his iPhone.

'Look, Mac, thanks for that. I'll have to go. Let me know how it turns out . . . if you can, and I'll be in touch when I'm done at this end.' She cut the line and sauntered back in to Bella's.

The guy's eyebrows shot up in a question, but Viv gave him nothing. 'Sorry about that. Now, I know it's a bit late to ask, but I don't think I caught your name last time we met.' She grinned.

His slim fingers fiddled with some salt spilled on the table, his unconscious need to gather it into a neat little pile a source of amusement to Viv. Then, as if making a decision he sat up straight and threw his hand across the table for Viv to shake. 'Jacob, call me Jacob.'

Viv took the soft hand. 'That's not what I imagined it would be. Mine's Viv, but you already know that. Just out of interest where did you get my email address?'

'Easy. I have my ways.' He smiled, parting full lips and exposing a set of straight gleaming white teeth. The kind Viv couldn't resist.

Now it was Viv's turn to fiddle with the salt, but she stopped herself. 'Now. Freud. What's not to like about him?'

Jacob's eyebrows knitted. 'God. You really are a disciple.' 'No. Not a disciple, but definitely keen to salvage his reputation. He's always getting a raw deal. Without him where would we be?'

'We'd be paying more well deserved attention to CBT.' Viv interrupted. 'Ah. But CBT wouldn't have developed the way it did without the Watsons of this world battling against good old Freud. They were desperate to find anything, and I mean anything, that wasn't Freud's. C'mon, admit it, rats and stats are not exactly relevant to us, are they. Freud is the father of all psychology today. Whether you like him or not is irrelevant. Before Freud we had the church. Psychoanalysis, and everything that comes after it, do as the church did, offer a place to confess but without the Hail Marys.'

Jacob sat with his mouth open, trying to get a word in.

Eventually Viv sat back. 'There. Freud's the man.'

He shook his head but smiled. 'My God, he really has got beneath your skin.'

'Look . . . ' She'd already forgotten his name.

He came to her rescue. ' Jacob.'

'Yeah, Jacob, only do a PhD on someone or something that you're passionate about. Trust me if you're not passionate, bordering on obsessive about Freud's women you're in trouble . . . Be prepared to look lumpy. You can't do a PhD and not let it get under your skin and everywhere else.' The aquiline head nodded as Viv continued. 'They've already got to you, haven't they. Which one are you working on at the moment? Let me guess . . . Salome, Bonaparte . . . or no, please don't tell me you believe that crap about Mina?'

He sat forward. 'As it happens I do believe what has been discovered about Mina.'

Viv took a huge breath in frustration. 'What? One man's speculation. He wasn't under the bed for fuck sake. If you knew how many letters Freud wrote you would know that having an affair with Mina, his wife's matronly sister, right under Martha's nose is too far fetched. His pen never left paper.'

Bella arrived and with raised eyebrows offered, 'Coffee anyone?'

Viv looked at her watch and shook her head. 'No thanks, Bella. Just the bill when you're ready.'

Jacob also shook his head. 'Not for me either.' But his eyes were screwed up as he glanced from Viv to Bella, sussing what their relationship was. As Bella moved away Jacob said, 'We can't leave the conversation hanging like that. How about . . . '

Bella laid the chit in front of Viv who already had her wallet out and quickly laid cash on the saucer. Not answering the question she stood. Jacob followed her to the door where Viv gently placed her hand on his back, allowing him to exit first. They took a left towards Viv's flat, but when they reached the stair door Viv turned. 'I've got stuff to do right now but what do you say we have dinner?' Then she remembered she was meeting Margo. 'Actually not tonight. But tomorrow night.'

'I'll check my diary.' Sarcasm oozed from his lips.

Viv looked at the ground, embarrassed, and scuffed an imaginary stone on the pavement.

He thawed. 'I'll email you if you promise to answer.'

'I promise.'

He smirked. 'I'm short of a fuck buddy at the moment.' Viv's horrified face told him everything he needed to know, and he jumped clear of her fist before it hit his solar plexus. He trotted up Victoria Street and threw an enormous grin back over his shoulder, as she stood, still dumbstruck.

Viv, finally gathering her wits, sighed and stuck her key in the door.

Chapter Twenty-Six

Viv entered the stairwell but didn't head up. She had a quick look in her mailbox before taking out her phone and trying Lynn's number again. This time the answering machine was on and Viv left a message. She waited a further couple of minutes then opened the door, checked the street for any sign of Jacob, and retraced her steps to the Grassmarket.

After such a generous lunch she felt snoozy, so decided it was best to leave the car and jog to Cluny, where the Mullans's cleaning lady, Shaz, should be hard at work. Shaz knew Viv. They had had many a chat while one or other of the Mullans had been washing their hair. Viv ran up the steps leading from the Grassmarket to Keir Street, disgusted by the amount of paper and plastic littering them. At the top she wove her way along the lane that separated tenements and a wall topped with ornate cast iron railings that was the boundary to George Heriot's School – once a refuge for 'faitherless bairns'.

A short way across Lauriston Place she got into a rhythm and picked up speed as she swept down Chalmers Place, the home of the old Eye Pavilion. The Meadows were busy so she had to dodge cyclists and other joggers sharing the same path to reach the Links, reputedly the oldest golf course in the world. She reached Bruntsfield within fifteen minutes. Edinburgh had loads of big green spaces, but Viv, having spent many a sunny day in her childhood putting on the Links with her dad, was particularly fond of this side of town. Beyond the Links Viv chose to stay off the main road and wove her way through the affluent back streets of Churchill, cutting through the grounds of Astley Ainsley Hospital, to reach Cluny.

The Mullans had been in their substantial semi-detached Victorian villa since they had come to Edinburgh ten years earlier. The property that they were attached to was a Catholic retreat centre. Occasionally Viv had seen nuns driving into their sweeping drive, and wondered why the Mullans only had space to park one car.

Viv turned into the wide leafy avenue and strolled toward their empty drive. So far so good. She felt in her inside pocket for the package that Mac had given her. She stopped while she separated out the phone and the USB, tucking them each into a front pocket. The bell echoed round the Mullans's cavernous hallway before she heard someone clattering downstairs.

The door swung back and Shaz, clearly expecting someone else, said, 'Oh, Viv. They're no here. Are they meant to be?'

'No. No, Shaz. I've been a bit of an idiot and left my scissors somewhere and I can't remember where. Thought it might have been when I was last here.'

Shaz beckoned her in and closed the door. 'I've no noticed anything. Where did you do it?'

This knocked Viv slightly off balance and she floundered for an answer that would keep her options open. 'Well, I cut his hair in the kitchen but he asked me to take a look at a book he was reading that was in his . . . ' She hesitated trying to remember whether he called the room he worked in his study or the library and decided just to point. 'Through there.'

'I'm in the middle of changing the beds for them getting back, but go ben and take a look.'

This was a gift and Viv made her way straight to the study. She scanned the room for his laptop but there was no sign of it and his desktop computer was off. How would she justify it being on if Shaz came back? No time to worry about that now. But as luck would have it, when she nudged the desk the computer sprang into life. As quickly as she could she found a USB port and began clicking at the keys. She wouldn't call herself a hacker but others might. She heard Shaz's footfall on the stairs again and ducked down beneath the desk scrabbling about on the floor pretending to look for her scissors.

Shaz stuck her head round the door and at first didn't spot Viv on the floor, then giggled when she did. 'I doubt they'll be doon there. I've hoovered in there the day.'

Viv bumped her head on the way up and Shaz erupted into laughter. 'My God. Yer scissors must be worth some.'

Viv walked round the desk and through to the kitchen. She leafed through a pile of papers and magazines on the worktop, clearly unable to find what she was here for.

Shaz rifled through a bleached-pine, linen press and picked out what looked like pillowcases, but then she hovered, 'If you're done here I'll show you out. I've got to get back on.'

'Don't worry about me. I'll check the bins. They might have slipped into the bins when I emptied my sheet out.'

'The only bin that hasnae been emptied is his. I'm no' allowed to touch anything in that room. You're privileged if he let you in there.' She nodded towards the study.

'Right. I'll just have one last scout around and then I'll be off. No need to see me out. I guess you've got enough to be getting on with.' Viv gestured at the pillowcases.

'Aye y'er telling me.' Shaz's undernourished, undoubtedly, at one time, over drugged frame, never stood still and she was off upstairs like a bolt. Viv breathed a sigh of relief and headed back into the study.

The computer hummed and a warning sign with an exclamation mark sat on the screen. Viv knew how to get round this but it could take a few minutes. The computer objected to her first attempts, then bingo she was in. Viv didn't try to make head or tail of anything she just copied the lot onto the USB. The machine was slow and she wiped her palms on her trousers, whispering at it to hurry up. Then she heard the thud of the front door closing and the click of heels on the parquet flooring. These footsteps did not belong to Shaz. As Viv hit the deck again she sensed that whoever was in the kitchen had heard her so she blasphemed loudly. 'Shit!'

'Hello!' Lucy Mullan, Ralph's wife, came round the door and tentatively squinted into the room. Viv scrabbled to her feet and brushed off her trousers.

'Hi, Lucy . . . Shaz let me in . . . I'm really sorry about this, but I've lost my scissors and wondered if I might have left them here.'

'What? In Ralph's library?' She furrowed her brow, and dropped the canvas overnight bag she was carrying onto the floor, and heaved her black leather medical case onto the table. 'Ralph hates anyone in here. So . . . '

Viv interrupted. 'He was showing me his copy of Patrick Stewart's memoir. We were both at the signing.'

Lucy's shoulders dropped. 'Oh that.'

'I'm sure I had my tapering scissors in my hand but I can't find them anywhere. This is the last resort.'

Lucy began to walk into the room and Viv swallowed. Then, completely out of character, she said, 'I'd kill for a cuppa.' As the words tumbled out of her mouth she could feel her face contort. But the request had the desired effect and Lucy stopped in her tracks, staring at Viv appraisingly. She walked over to Ralph's desk and as she squeezed round his chair the computer sprang back into life. Viv imagined that a message saying that her task was complete would be sitting on the screen.

Lucy looked at Viv. 'Are you sure you didn't find what you were looking for?' The ambiguity of the question hung between them. Viv shook her head and backed out towards the kitchen.

But Lucy had other ideas. 'Take a seat, Viv. I'll get you that cuppa.' Her voice was too high for Viv's comfort. Then Viv realised it was probably for Shaz's benefit. Viv couldn't now deny she'd like a cuppa and pulled out a chair from the kitchen table.

As the kettle boiled Lucy called up to Shaz. 'I'm home, Sharon. You must be almost through.' This was more of a command than a question.

Shaz came bombing downstairs. 'I didnae hear ye comin' in. I've jist the one mair thing to . . . ' She glanced from Lucy to Viv.

Lucy interrupted her. 'Don't worry about that, Viv and I are about to have tea. You just head off and I'll see you day after tomorrow.'

This all sounded perfectly amiable, but a strange glint in Lucy's eye didn't bear this out.

It took a few minutes for Shaz to get changed into her outdoor kit and for the front door to close behind her with a threatening clunk.

Lucy spun round. 'Now, Viv, you and I know each other pretty well. In fact how long have you been coming here and never left anything behind except for hair? I suspect you're way too efficient to leave your scissors behind.'

Viv snorted. 'Believe me, I'm astonished if this is the first time I've left them here. I'm always leaving them somewhere.'

Lucy shook her head. 'Nah. I'm not convinced. Let me guess what you're really here for.'

No one spying on this scene of domesticity could imagine the tension between the two women. Lucy banged two beautifully hand-painted mugs onto the worktop. Then after she collected milk from the fridge she closed the door with the tip of an impressive pointed shoe-tip. Her eyes began to bulge. Adrenaline, Viv guessed. She poured the tea in a theatrical gesture from a great height, but didn't pass a mug to Viv. Lucy walked to the end of the table, never taking her eyes off her guest, and rummaged around in her medical bag.

Viv watched as the USB's light flickered in the back of Ralph's computer and glanced from it to Lucy. Surely that would give her away. Lucy was a GP and certainly no bimbo.

Lucy interrupted Viv's rising panic. 'Either you are up to something with Ralph . . .'

Viv spluttered her defence. 'Oh, my God, you're kidding.' The revulsion in her voice hit the wrong note.

'Well, if my husband,' Lucy spat the last of these words, 'is so disgusting to you there must be another reason for you being here.'

'I've told you . . .'

Then, in a voice that Viv wouldn't have believed could come from Lucy, she said icily, 'Don't you dare patronise me. You're not here for scissors.'

Viv began to interrupt. 'But . . .'

'Don't. Just shut up.'

None of this had been in Viv's plan, and she rubbed her palms down the sides of her thighs. She gulped involuntarily as Lucy, still not taking her eyes off Viv, opened her medical case and took out a syringe along with a small bottle, from which she drew a clear liquid. Viv scraped her chair back noisily over the terracotta tiled floor and moved towards the door.

But Lucy yelled, 'Not so fast!'

Viv's survival instinct was pretty robust but before she was halfway across the hall, Lucy had darted in front of her still grasping the syringe. 'Now come back in here and join me for tea.'

Viv stepped backward to the kitchen and bumped into the table.

'Careful now!' Lucy sounded as if she was speaking to a naughty child. 'We wouldn't want any accidents now, would we?' She smiled but it wasn't the kind designed to comfort.

Nor did her question require an answer. Viv sat as directed by a nod from Lucy.

'Now place your hands on the table in front of you where I can see them, and don't try anything stupid.'

'Look, Lucy, whatever you think is going on you'll need to fill me in. I'm here to look for my scissors.'

Lucy shook her head. 'Nice try, Viv. You must think very little of me. Your scissors aren't here and you know it. Now why don't you start by telling me why there's a USB in the back of Ralph's Mac?'

'I've no idea. Maybe he left it there.'

Viv watched as Lucy clenched her jaw then spoke through gritted teeth. 'Don't take me for an idiot. Now why?'

'Maybe it was Shaz.' Enough of a shadow flew across Lucy's face for Viv to know she'd planted a seed of doubt. Viv felt bad about accusing Shaz, but no matter, she'd never know. Lucy looked at the computer as if it would reveal the answer.

'You're clever, Lucy. Why don't you tell me what's going on and maybe we can put our heads together.'

Viv watched as the hand holding the syringe relaxed its grip slightly, but Lucy then pointed it at Viv smiling. 'You're good, you know. But not that good.'

Viv wondered what might be in the syringe, knowing that it was a medicine designed to cure someone. She ran through the possibilities from the contents of the bag that could prove lethal. That Lucy had filled the syringe was a good thing. An empty one could do a lot more damage. Viv gave an imperceptible shake of her head but Lucy noticed and grinned. How could this woman, who had sat here at this very table with Viv and poured her heart out, look as if she was possessed?

'God, Lucy, I'm guessing for you to behave like this you must have had the worst day possible. Surely we can talk it through.'

Lucy laughed loudly. 'What would you know? You'd never understand. The thing is, Viv, I like you, but I can't let you leave here knowing . . . '

Viv raised her voice. 'Knowing what? That my scissors aren't here?' She expelled a huge breath. 'For heaven's sake I don't know anything . . . ' She hesitated as if an idea had just struck her. 'But we could find out from the USB if there's anything on it that there shouldn't be.'

Again a shadow crossed Lucy's eyes. But she still hovered too close to Viv with that needle.

'Don't move.'

Viv dropped her eyes.

'I mean it! Don't move.' Lucy backed out of the kitchen, into her husband's sanctuary, towards his computer.

Viv had to decide whether to make a break for the front door, or to accomplish what she came for. She followed Lucy into the study.

Lucy screamed at her. 'Get back in there!'

But Viv had reached the desk and rolled the mouse. A 'disc eject' alert leapt on to the screen. 'Looks as if whoever tried to use that USB hasn't had any luck.'

Lucy, sweating, and confused, grabbed for the USB but Viv beat her too it. Lucy lunged at Viv with the syringe and Viv leapt back into the kitchen. Viv called her bluff and continued backwards towards the front door.

Lucy yelled, 'Don't make me do this!'

But Viv reached for the handle. Lucy lunged again. Viv managed to leap out of the path of the needle, but stumbled on the curved edge of the bottom step and rolled away from the front door. Viv was up quicker than she went down. Lucy recovered her composure, even straightening her suit jacket, and walked towards Viv. Watching the advance of the needle, Viv wheeled her right leg up, crunching the heel of her boot into the elbow of Lucy's offending arm. Lucy squealed but didn't drop her weapon. She was tough and fit and ran at Viv like an angry bull. Viv leapt onto the staircase. Now at an advantage she kicked out again, this time aiming not at the arm but at Lucy's knee-cap. Lucy yelped but Viv could see that the other woman had passed the point of no return. Viv was acutely aware that she might have taken something, she'd seen the effects of substance abuse many times.

Lucy was slightly taller than Viv and not dissimilar in build, so they were well matched. She lunged again, her only mission to stick the needle in anywhere. Viv stumbled backward and lost her footing giving Lucy the chance to reach her. Viv felt a tiny prick through her boot against her ankle, but kicked out and watched, relieved, as the syringe went flying over the hallway floor. She steadied herself on the next step but Lucy grasped at her trouser-leg. If Viv could have seen a film of this she'd have laughed out loud. It was pure slapstick. Only the look on the other woman's face convinced her otherwise.

Lucy took a swipe with her fist and connected with Viv's upper arm. Viv cried out almost releasing the memory stick but was still able to ball her other hand and land a punch in Lucy's gut. Winded, Lucy staggered and looked as if she was about to fall, then in another burst of energy she grabbed the edge of Viv's jacket and hauled Viv down with her. They were like two boys scrapping in a playground, but doing more damage to each other. Lucy was first to regain her feet and she kicked Viv in the back with the pointed toe of her Jimmy Choo. Viv screamed, but suddenly Lucy was back on the floor with another body pinned on top of her. Viv rolled into a foetal position, vomited, and passed out.

Chapter Twenty-Seven

Viv came to on a moving stretcher. She immediately tried to sit up. 'What the hell's going on?'

Jacob was holding her hand. Viv withdrew it, and asked again, 'What the hell's going on?'

'Well, at least whatever was in the syringe hasn't dulled your senses. We're on our way to the Royal to have you checked out. I'm guessing she didn't manage to puncture you enough to cause any real damage.'

The paramedics slid Viv onto secure runners within the ambulance before they were on their way. Viv tried to wipe something from her lip but her arm wouldn't co-operate and she dropped it back by her side. 'I'm lost. What the hell are you doing here?'

Jacob grinned. 'You did a great job. You got the stick.'

Everything flooded back into Viv's mind. 'You might have the stick but we don't know if there's anything on it yet. She . . . ' Suddenly nauseous, she swallowed.

'It can wait, Viv.'

One of the female paramedics handed Viv a bottle of water. 'Here. You can sip this.'

Viv looked at it suspiciously. Clear liquid now had a different meaning.

Jacob nodded. 'Go ahead . . . Lucy isn't going anywhere soon and you've had a good kick in the kidneys so shouldn't be doing too much chatting.'

The ambulance slowed and the doors swung open to reveal the chaos of

A&E. The combined smell of disinfectant and hospital food made Viv retch. She clung to an empty cardboard bowl then handed it back to the same female who had given her the water. Her eyelids drooped, but she was conscious of Jacob walking at her side as the trolley made its way through bustling corridors towards a cubicle. Moments later a doctor appeared and Viv became vaguely aware that the account of events that Jacob was giving him wasn't exactly as she would have described them. The doctor gently checked Viv's ankle, where a tender swelling had appeared. He didn't seem overly concerned. However, when he rolled her onto her side and gently prodded her back, Viv shrieked.

'We'll need to have that X-rayed. You've had a fair puncture with something . . . ' He looked round at Jacob who responded, 'Who'd have thought a pointy shoe could be such a lethal weapon?'

The doctor tutted and shook his head. 'There could be some internal bleeding.'

Viv struggled onto her back. 'I'll be fine. It's only bruising.'

The doctor sharply replied, 'You're not here to ignore my advice . . . Nurse, see that this patient is X-rayed.' The nurse raised her eyebrows but unclipped the brake on the trolley and steered Viv back out to the corridor. Viv glanced at Jacob, who just nodded. 'You'd better be completely checked. We'll need to write a detailed report.'

Writing any kind of report had never been high on Viv's priority list, especially one that was supposed to be a priority, but Jacob's look made her realise that agreeing to secure those files had also secured her the headache of bureaucracy. The next couple of hours were spent lying waiting for whatever treatment was next., giving Viv time to quiz Jacob about his role. Jacob, a consummate professional, managed to skirt round the detail of how he actually became involved. But he did say that following her to the Mullan's was a precaution since it was her first assignment.

Grateful for his intervention Viv lay back and winced at the pain in her back, which was sufficient to inhibit further questions. But eventually she mustered the energy to ask, 'Was this all part of your game plan? I mean, the night we met. Was that already part of this mission?'

He grinned, exposing his beautiful white teeth, and nodded. 'It's okay to have fun on the job you know.'

'Does that mean you're not an academic . . . and for that matter are you even remotely interested in Freud?'

He laughed. 'No, I'm not remotely interested in Freud.'

'But the books on your desk . . . the notes?'

'Viv, you'll get the hang of us if you want to. But if we're involved it has to be good. We have to know how to get what we want.'

A draught came howling down the corridor, and with it Mac, searching in each cubicle and on each trolley until he spotted Jacob waving.

Viv was mortified to feel tears begin to roll down the sides of her face. Mac bent down as if he was about to kiss her but instead he gently pushed her hair back off her forehead. The intimacy of the gesture caused Jacob to raise his eyebrows.

'You okay?' He shook Jacob's hand. 'Hi. I believe you got what you needed.' He nodded at Viv. 'You make a habit of this and I'll get ideas. Hospitalised twice in one week. A girl could get a reputation.' He grinned. Then turning to Jacob. 'What's still to be done?'

Jacob, entirely professional, said, 'We've been waiting for ages to have a second X-ray. The first one had a shadow that they're not sure about. It could just be that Viv moved a fraction, but they want to take a another look.'

Mac nodded. 'I'll take over here if you like.'

At this Viv interrupted. 'Eh hello, I'm here. I don't need a minder. I'm sure . . . '

Both Mac and Jacob turned their backs on her. Not interested in her bravado.

Jacob smiled at Mac. 'How about I go and get some caffeine and supplies? We can take it from there.'

Mac nodded and Jacob took off down the corridor.

Viv wiped her eyes and nose. 'What is it with me? Every time you turn up in a crisis I'm guaranteed to start blubbing.'

'Go figure, Viv . . . ' Then, realising she was struggling, he continued more softly, 'Call it empathy, Viv. Empathy and me, we're like that.' He crossed his fingers and she glared at him. 'You did a good job, Viv. We'd no idea she was quite so unhinged . . . or would behave like that.'

'What exactly did you find out from that memory stick?'

He ran his hand across his throat. 'Classified now.'

'Fuck that! I'm lying here with a damaged kidney. The least . . . '

He cut in. 'Calmly, calmly. I'll fill you in when we do the debriefing.'

'For God's sake! There doesn't need to be a debriefing. She attacked me, we fought and eventually d'Artagnan there,' she flapped her hand in the direction that Jacob had gone, 'jumped in and retrieved the USB. End of!'

Mac stuck his long slim fingers into his dark hair. 'You are unbelievable. For now let's just focus on what damage has been done.'

Before he had finished, another nurse let the brake off the trolley and deftly wheeled Viv back into the X-ray suite. Viv smiled, recalling how academics bang on about linguistic hygiene: a room less like a suite she'd never seen. Mac waited outside until she was wheeled back, then strode beside her as the nurse picked up her pace.

'I read recently that perception is the leader of the human dance.'

Viv looked at him quizzically. 'Did you say deception?'

'No. Perception . . . But you know what? I think you're right. Deception's more accurate.'

They fell into a companionable silence and Viv's exhausted lids fell over her eyes as she was trundled toward sleep.

Chapter Twenty-Eight

During the next few days Viv was supposed to be convalescing, but Mac pitched up one morning to share some surprising news about the debacle in Aberdeen.

He sat nursing a cup of espresso and launched. 'God, Viv, I'm struggling to get my head round this one.' He sipped his coffee, as Viv's frustration grew. 'Simon, it transpires, was, is even more twisted than we thought. According to his birth certificate he isn't . . . wasn't a man at all, but born female, now in the early stages of gender reassignment. I'm not sure which tense to use. It's all got a bit confusing.'

Viv nodded. 'You know, that makes complete sense to me. When I was up that glen, lying in the heather watching them . . . oh my God, it was so sensual and natural to me . . . what you've just said makes total sense.' She nodded again emphatically.

Mac stared at her as if she might continue but she didn't, so he said, 'Don't suppose you'd like to enlighten me?'

'Nah. You'll get there in your own time . . .' She glanced towards the window. 'I feel sorry for Rebecca, though. She's just been an extra in their drama.'

Mac stood to leave. 'There's more to this gender stuff than I've been willing to learn.'

Viv smiled. 'You're doing okay, Mac, you can't be good at everything.'

He ran his hands through his hair and gestured for her not to get up. 'Sit where you are. I'll stick these in the kitchen.' He held up their cups.

But there was no way she'd let him. She unfolded her legs from beneath her and took them from him. 'Thanks, Mac. You're a good man.'

'Yeah, but a man nonetheless.'

She giggled. 'There's no denying that.' She rubbed his upper arm as he made for the door.

That same day, Viv received a letter from Lynn. Although surprised that Lynn had her address, Viv was even more surprised at what she read. She lifted the phone and pressed Lynn's number.

'Hi, Lynn, it's Viv.'

'Oh, Viv. Thanks for ringing. I'm desperate to talk to someone and I know how good you are at keeping things to yourself.'

'But Lynn if you need professional help . . . I mean counselling, I'm not your woman. You should go to your GP and . . . '

Lynn interrupted. 'No. No. I can't . . . I can't really speak on the phone but could you meet me for coffee?'

'Okay. Will I come to the house?'

'No. No . . . it's shambolic. I'm selling up.'

Viv remembered the ESPC photograph. 'But . . . why?'

'I'll tell you when I see you.'

Viv ruffled her hair and sighed. 'Okay, where?'

'How about the Dakota?'

'Sure. When?'

'ASAP.'

'It'll take me half an hour to get ready and the same to drive out. Say, eleven o'clock?'

'Great. See you there . . . and thanks, Viv.'

She stood looking at the phone; the relief in Lynn's voice was hard to fathom. What the hell had been happening?

Viv showered tentatively. After five days the purple and yellow hues on her back and sides were still impressive although the colour of her neck had faded so that she now only looked jaundiced. She gently drew a towel over her shoulders and patted her wounds before pulling on jodhpurs and boots and heading out.

The Dakota looked more like a correction facility than a trendy boutique hotel, but the bonus was heaps of parking. Viv swung the Rav into a space right by the door. Lynn rose unsteadily from a leather armchair when she spotted Viv. Alarmed at how wobbly Lynn was, Viv took her arm and guided her through reception and into another lounge.

'My God, Lynn, we're the walking wounded. What's happened to you?'

Lynn winced as she shrugged her jacket off and plonked herself down. 'It's a long story.'

Viv slipped her own jacket off and gently took a seat opposite. 'That's why we're here, so why don't you take your time and tell me what's happened.' She was keen to hear about the flat first but held her tongue.

A waiter laid down napkins and a small bowl of salty bites, asking what they'd like. The morning menu had endless varieties of coffee but they both opted for cappuccino.

Lynn fiddled with her napkin and said again, 'It's a long story.'

Viv nodded then said, 'Excuse me for a second.' She reached for her mobile as it vibrated, checked the caller's ID, then put it back in her pocket. 'Sorry. I've switched it off now. And here we are with as much time as we need.'

Lynn stared back, let out a breath and set off. 'When Thurza first came to Newhall, Toddy was under a load of pressure. Being the second son he hadn't been primed to take on the big house; it was supposed to go to his brother Alexander. But then he was killed in that terrible climbing accident in the Alps. Toddy had to step in. Toddy, grieving himself, was left to look after his distraught mother while having to get his head round being the new Earl. Ben knew the estate and how things work, so he was invaluable to Toddy and they'd always been close.

When Sandy died Toddy said to Ben that he was relieved it hadn't been him, Ben. Between them, Toddy and Ben gradually got estate business back into a rhythm and all was well for a while. When Thurza came along things began to change . . . well it sounded as if she injected a bit of cash into building work and Toddy eased off the physical stuff and retreated to the office. The pressure for him and Thurza to produce an heir began to mount.'

Viv had known all of this, until the part about the heir. 'Look, Lynn, I already knew about all that stuff, but I haven't any knowledge about Thurza not being able to have kids. And I'm not sure that I want to know.'

Lynn continued staring at Viv. 'Thurza had loads of tests . . . It turned out to be him, Toddy. That's when the shit really did hit the fan, the drinking increased and . . . Well you've probably seen her . . .'

Viv nodded. 'Sure. I have, all too often.' She sat forward in her seat then immediately back again as the waiter arrived with their coffees.

When the waiter retreated, Viv lifted her cup and cradled it in her hands. She blew over the top of it then signaled with her eyebrows to Lynn to go on.

Lynn took a deep breath then tentatively looked round as if worried that someone might over hear her and as if to reassure Viv. 'Toddy couldn't have children.' She paused, letting Viv digest what this meant.

'Yeah yeah I get that. But how come . . .? So, if they didn't have IVF, which I'm sure I'd have heard about, someone must have come to the rescue.'

'That's just what I'm about to tell you.' Lynn looked at her neat pink fingernails, then lifted her coffee. 'I wasn't around full time then so I'm only repeating what Ben told me . . . Ben had inherited the lease of his dad's cottage on the estate. He'd grown up with Sandy and Toddy. And spent lots of time with them, at least through primary school. Even during their holidays from Eton they'd get together and shoot rabbits and go ferreting. That kind of stuff . . . What I'm trying to say is that Ben knew them as well as his own family, so when Thurza approached him to be a donor, it didn't sound as if it would be all that difficult. Ben was young and virile with no problems . . .'

Viv was having difficulty thinking through the long-term ramifications of this. But Lynn continued, 'Obviously it all had to be completely hush hush, but Ben let it slip one night when we'd had too much to drink, and I pressed him for the details.' She looked at Viv to see what effect her story was having.

Viv tried not to look as perplexed as she felt, and nodded her understanding.

Lynn went on, 'You know what that means though, don't you? It means that my boys are brothers to her boys.'

'Yeah. Yeah. I get it . . . how long have you known?'

Lynn shook her head. 'A long time. When he first told me I was outraged, but the more he explained the more I felt sorry for Thurza. Toddy isn't exactly a looker. Even if he'd had a personality, you know a great sense of humour or something, it would have made up for the . . . ' She shook her head. 'Well, never mind.'

'What, Lynn, you think I'm not outraged every time she's hiding bruises? I don't get it.' Then she whispered, 'I suppose I do get it, but it's pathetic that she stays with him.'

'But, Viv, it was Thurza's idea to get Ben involved. Toddy would never have suggested it. So she's hugely grateful to have healthy twin boys. But I'm guessing that every time Toddy sees them he thinks of Ben. They look like Ben. My own boys could be Thurza's. There's no mistaking that they all came from the same gene pool.'

The waiter hovered. 'Can I get you anything else?'

They looked at each other and nodded in unison. Viv said, 'Same again, please.'

Lynn whispered, 'I'll regret this.'

Viv's sense of ethics also began to tickle at the edge of her conscience. 'If you feel that way maybe we shouldn't say any more.'

'No. I meant the caffeine. But I expect you're right. Not that there's much more to say anyway . . . Although Thurza came round and apologised unreservedly. She's going to recommend Marty for a holiday job at a friend's farm. She knows which buttons to press with him. He'd love that.' Lynn moved awkwardly in her seat.

'So how come you're in so much discomfort?'

The hotel was quiet and the waiter soon returned with their new cappuccinos. Lynn scraped bits of cocoa off the top of hers and continued her story as she licked her spoon. 'The day that Thurza came to speak to Martin, she stayed on after he left . . . Things got out of hand.'

Viv kept her voice steady. 'In what way out of hand?'

Lynn looked sheepish. Then her face broke into a grin. 'I slapped her. I slapped her good and hard round the face.'

Viv was so taken aback that she also smiled. 'But why? She'd just apologised and that's what you wanted.'

'She sounded smug. High and bloody mighty. It just got to me.'

'But what did she say?'

'Oh, she didn't say much. She slapped me back.' Then Lynn giggled. 'So I slapped her again.' She stared at Viv. 'You know how it goes. One punch leads to another and soon we were like bitches in a bar room brawl . . . and let's say we were less than polite.'

'But you're in pain. You can't have that.'

'Oh I did that when . . . well after two or three goes at each other we both got hysterical and I staggered back and whacked my thigh on the corner of the HiFi.'

Viv shook her head. 'When was all this?'

'A few days ago. Believe it or not, by the time she left we'd had a cup of tea, and made up.'

Viv's mouth was wide open in utter disbelief. 'But I don't get it . . . Why would you sell the flat, Lynn? It's your castle. That view, my God, where else would you get a view like that?'

Lynn's eyes filled. 'I just can't live with them so close by.'

'But if you move, they'll have won . . . Not that Thurza's exactly sitting on the jackpot.'

'She helped with the flat.'

Viv nodded. 'So what? That was then and this is now. It's your home and presumably you own it?'

'Oh, sure. Thurza saw to that when the boys and I had to leave the cottage. But it's awkward for everyone.'

'The boys . . . ?'

'Oh, God, no. They don't know and never will.' She looked at Viv pleadingly.

Viv drew in a deep breath. 'I'm not going to talk to anyone about any of this so you can relax. But knowing this goes some way to understanding their relationship.'

Lynn threw Viv a questioning look. 'You mean Thurza and Toddy?'

'Yeah. It must be hard for him. Not that that excuses his behaviour. She must feel beholden to him. My godfathers, how could they have imagined that doing something so dramatic wouldn't have major consequences?' Viv stared across at Lynn. 'How are the twins?'

'Really nice boys. But they were bound to be. Their dad was a really good man.'

It was Viv's turn to give a questioning look. 'And the accident?'

'We'll never know. Ben was doing tree work . . . in the days before harnesses and health and safety freaks. He fell off a sequoia, raising the crown apparently.' Her eyes filled again and she stared toward the tinted windows at the end of the room. 'Toddy was with him, and unless he's an excellent actor, was absolutely devastated. Thurza said the other day that Toddy had always loved Ben more than he ever loved her. Imagine living like that, Viv? It must be horrible.'

After all that Lynn had been through her attitude towards the Newhalls was admirable. If Viv had found herself in those circumstances she was not sure she'd have handled it so well.

'What do you mean exactly?'

'Toddy's temper has got to have something to do with all his grief. That stiff upper lip stuff must be killing him.' She nodded. 'His temper's certainly not getting any easier.'

Viv recalled Toddy and the relationship between him and Ben. Since they were childhood friends, good enough friends for Ben to agree to help them with a family, there must have been all manner of conflicting emotions flying around. Viv wanted to ask more questions but she remembered the 'need to know' rule, and guessed that over time she'd get the details.

Lynn interrupted Viv's musings. 'So you see Ben was responsible for . . . '

'Nothing beyond helping out his childhood friend and his wife.' Then tentatively, 'I guess there was an inquiry at the time of Ben's death?'

'Not that you'd believe. It became the elephant in the room. I think that's why Thurza wanted me off the estate. Me and the boys were a constant reminder . . . What a mess.'

Viv's head shot up at this. 'You can't take the blame for any of this. You weren't even around when Ben . . .' She left it hanging, seeing that Lynn was too upset to go there.

They sat quietly, Lynn looking out towards the car park and Viv appraising the décor.

Then Lynn blurted, 'He didn't sleep with her . . . they had some kind of medical implement like a turkey baster.' She grimaced and shook her head. 'No point in going over it now, but after this recent debacle I don't want anything more to do with them, and the house is a constant reminder.'

'But, Lynn, promise me you won't do anything until you sleep on it for a couple of weeks. The flat is so perfect for you. Beside where would you go?' Then smiling. 'Who'd you get to cut your hair if you left the area?'

This brought a smile to Lynn's face. 'I hadn't thought of that.'

Viv pressed. 'Promise me you'll think about it for a while. No one ever regrets thinking time when making a decision as important as this.'

Lynn nodded. 'Okay. I'll give it a couple of weeks . . . Thanks, Viv.'

Viv reached into her jacket and took out some cash. Immediately Lynn started fussing in her own purse.

'It's coffee, Lynn. It'll not break the bank.'

Lynn conceded. 'Thanks. I owe you . . . and more than a cup of coffee.'

Viv stood and scooped her jacket off the back of the chair. Lynn followed her lead.

As they walked back through reception to the car park Viv said, 'There ain't nothing stranger than folk.'

Lynn pushed open the door. 'You're telling me. Thanks for listening, Viv.'

Viv waved as she stepped up to the Rav then returned the call she'd missed before heading back into town. 'Hi, Red. What's up?'

'We should have a chat.'

'Sounds ominous.'

'Well you know the girl from the canal?' She waited for Viv's reply.

'Well I know the case you're talking about but I don't know the girl.'

'You sure about that, Doc?'

Viv hesitated. 'Yes. Why? You going to tell me otherwise?'

'Funny you should say that 'cause we have a photograph of you with the deceased.'

Viv was gob-smacked. 'A what? How . . . I mean, who is she?' All manner of possibilities ran through Viv's mind. Confusion was evident in her tone.

'The girl's name is Nancy McVee.'

'What? You must be kidding. Nancy McVee?'

'So you do know her? You'll have to come in.'

'I don't actually know her, but I . . .'

Red sighed. 'Viv, this is serious. I'll need your full co-operation.'

'Of course, it's just bizarre. You're right. I'll have to see you to give you the full story. I'll head in now.' She looked at her watch. 'See you in twenty minutes.'

'And Doc, don't get creative on the way.'

Viv jumped into the car, gripped the steering wheel, and stared straight ahead. If Nancy McVee was dead, what did that mean for Walter? She tried to remember the timeline. Nancy had sent Viv an email, days after that body was fished out of the canal. Okay, so someone else could have sent the email, but why would they bother? This thought tickled at something uncomfortable inside her. What if Walter was involved, and wanted to make it look as if Nancy was still alive? He'd even said that she'd been in touch again. But Walter? He wouldn't hurt a fly. Oh boy, this could be interesting. She started the engine, pulled out of the Dakota car park and headed for Fettes.

Red was pacing in the foyer when Viv arrived. She gestured towards a door on the right. The look she threw Viv was not encouraging. Red strode down the corridor and Viv followed on her heels.

When they reached the office Red turned. 'Couldn't believe my eyes when I saw these.' A large table in the office was obscured by photographs. Viv recognised the event they showed immediately. They'd been taken at a staff party in her early salon days. She could name everyone in them. Face by face she gave Red their names. She pointed to Mazza, aka Mary Smith – who wouldn't want to lose that name?

Red nodded. 'That's her. That's Nancy McVee.'

After a few minutes of bending over the photographs Viv slumped into a chair and Red said, 'How you doing? I'd forgotten about last week's shenanigans.'

'I'm okay. I can't believe this, though. You see, only week before last someone, a friend, asked me to talk to Nancy McVee, clearly not her real name . . . have you found other pseudonyms?'

'Yes. She's obviously been changing her name like you change your socks. You think that back then she was called Mary Smith?'

'I can see why she'd want to ditch that. But why change it to Nancy McVee? That wouldn't exactly sweep the nation with excitement. Anyway I emailed her and got a reply that made me think that whatever my friend was concerned about there wasn't anything I could do to help him.'

'And your friend's name?'

Viv hesitated and Red pressed. 'C'mon. Don't you go holding out on me.'

'Dr Walter Sessions. But he won't have anything to do with this.'

Red raised her eyebrows and Viv smiled. 'He can't have. He's a friend of mine.'

'What – you think that all the guys we have banged up are friendless?'

Viv tutted. 'Of course I don't. But Walter?'

'Go on. Walter. What about him?'

'Well, he's a desperate man at the moment.' She glanced at Red. 'But not desperate enough to kill anyone.'

'You've got his details and we'll follow this up. No need for you to be involved any more. In fact, if I were you I'd lay low for a bit.'

When Viv looked up at Red there was compassion in her face. She really did seem concerned about Viv's wellbeing.

She took out her phone and scrolled through for Walter's details, handing the phone to Red when she found them.

As Viv drove back to the West Bow she considered how complicated silences were. Often the weight of their content became the most powerful of motivators. One act, swept under the carpet, could, years later, jump out and wreck a life. She recalled how many times she had leapt into something without thinking through the repercussions? Too many . . . and yet she'd lived to tell another story.

She parked in a residents bay and strode back towards the flat. No sooner had she closed the door and slumped against the back of it than her phone rang, it was Mac. 'Hi Viv, we're having a wee get together tonight and wondered if you're up for it. Nothing fancy, but since we've put a few tricky things to bed in the past week we thought we'd celebrate . . .'

Viv, exhausted, checked the clock. 'What time are you thinking of?' The idea of going back out filled her with dismay. She'd fantasised about a long hot soak and a night by the telly, but she was torn, he sounded really keen.

As if sensing her reluctance he added. 'We can make it early if that suits you.'

She heard herself agreeing to go, and grimaced with annoyance. 'Okay. Seven o'clock and I'll just stay for one.'

'Great! Sal and Sandra need to have an early night so that's ideal. Want me to pick you up?'

Still without enthusiasm she said. 'Can you be bothered?'

'Sure. For you dear anything.'

She imagined him grinning at the other end of the line. 'You taking the piss?'

'No . . . No actually I'm not. So I'll see you at five to seven.'

He hung up before she had time to renege. She punched the cushion on the sofa and blasphemed. Then sat for a few minutes thinking of a viable excuse to back out. But by the time she'd had ten minutes tussling with what she could say the idea of getting changed wasn't so drastic. She had an hour and a half before he'd ring the bell so she pulled her feet up onto the sofa and dragged the heavy velvet throw over her legs and fell into a deep, dream-disturbed sleep.

When she woke she lay still, the noise of Edinburgh going about its business virtually imperceptible in its familiarity. She looked around her eccentric little sitting room, its walls concealed by paintings and prints so that the red wallpaper was barely visible. A series of six Victorian cartoons of Dr Syntax, arranged above her desk, reminded her of how much the room had become her own. Sal had surprised her by offering her the chance to buy the flat and Viv hadn't needed to be asked twice. The proud owner of a garret in the West Bow with its contents thrown in, she'd set about giving it her stamp.

The buzzer going made her jump and seek out the clock. She answered it thinking that Mac was early so would have to wait while she got ready. As she pressed the door release she heard footsteps on her landing.

The shock on Viv's face made Sal laugh. 'I know you weren't expecting me but I'm not that scary.' When Viv didn't reply immediately she hesitantly moved back.

Viv stepped forward and embraced her. Dropping her head onto Sal's shoulder. 'Sorry I was . . .'

'It's okay Viv.'

They turned and walk down the hallway into the sitting room. 'I fell asleep.'

Sal stepped over the red velvet throw lying on the floor. 'You sure you're up to a night out?'

Her gentle voice touched a place in Viv that made her defences rise. 'I'm fine.' She said, her tone too high. 'I'll just get changed.'

Sal ran her hand down Viv's arm and squeezed her hand. Viv looked away but returned the squeeze. Still holding hands they stood in silence until Viv wiped her cheek with the back of her free wrist. Sal rubbed Viv's back then pulled her onto the couch where she held her until the sobbing had run its course.

Viv pulled away and leaned back, then grabbing a cushion she held it like a transitional object. 'Sorry Sal, what a mess I am. I'm such a bubbly bairn.' She laughed. 'It's a disaster if someone's nice to me. You should be majorly pissed off.' She stared at Sal, whose generous blue eyes were more than she could cope with.

'I've been keeping track of what's happened the last couple of weeks and decided you didn't need a limpet clinging to you. So, difficult though it was, I took a step back to give you space and see what emerged.' She nodded at Viv. 'And this is it.'

Viv took Sal's hand again and rubbed it over her lips. 'Thanks. I feel as if there's light at the end of the tunnel with the proverbial train coming my way.'

'One day at a time Viv. Remember, how do you eat an elephant?'

Viv's shoulders dropped and she smiled. 'You're right, but I've been a real ass and stuffing huge lumps in.'

Sal took out her mobile phone and while dialing said. 'Haven't we all? Now, I'll ring Mac and tell him we're not going to make it. Then I'll get the kettle on. How does that sound?'

Viv drew her legs up beneath her and pulled the velvet throw back over her knees. 'Music to my ears.'

To find out more about upcoming releases go to www.vclifford.com

Made in the USA
Monee, IL
18 August 2020